HARVEST
BOOK EIGHT OF
ABNER FORTIS, ISMC

P. A. Piatt

Theogeny Books
Coinjock, NC

Chris Kennedy/Theogeny Books
1097 Waterlily Rd.
Coinjock, NC 27923
https://chriskennedypublishing.com/

Publisher's Note: This is a work of fiction. Names, characters, places, and incidents are a product of the author's imagination. Locales and public names are sometimes used for atmospheric purposes. Any resemblance to actual people, living or dead, or to businesses, companies, events, institutions, or locales is completely coincidental.

Cover Design by Elartwyne Estole.

Ordering Information:
Quantity sales. Special discounts are available on quantity purchases by corporations, associations, and others. For details, contact the "Special Sales Department" at the address above.

Harvest/P. A. Piatt -- 1st ed.
ISBN: 978-1648556784

DINLI

DINLI has many meanings to a Space Marine. It is the unofficial motto of the International Space Marine Corps, and it stands for "Do It, Not Like It."

Every Space Marine recruit has DINLI drilled into their head from the moment they arrive at basic training. Whatever they're ordered to do, they don't have to like it, they just have to do it. Crawl through stinking tidal mud? DINLI. Run countless miles with heavy packs? DINLI. Endure brutal punishment for minor mistakes? DINLI.

DINLI also refers to the illicit hootch the Space Marines brew wherever they deploy. From jungle planets like Pada-Pada, to the water-covered planets of the Felder Reach, and even on the barren, boulder-strewn deserts of Balfan-48. It might be a violation of Fleet Regulations to brew it, but every Marine drinks DINLI, from the lowest private to the most senior general.

DINLI is also the name of the ISMC mascot, a scowling bulldog with a cigar clamped between its massive jaws.

Finally, DINLI is a general purpose expression about the grunt life. From announcing the birth of a new child to expressing disgust at receiving a freeze-dried ham and lima bean ration pack again, a Space Marine can expect one response from his comrades.

DINLI.

* * * * *

Chapter One

Octavia Gutiérrez-Ramirez—Ogre, to her friends—entered *Fortuna's* control station to the blare of sirens and flash of emergency lights.

"What's up, Shade?"

Shade, full-time mechanic and part-time control station watch stander, looked up from his console and shook his head. "I don't get it, Captain. We're in hover. There's nothing on the scope, but the collision alarm went off. I can't get it to reset."

"Huh." Ogre checked her screen. The readings showed they were three kilometers clear of the gap in the asteroid field they'd been hovering next to for the last two weeks. "What about Elvis?"

"Elvis" was the nickname for the artificial intelligence Ogre used as her assistant to pilot *Fortuna*. She didn't like turning control of the ship over to something she didn't fully understand, but having Elvis meant she could sleep at night, and there was one less crewmember to share the profits with.

"I put him to sleep when I took the watch," Shade said. "He talks too damn much."

Ogre flipped her display from sensor input to the exterior cameras, and her eyebrows shot up in shock at what she saw.

The unmistakable shimmer of an impending warp jump surrounded *Fortuna*.

"What the fuck?" Shade blurted. "We're not jumping, are we?"

"No. There's no gate here. It's got to be an anomaly or weird harmonic." Ogre paged through her command screens but saw nothing unusual. "This is bizarre. We're ninety-seven Terra hours from the nearest jump gate." She stared at her console for another second before she made her decision.

"We need to move," she said. "We'll use the thrusters to reposition clear of the shimmer."

"You think that shimmer is legit?"

Ogre shrugged. "I don't know what it is, but I don't want to find out the hard way. Call DeeDee and tell him what we're doing."

DeeDee was Demonte Durant, foreman of the wildcat miners working in the nearby asteroid field. Ogre didn't have to inform him when she repositioned *Fortuna,* but it was a courtesy she extended to keep relations cordial. She had been on ships where the drilling support ship crew and miners were in constant conflict, which only added to the misery of extended prospecting missions in deep space.

While Shade hailed DeeDee, Ogre turned on the all-sensor collection system before she plotted a new position for the ship. They only had to move two kilometers to be clear of the shimmer, but she doubled that distance, just to be sure. Maneuvering near an asteroid field was a chancy proposition, and the collection system would help cover her ass if anything went wrong during the move. She had chosen her hover position because of the gap in the asteroid belt, which should have meant they didn't need to maneuver for at least two weeks.

Until the warp showed up.

"DeeDee told us to have a nice trip," Shade said.

"Here we go."

The thrusters moved the ship while Ogre watched to ensure they were clear of the shimmer.

"Fucking space, man," Shade said as *Fortuna* glided into position. "Just when I think I've got it figured out, some shit like this happens."

Ogre laughed. "Nothing surprises me out here anymore. I've been—whoa!"

A ship popped out of the shimmer. The vessel was a strange shape, unlike anything Ogre had ever seen before. Three propulsion pods hung in a vertical stack below the main fuselage, and stubby wings protruded on both sides. What made the craft remarkable wasn't the unusual propulsion arrangement or boxy body; it was the size. It was the biggest spaceship Ogre had ever seen during her years in space. It was larger than the biggest Fleet flagships.

"That's a big bastard," said Shade. "Where did it come from?"

Before Ogre could answer, another ship emerged through the shimmer and then a third. Two more followed. Ogre and Shaft sat in stunned silence while the five ships maneuvered into a tight formation and then accelerated out of sensor range.

"Where do you think they're going?" Shade asked.

Ogre turned off the data collection system and entered a series of commands to archive and compress the information for transmission.

"I don't know, but I'm sending this to the fleet in orbit around Maltaan. I'll let them figure it out."

* * *

As she orbited around Maltaan aboard the Fleet flagship *Giant*, Commodore Eloise Allard pursed her lips and stroked her chin, a sure sign of her indecision. Five unidentified contacts had just appeared on the strategic display in the Flag Operations Center, or FOC, and there was a great deal of speculation about their identity.

One of the watch standers suggested the contacts were Fleet ships arriving from Terra Earth, but they were approaching from the wrong direction. Fleet Scheduling didn't expect any ships to arrive in orbit around Maltaan for at least another week. Another said they were mining vessels traveling together, but they flew in a precise formation unlike any civilian craft Allard had ever seen.

"Wasn't there a report about some unidentified ships in the last few days?" she asked Commander Deland, her staff operations officer seated at the console next to her.

"Yes ma'am, there was. An asteroid mining outfit way out in the middle of nowhere reported that some ships jumped through an unmapped warp two days ago. Those guys are always reporting star maidens, sun gods, and all manner of other craziness. We acknowledged receipt, but I didn't give the report much credence."

"Hmm. Perhaps, this time, we should have." Commodore Allard pointed to one of the screens mounted on the forward bulkhead of the FOC. "Display the report up there, Commander."

While Deland fumbled to find the miner's report, Allard slipped on her headset and keyed her mic. "Staff Watch Officer, which destroyer is the duty ship?"

"Comte de Grasse, ma'am."

"Send her out to intercept and investigate. Tell her to make best speed. I don't want any aggressive maneuvers, but she should be prepared for anything. Instruct her to broadcast hails on all channels."

By then, Deland had the report and video cued up on the screen. "Commodore, this report is from the mining support vessel *Fortuna*. They detected what they thought was a warp gate shimmer near an asteroid belt they were prospecting."

"That looks like warp gate shimmer to me," Allard said.

The view shifted as *Fortuna* moved clear of the shimmer. A few seconds later, five indistinct blobs popped out of the shimmer, one at a time. Several seconds later, they disappeared.

"The video was captured by *Fortuna's* docking cameras," Deland explained. "The resolution on them at this range is poor, and she's not equipped with long-range visual sensors."

"Pity. They looked rather large."

"The master reported they were the largest spacecraft she's ever seen. Larger than Fleet flagships, even."

"You dismissed this report, even with the video evidence?"

"What video evidence, Commodore? That shimmer could have been atmospheric reflection, a hydrogen cloud, or a hundred other things. Same with those blobs. The resolution makes it impossible to tell."

"Watch Officer, how long before they are in range of our rail guns?"

"At their current speed, four hours, Commodore," the watch officer said.

"And how long until Comte de Grasse intercepts?"

"Comte de Grasse will be within weapons range in one hour and twenty-six minutes and visual sensor range in two hours and ten minutes."

"Very well. Set Alert Condition Bravo throughout the fleet. Send potential threat warnings to the Maltaani ships in company and MAC-M, too."

"Is all of this necessary, ma'am?" Deland asked.

The FOC watch lurched into action. They had done nothing but vessel control during the past twelve months on Military Assistance Command—Maltaan (MAC-M) support and there was confusion over how to execute Allard's orders. Battle watch consoles that hadn't been manned in over a year had to be powered up, and two of them failed to boot. Watch manning had been reduced to the bare minimum required to manage the ships arriving and departing the space around Maltaan, and bewildered personnel filtered in to take their assigned watch stations. Calls for confirmation of the alert condition came over the net, evidence of similar confusion across the fleet.

Allard gestured at the commotion. "What do you think, Commander? Is it necessary?"

Deland, whose responsibilities included the FOC, frowned but didn't respond.

"I have assumed Battle Watch Captain," Major Sussman, one of Deland's assistants, announced. "All stations manned and ready. Threat warnings have been acknowledged by the Maltaani flagship and MAC-M."

"What of the fleet?" Deland asked, seemingly anxious to deflect some of the commodore's criticism toward the other ships.

"I've received readiness reports from all but *Sao Paolo*, sir."

"Tell her to hurry up," Deland said.

"Didn't she just have a generator fire?" Allard asked.

"Yes ma'am," Sussman said. "Her operations center is inoperative until they complete repairs. She gave an estimated time for repairs of eight hours."

Allard saw another frown from Deland, along with some reddening of his ears.

Good. Perhaps he'll remember that I shouldn't have to tell him these things.

The tension grew as the minutes ticked away. The BWC posted a countdown timer on one of the screens displaying time to *Comte de Grasse's* weapons range, visual sensor range, and *Giant's* rail gun range.

Commodore Allard went to the back of the room to pace and watch the clock.

* * *

"Commodore?"

Allard snapped out of her rumination and looked up. "Go ahead."

"Ma'am, the Maltaani fleet is leaving."

"What?"

The BWC pointed to the strategic display. The symbols for the Maltaani fleet had left their assigned orbit sectors and were headed away from the planet.

"Where the hell are they going?"

"They didn't say, ma'am. They transmitted a one-word response to our threat warning. 'Badaax.' Then they turned and left."

"What does 'badaax' mean?"

"None of our interpreters recognized the word, and when we ran it through our software, it came up as 'harvest.'"

"Are you certain their transmission was a response to our warning?" Deland asked.

"Not certain, no, but they won't respond to our request for clarification."

Deland joined Allard in the back of the FOC. "It might mean nothing," he said in a low voice.

"That's true, but it would be quite a coincidence. The Maltaani fleet hasn't sent more than two messages to us in the last month, and they choose this moment to send us an unrecognizable word and depart their assigned orbit? Maybe they know something we don't."

"I'll have the transmission sent down to MAC-M and see if their interpreters can figure it out. It might have been garbled."

Allard nodded. "Very well." She called to the BWC. "What has *Comte de Grasse* reported?"

"Nothing yet, ma'am. They're not receiving any emissions from the unknowns. She is forty-minutes from rail gun range and an hour and thirty-two minutes from visual sensor range."

"Thank you."

Commodore Allard returned to pacing, pausing to cast an occasional glance at the countdown timer.

* * *

Commander Jules Després, commanding officer of *Comte de Grasse,* stared at his tactical display and willed time to speed up. His console displayed the maximum weapons range as a ring around the ship, and it crept toward the five unknown contacts with maddening slowness. He didn't anticipate an engagement, but the tension increased with every passing second, and the potential for a misstep increased with it.

"Weapons Control, verify weapon and safety status," he said over the intercom.

"This is Weapons. All weapons are in Alert Condition Bravo and safeties are engaged."

"Very well."

"Captain, that's the fourth time you issued that order in the last ten minutes," the executive officer said over the private command channel.

"I know!" Després hissed.

"I didn't mean to offend you, sir, but you're making the watch nervous."

Després looked up from his screen, and several watch standers who had been watching him ducked and turned their heads back to their consoles.

"I have the weapons status pulled up on my screen," the XO said. "I'll let you know if anything changes."

Després took a deep breath, and a trickle of sweat running down one of his armpits surprised him. "Thank you, XO."

Without warning, his screen went blank. The entire space went dark, and a second later, battery-powered emergency lighting flickered on.

"What happened?" Després demanded over the intercom, but his headset was dead. The operations center erupted into chaos as watch standers stood and added their voices to the confusion.

"Silence!" the XO shouted. "Watch Officer, report!"

"We've lost power to the operations center," the watch officer reported. "I sent a runner to the engineering control center because we have no communications."

"Then what do we have?" Després demanded.

The XO looked around at the frightened faces of the watch standers standing among the dark consoles. "We have nothing, Captain."

The air in the space began to grow stuffy because the ventilation had shut down, and a trickle of sweat down Després's back joined the ones in his armpit.

"Evacuate the space," the captain ordered in a calm voice.

Comte de Grasse lurched and shook as if someone had thrown the engines into reverse thrust. The atmosphere in the operations room went from stuffy to unbearably hot.

"Get out!"

Watch personnel scrambled over consoles and pushed past each other in the rush for the door. The bulkheads glowed red, and the soles of Desprès's boots stuck to the superheated deck. The XO stumbled and fell, and Desprès watched in horror as he burst into flames and the skin melted from his face.

Desprès took one final breath of scorching air before he too went down. He was dead before his body hit the superheated deck and began to sizzle.

* * * * *

Chapter Two

Gunnery Sergeant Petr Ystremski walked out of the Fleet hospital into the bright African sunshine and smiled. Even the oppressive humidity and funk of the swampy ISMC training grounds couldn't suppress his ebullience, and he practically bounded down the steps to the sidewalk.

Twelve months earlier, Ystremski had been more dead than alive when he returned to Terra Earth from a combat tour on Maltaan. The gunny had suffered a massive overdose of radiation from a nuke explosion during the initial invasion. After he had recovered from that and returned to the fight, the leader of the Maltaani insurgency had thrust a sword through his guts before Ystremski killed him with his kukri.

The severe damage caused by the sword had been exacerbated by the onset of a persistent fungal infection common to wounds suffered by humans on Maltaan. Known as the "Maltaani mushrooms," the infection was fatal if left untreated.

The nanobots injected into Ystremski's bloodstream to combat the effects of his radiation poisoning had held off the fungal infection long enough for Fleet doctors to find the right combination of antibiotics and other drugs to defeat it. It had been a long and painful process, but at long last, the doctors had determined that Ystremski was ready to return to full duty.

"Gunnery Sergeant Ystremski?"

A first lieutenant approached, and Ystremski saluted. "Yes sir. Do I know you?"

The lieutenant gestured to a nearby van with heavy tint in the windows. "We've never met, Gunny, but you know the general."

The van door slid open. "Come on, Gunny," a familiar voice called from the dim interior.

As Ystremski approached, he recognized General Nils Anders.

"Hello, General," Ystremski said as he slid into the vehicle, and the lieutenant closed the door behind him. "This can't be good."

Anders laughed, and they shook hands. "Good to see you too, Gunny." He leaned forward as the lieutenant climbed in behind the wheel. "William, take us over to the proving grounds."

When the van was in motion, Anders looked back at Ystremski. "How have you been, Gunny?"

"The doctors just released me to full duty, so things are looking up, sir. Congratulations on the promotion, by the way. I saw your name on the list."

"Thank you. Gunny, how would you feel about coming to work for me in the Science and Technology Directorate?"

"With Captain Fortis, sir?"

Anders nodded. "With Captain Fortis."

"My wife is going to kill me, but where do I sign?"

"Easy duty, Gunny. Home every night. Well, most nights."

Ystremski scoffed. "Tanya knows there's no such thing as easy duty with Fortis, sir. Since I linked up with him, I've been shot twice, stabbed, and roasted by a nuke."

It was Anders' turn to scoff. "You're not afraid of a challenge, are you Gunny? Besides, I heard Manpower wanted to send you on deployment with 3rd Division."

The banter continued while the van crossed the sprawling ISMC base. Anders knew Ystremski wouldn't turn down the chance to serve with Captain Fortis, and Ystremski knew he was fortunate to have someone like General Anders looking out for him. Duty in a regular Space Marine infantry unit, even a deployed unit like 3rd Division, would be almost unbearably boring compared to service with Fortis anywhere else.

The van braked to a stop in front of a large hangar.

"Here we are," Anders said. Before the lieutenant could open the door, Anders climbed out, followed by Ystremski.

"You're getting here at a good time, Gunny," the general said as he led Ystremski into a low concrete building that squatted next to the flight line. "Today is the first full-mission profile test of the IEBS."

The Integrated Exoskeletal Battle System, or IEBS (pronounced, "eebs"), was the latest product of UNT military research and development, and it represented a huge leap forward in infantry troop protection and force multiplication. Since his own return from Maltaan, Captain Fortis had commanded the 107 Space Marines assigned to test and evaluate the IEBS.

Ystremski followed Anders into a darkened room equipped with three rows of consoles facing an array of monitors that covered the front wall. Civilian technicians manned the first two rows while the third was occupied by uniformed personnel. A colonel rose from her console, gave the major next to her an annoyed look, and smoothed her uniform.

"Welcome, General," she said with a pained smile. "I wish you had told us you were coming, sir. I would have arranged a suitable reception."

Anders waved off her apology. "It's not necessary, Colonel." He gestured to Ystremski. "Colonel Moultrie, this is Gunnery Sergeant Petr Ystremski, the Space Marine I told you about. Gunny, Colonel Moultrie is the Test Director for the IEBS program."

Moultrie smiled and extended her hand. "Gunny, welcome." She motioned to the major who stood behind her. "May I introduce Major Wright, my deputy."

The gunny couldn't help but note the look of distaste on Wright's face as they shook hands, so he tightened his grip and held Wright's hand for an extra beat. Wright's eyes widened when he felt the squeeze, and Ystremski smiled when he saw the major flex his hand.

"Do you have a couple consoles for me and the gunny to observe the exercise, Colonel?"

"Uh, well sir, your console is waiting for you." She gestured to the three consoles of the back row. "I'm afraid there's no room for the gunny." Moultrie blushed. "I wish I had known you were coming, sir."

Anders pointed to a vacant console. "I know this one is me. What's that one?"

"That's me, General."

"How about that other one?"

Wright spoke up. "That's me."

"You've seen them drop before, right?" Anders asked the major. Wright nodded. "I'd like Gunny Ystremski to watch the whole thing, if you don't mind sitting this one out. In fact, Colonel, if you wouldn't mind sliding over so the gunny can sit next to me, I'd be very grateful."

Moultrie and Wright exchanged confused looks, and the colonel's hands fluttered in the air.

"Of course, General. Devon, move your binder and let me slide in there. General, are you sure you wouldn't be more comfortable in the middle?"

"My regular console is fine."

Ystremski chuckled inside at the headquarters warfare Anders waged on Moultrie and Wright as the trio slid into their seats. Major Wright clutched his binder to his chest and leaned against the back wall.

"What's the status of the drop?" Anders asked.

"The company was boarding the shuttle when you walked in, sir."

* * *

Captain Abner Fortis stood on the tarmac and greeted each of his Space Marines with a nod and a slap on the shoulder as they lined up to load the shuttle that would take them to the ragged edge of space. It was a tradition that went back to the earliest days of soldiers throwing themselves out of perfectly good aircraft, when leaders gave their soldiers one final visual inspection before they loaded.

The IEBS worn by the Space Marines were self-contained and made his inspection unnecessary, but Fortis liked to make the connection with his Space Marines. He respected the many traditions in the ISMC that were written in the blood of those that came before, and he liked to observe them. Technology might have made his inspection obsolete, but there were humans inside those suits.

When the final Space Marine was loaded, Fortis followed them up the boarding ramp and gave a thumbs up to the loadmaster. Motors whined as the ramp closed, and the shuttle began to roll down the runway. Fortis backed into his position as jump leader and heard a *click* as the mechanical jaws secured his IEBS to the bulkhead. Master Sergeant Brooks, Assistant IEBS Test Director, assigned as the company senior NCO, was locked into the position next to Fortis. He gave the jaws a quick once-over.

"You're good to go, Skipper," he told Fortis over the command circuit.

"Thanks, Top."

After a steep climb, the shuttle leveled out.

The shuttle pilot's voice crackled in Fortis's ear. *"We're at jump altitude. Standby to open the ramp."*

As the ramp opened, Fortis could see the bright blue curve of Terra Earth and the darkness of space above.

"Three minutes to drop," the pilot announced. Amber lights flashed. *"Releasing hooks."*

The jaws of the rack clicked open, and Fortis was free to move. He stepped to the center of the aisle and made the hand signal for buddy checks. Buddy checks were as unnecessary as his greeting was during onload, but it was another tradition Fortis liked to observe. The Space Marines were about to throw themselves out of the shuttle forty kilometers above Terra Earth without parachutes, and the final bit of encouragement from their comrades might help steady a last-minute case of nerves. This was their highest jump yet, and although the IEBS had performed flawlessly so far, in the view of the Space Marines, that just meant somebody was due.

A red light over the ramp illuminated, indicating one minute to jump. Fortis signaled for the jumpers to line up in two sticks facing the open ramp. His IEBS was in Leader mode, and he could see elevated heart and respiration rates throughout the company.

Good. They're smart enough to be a little scared.

"Stand by for drop," the shuttle pilot's voice crackled in Fortis's ear. *"Drop in three... two... one..."*

Fortis raced down the ramp and threw himself free of the shuttle. He performed a slow backflip, and the retro rockets on his IEBS slowed his descent so he could observe the other Space Marines as they dropped. He was satisfied to see them begin to maneuver into squad-sized formations.

All except one, who plunged past him toward the surface.

Beep-beep-beep-beep...

* * *

"What's that alarm?" Moultrie demanded.

The piercing tone of the alarm blared in time with a flashing red screen on one of the monitors. A technician typed furiously on her keyboard, and the alarm silenced, but the screen continued to flash.

"Low Retro Rocket Fuel Level on Unit Eight," she reported.

"Low fuel? How?"

Anders leaned over to Ystremski. "The IEBS uses a system of retro rockets to control the rate of descent. It's much lighter and more maneuverable than traditional parachutes, and up until now, more reliable."

* * *

An alarm sounded in Fortis's ear, and a warning light flashed on his visor. He navigated to the advisory page on his heads-up display and saw a red status for Unit Eight, worn by Sergeant Connolly.

What the fuck?

"Mayday, mayday," Connelly transmitted over the emergency circuit. *"This is Romeo Echo Eight, declaring an emergency. Retro Rocket Fuel Level (RRFL) at eight percent."*

The ground station observing the drop responded immediately. *"Romeo Echo Eight, this is Exercise Control, have you reset the alarm?"*

"Affirmative. I've attempted reset twice but it won't clear."

By that time, Connelly was far below the group and falling fast. Without the rockets to slow his descent, Connelly would freefall all the way to the surface and experience what the Space Marines referred to as a "kinetic landing."

"This is Exercise Control. Test fire your rockets manually. There might be a fault in the alarm."

"Roger." Connelly's voice was tight with tension and fear. *"Retro rockets are functional."* A second later, he continued. *"Fuel level zero. I'm out."*

Fortis flipped his own rockets to manual, bent his knees, and goosed the control until he was head down.

"This is Romeo Echo One, nose down and full burn."

He fired his rockets and felt them accelerate him toward the surface.

"One! What are you doing?"

"Going to see if I can help my guy," Fortis said. He flipped to the infrared display on his visor and saw Connelly as a bright spot three thousand meters below him.

"Negative, One. Abort your maneuver."

Fortis ignored the order and continued his high-speed dive toward the surface. He pulled up the Master Control Page and turned off the remote override, just in case Exercise Control tried to stop his maneuver.

* * *

"What the fuck is he doing?" Moultrie shrieked. The technician threw up her hands, and the colonel scrambled to don her headset.

"This is Exercise Control Actual. Abort your maneuver. I say again, abort your maneuver."

The circuit was silent.

"He just turned off the remote override, ma'am," the tech announced. "Romeo Echo One is in powered descent."

Moultrie slammed her fists onto the console. "They're both going to die."

* * *

"*Romeo Echo One, this is Exercise Control Actual. Abort your maneuver. I say again, abort your maneuver. That's a direct order.*" Colonel Moultrie sounded furious.

Fortis didn't respond. Instead, he maneuvered to return to the upright position when he got within one thousand meters of Connelly.

"Eight, this is One. I'm a thousand meters above you and closing. What's your flight attitude?"

"Upright, sir, but I'm falling fast."

Fortis feathered his rockets to slow his descent as he approached Connelly. The closure rate slowed and he reached out to grab Connolley's IEBS. He misjudged the angle and slammed into the sergeant. Both Space Marines went into uncontrolled spins.

"What the fuck, sir?"

"Shit! Sorry about that. Harder than it looks. Let me try again."

Fortis tried to ignore the altimeter racing to zero as he got his descent under control and maneuvered for another intercept. There wasn't much Connelly could do to control himself, so Fortis had to time it perfectly. They collided a second time, but this time he managed to grab Connelly's IEBS.

"Gotcha. Grab my chassis and hold on tight, my rockets are about to fire."

Fortis flipped his retro rockets to automatic, and they immediately fired at full power. Even though Fortis was strength enhanced to level ten, Connelly started to slip out of his grasp. The sergeant wrapped his legs around Fortis's waist and hugged his helmet to his chest. The rockets roared, and the altimeter slowed its countdown to a survivable rate of descent.

"Almost there," Fortis said.

Another red warning light flashed in his visor and Fortis saw his own RRFL was at ten percent. He cut off the rockets and the pair began to fall faster.

"What happened?" Connelly blurted, unaware of the alarm.

"Low fuel," Fortis said. "Gonna have to wait until the last second and give the jets one final blast to slow us down."

By then, they had drifted far off target. Under normal circumstances, Fortis could have maneuvered himself back over the drop zone with small rocket bursts, but with almost no fuel left, it was more important to land at a speed they could survive than win points for accuracy. They weren't falling straight down, and Fortis realized that they could use that to their advantage.

Fortis's altimeter fluctuated as it read the peaks and valleys of the mountains sweeping by below. If he timed the final engine burst correctly, they would land near the top of one of the peaks. If he mistimed it, they would run out of fuel over a thousand-meter valley and fall to their deaths. He pushed the thought from his mind and concentrated on firing at the right moment.

"Hold on," he said through gritted teeth and then hit the ignition.

The retro rockets fired at full power, the altimeter slowed to almost zero, and the rockets flamed out. The pair slammed down on the side of a steep mountain. Fortis lost his grip on Connelly as they tumbled down the mountain in an avalanche of rocks and boulders. The world went by in a jumble of rocks and dirt and sky. He had managed to avoid the largest tree trunks when he entered the tree line, and the scrub brush was no match for the weight of his IEBS as he continued his tumbling descent.

Fortis was on the verge of unconsciousness from the slamming and banging when he fell the final ten meters and splashed down in a stream at the foot of the mountain. A few seconds later, Connelly splashed down next to him in a cloud of rocks, dust, and tree branches.

Fortis was dazed for a moment, but he knew he had to get moving.

"Connelly, can you hear me?"

The sergeant groaned in response.

"Connelly, talk to me. Are you okay?"

"We missed the drop zone," Connelly said, and the two Space Marines burst into laughter. *"And yeah, I'm okay."*

Fortis activated his emergency transponder. "Exercise Control, this is Romeo Echo One. One and Eight are on the surface. Request hovercopter extract."

"This is Exercise Control, roger, we see your beacon. Search and rescue are on the way."

* * * *

Chapter Three

The exercise control room technicians erupted in cheers when they heard Fortis's call for extraction. Even Moultrie had a big smile on her face when she turned to General Anders.

"They're alive!"

Anders nodded. "There will be time to celebrate when the other ninety-eight are on the ground, Colonel."

Chastened, Moultrie turned her attention to the room. "Maintain discipline!" she shouted over the noise. "We still have Space Marines in the air."

Ystremski stifled a smile as the technicians went back to their consoles. He had felt a stab of fear when Fortis began his pursuit of the out-of-control Space Marine, but as the situation played out, the fear had become excitement and then relief when he heard Fortis call for extraction.

His first instinct was to meet the search and rescue bird when it returned with Fortis and Connolly, but he knew the pair were safe, and he needed to focus on the task at hand. There was still an exercise to observe and learn as much as he could about the IEBS.

The colonel suggested they end the exercise when all the Space Marines were on the ground, but Anders refused.

"Let's see how the company handles the situation," he told her. "Who's going to step up and take charge?"

The exercise scenario was a simple insertion and assault, but the retro rocket casualty demonstrated that nothing was ever simple when it involved live fire and all the hazards that entailed. Master Sergeant Brooks took control of the command element while the two platoon commanders, Lieutenants Sergio Penny and Harold Young, continued the mission as assigned. Penny was the next ranking officer in the company, but the middle of a high-risk insertion was no time to assert seniority.

As soon as the Space Marines landed, the scout-snipers deployed to cover their approach. Fifteen-millimeter ballistic rifles barked as they eliminated enemy soldiers visible at the target compound. Grenadiers from both platoons showered the compound with a combination of high explosive and fragmentary grenades while the rest of the Space Marines closed in. Sappers blew holes in the compound walls, and the Space Marines poured inside.

Everyone in the exercise control room monitored the action via miniature cameras mounted on the platoon leaders' helmets. It pleased Ystremski to see the movement of the Space Marines as they assaulted the buildings inside. Although the IEBS was bulkier than the heaviest battle armor he had ever worn, it didn't seem to hinder them at all. Overall, it was an impressive display.

Colonel Moultrie announced the end of the exercise, and the Space Marines filed out of the compound to await extraction by hovercopter.

General Anders turned to Ystremski. "What do you think, Gunny?"

"Quite a display, sir. The grenadiers are devastating."

"Forty-millimeter grenades, delivered at ranges up to one thousand meters," Anders said.

Ystremski gave a low whistle. "I can't wait to play with that."

"You'll get the full rundown on the IEBS over the next couple days. There is a nighttime full mission profile exercise scheduled for next week, and I expect you'll be a full participant."

"Any chance I can use a regular chute, sir?"

The general chuckled as he stood. "Let's go see how Fortis and Connelly are doing."

As they stepped outside, the first load of Space Marines from the exercise touched down by hovercopter. A passenger van pulled up, and Fortis and Connelly emerged.

"Hello, Abner," Anders said. "I'm glad to see you in one piece."

"You and me both, General," Fortis said as he saluted the general. He noticed Ystremski standing next to Anders. "Hiya, Gunny." The two men shook hands. "Have you come to see the future of the Corps?"

"I've come to *be* the future of the Corps," Ystremski said.

"You're joining the company? Outstanding."

"From what I just saw, it looks like you need all the help you can get."

It wasn't long before all the Space Marines were formed up on the tarmac. After a few brief remarks by Anders and Moultrie, Fortis dismissed the company to remove their IEBS, stow their gear, and conduct debriefs with various IEBS support personnel. The gunny waved off the offer of a ride from General Anders and followed Fortis to the command element debrief instead.

Fortis introduced Ystremski to the command element before Master Sergeant Brooks took charge of the debrief. There wasn't a lot to talk about. The exercise was a textbook assault, and despite the sudden loss of the company commander, the platoons had executed their responsibilities with speed and precision.

The only issue that warranted any discussion was the time delay between the grenade barrage and the assault. Several Space Marines felt it had been excessive and would have given the defenders a chance to regroup and mount a defense, while others thought the fifty-meter kill radius of the frags required the attackers to remain well clear of the target until the barrage was over. After some spirited debate, Fortis assigned both camps to put their cases in writing and submit them up the chain of command for consideration.

"Any further discussion?" Fortis asked. Nobody answered. "That's it then, thanks."

"I'm glad you're here," Fortis told Ystremski as they walked to the company barracks. "The IEBS will be a huge boost to regular battle armor. The testing can be tedious at times, but now that we're executing missions, it's a lot more fun. And you're right, I could use the help running the company."

Ystremski nodded at Brooks, who was climbing the steps to the training command headquarters building. "What about Master Sergeant Brooks?"

"Brooks is an Assistant Test Director. He doesn't work for me; he works for the colonel and Major Wright. He's been filling in as company NCO because the billet was empty."

"Is he a good Marine?"

"Yes, he is. He's got a lot of experience bug hunting, which is what the IEBS was originally designed for. He spent the Maltaan invasion in orbit like a lot of other guys, but he's tactically sound. Sometimes, I think the colonel assigned him to the company to be her inside man, but I let him run the day-to-day and he doesn't meddle with the other stuff. He took the billet to set himself up for a job with the program after he retires, and that's okay with me."

"Do you think he'll have a problem being replaced by a mere gunny?" Ystremski asked.

Fortis scoffed. "If you think I'm going to Boudreaux to get you another promotion—"

"Captain Fortis!" The pair turned and saw Brooks trotting toward them. "Sir, Colonel Moultrie wants to see you in her office."

* * *

Fortis stood in front Colonel Moultrie's desk and waited for her to look up from the screen in front of her. Standing to her right, Major Wright glared at Fortis. Doctor Dunker, the civilian director of IEBS testing and evaluation, sat on her other side. Master Sergeant Brooks stood by the door.

Moultrie looked up. Her face was bright red, and veins stuck out on her neck and temple.

"I should ground you, Captain. I should kick you out of my program."

Wright sneered and Dunker cleared his throat. Fortis didn't respond.

"Do you have anything to say for yourself? What the hell did you think you were doing with that stunt?"

"Saving my Space Marine, ma'am," Fortis said.

"You deliberately disobeyed my direct order to abort."

"Yes ma'am, I did. I was on the scene, and from what I saw, I thought I could save Connelly. I was right."

"You were lucky!"

"I can't deny we were fortunate to make the landing, but it was necessary that I try."

The colonel rubbed the bridge of her nose between her thumb and forefinger. "I was warned by other officers about you, Fortis. They said you have a penchant for making it up as you go along, and a structured test environment isn't the place for you. I took you because of your record, and because I didn't believe all the stories. Your performance has been satisfactory so far, but it appears your old habits are resurfacing. What message does it send to the company when their commander disobeys a direct order?"

"What message does it send to the company when you allow a sergeant to fall to his death?" Fortis asked. "Connelly was going to die if I didn't do something, and everyone knew it. I could have let him die, and when asked about it later said, 'Orders are orders.' But that's not how it works in an infantry company, ma'am. If I had stood by and watched him fall without at least trying to save him, the trust between me and those Space Marines would have been destroyed. In battle—"

"This isn't wartime!" Moultrie slapped her desk. "You're not capturing a hill; you're testing equipment that will someday save those very same Space Marines you're so concerned about. I don't care if they follow you or not. I care that you have them ready to go in the proper uniform at the proper time. The testing program is on a tight schedule, and we don't have time for delays because of your conscience."

"Did our drop put us behind schedule, ma'am?"

Moultrie looked at Dunker, who shook his head. "One hundred and eight IEBS dropped today. One hundred and six IEBS completed the test sequence."

"The other two IEBS were damaged, weren't they?"

Dunker read from a paper in front of him. "Unit One suffered a racked visor and one bent leg support. Unit Eight's weapon interface scrambled on impact, and there are two pulse rifles missing, plus the original problem with the retro rockets. My technicians are making repairs as we speak."

Fortis shrugged. "We fell down a mountain. What do you expect?"

Moultrie seemed displeased with Fortis's attitude, and she turned to Major Wright. "Do you have anything to add?"

"The insubordination is inexcusable. I don't believe he belongs in the program."

The colonel glared at Fortis again. "The *general* was here, Fortis. How do you think your actions reflect on the program when you willfully disobey direct orders in front of someone like him?"

"Knowing General Anders, he's probably happy I tried, ma'am."

Her nostrils flared and her already red face turned several shades darker. "Captain Fortis, I'm grounding you for the next test series. I will not tolerate your blatant disrespect for the chain of command. You will continue to function as the company commander in an administrative role until I say otherwise. Until then, you will not suit up. Understood?"

"Yes ma'am."

"Carry on."

* * *

Fortis stepped outside and took a deep breath of the humid African air. He was greeted by Lieutenants Penny and Young, Gunny Ystremski, and Sergeant Connelly. "What happened, sir?" Penny asked.

Fortis shook his head. "Nothing. She grounded me for the next test series, but that's it."

"What the hell for?"

"I disobeyed her order to abort."

"I'm sorry she's busting your balls, sir, but I'm glad you didn't abort," Connelly said. "I was having trouble coming up with something epic to say for my last words when you showed up."

"Sounds like bullshit to me," Young said.

Fortis shook his head. "Don't worry about it. I'm not grounded forever. If she changes her mind and makes it permanent, DINLI."

* * * * *

Chapter Four

"Commodore, *Comte de Grasse...*" The BWC's voiced trailed off.

"*Comte de Grasse* what?" Allard demanded.

"She disappeared."

"What?" She searched the strategic display but didn't see the ship. "Where is she?"

"I don't know, ma'am. One scan she was there, and the next scan, she was gone."

"Did she make any reports?"

"Negative. Nothing. It's like space opened and swallowed her whole."

Allard was aware of how little humans knew about the phenomena that existed in the infinite reaches of space. It was rare, but ships sometimes vanished without a trace. It was a hazard that all spacefarers accepted as part of their job, but few talked about.

"Did we detect anything from the unknown contacts?"

"No ma'am. They're continuing to close, but we haven't intercepted anything from them."

Allard slipped her headset off and leaned over to Deland at the next console. He slipped his own headset off and leaned in.

"I don't like this," the commodore said in a low voice. "Something doesn't feel right. *Comte de Grasse* disappearing right now is too much of a coincidence for me."

36 | P.A. PIATT

"Do you think she was engaged?"

"I don't know. Possibly. Have the systems operators save the last three minutes of contact we had with her and send it to me for playback."

"Would you like me to put it on one of the big screens, ma'am?"

"No. I don't want to alarm the watch any more than they are. Keep this between us for now."

"Roger that, ma'am."

A few minutes later, a playback file appeared on Allard's screen, and she hit "play." It was exactly as the BWC had said: *Comte de Grasse* was there, and then she was gone. After she watched it twice, she cued the recording up to a few seconds before *Comte de Grasse* disappeared and replayed it at the slowest playback speed.

Just before the ship vanished, the scan showed a strong return for the ship. The next scan was less distinct, and the next scan was an unrecognizable ball of reflected energy. Each scan after that showed vacant space.

It looks like she melted.

"Ops, look at this."

Allard played the recording at regular speed and then slow speed. Deland stared, open-mouthed.

"Play that again, please."

Allard ran it twice more.

"She didn't drive through an undiscovered warp," he said. "I remember when we tested sensors on ships passing through the warp gates, and the shimmer was visible for several seconds. Plus, the ships disappeared in an instant. I don't know what that was, but that wasn't *Comte de Grasse* going through a gate."

"Exactly. She didn't collide with anything or explode, either. We would have seen a debris field."

"It's like she…" Deland said.

"Melted."

"Yeah. Like she melted. But why?"

"An enemy weapon." Allard keyed her microphone. "Battle Watch Captain, set Alert Condition Alpha throughout the fleet. All ships prepare for hostile action. Designate the five unknowns as Hostiles One through Five."

Every head in the FOC turned to look at her, including the BWC.

"Alpha?" he asked.

"Do it!" Allard snapped. She looked at Deland. "Contact MAC-M and get Colonel Wisniewski on the line for me."

A muted klaxon sounded, and the FOC lights changed from white to red. All over *Giant*, and every other ship in the fleet, Allard knew personnel were running for their battle stations.

And maybe their lives.

* * *

Colonel Terrance "Toro" Wisniewski gave his operations officer an annoyed look as he handed the threat warning back to her. "What the hell am I supposed to do with this, launch the alert mechs?"

Major Kris Anchrum stifled a smile. In her five months as MAC-M Ground Operations Officer, she had learned that Toro didn't like it when the staff laughed at his hyperbole.

"It's an advisory, sir. It's probably nothing. It looks like the commodore is using it as an opportunity to exercise the fleet. Perhaps we should do something similar down here."

"What do you mean?"

"It's been a long time since we exercised the troops, Colonel. I haven't seen anything larger than a company-sized field maneuver since I've been here."

Toro nodded. "Me neither."

"So, let's shake things up with an unannounced security drill. 'Daarben space port invasion is imminent.' That sort of thing. Full mission profile—everybody plays. Infantry, mechs, aviation. We have an OPORD for it; let's see which of the battalion commanders have read it and know what their role is."

Toro thought for a moment. "It *has* been slow around here lately. What about exercise judges?"

"Who better to judge their performance than you, sir? I'll arrange with Air Ops to provide a hovercopter to transport you anywhere you want to go, and you can see firsthand how everyone performs."

Toro swiveled around to look at the holo of Maltaan hovering over the table next to his desk. All the troops, mechs, and hovercopters assigned to MAC-M appeared on it.

Major Anchrum could tell the colonel liked her idea, but he didn't seem one hundred percent convinced.

"The men are getting too comfortable in garrison, Colonel. The troops have been idle since we hunted down the last of the test tubes and stopped riding security on the train. Disciplinary incidents are increasing, and I believe it's because they're bored. Let's get them out in the field where they belong. I'll have my people activate the live fire areas so they can send some ordnance downrange and maybe conduct some combined arms exercises, too."

"Hmm."

"Sir—"

Toro cut her off with a raised finger. "Give me a second to think about this, Major. I like the idea, but we can't go off half-cocked or someone's going to get killed."

Anchrum suppressed her impatience as she waited for Toro to finish mulling over her idea. Finally, he nodded.

"Okay, let's do it. Forward the threat warning to the battalion commanders, but I want it made clear to everyone, from the commanders to the privates, that this is an exercise."

"Will do, sir."

* * *

Major Jan van der Cruyff, commander of the Second Mechanized Infantry Battalion (2MIB) stationed in Ulvaan, read the message from MAC-M twice before he handed it to his deputy, Major Moon Li.

"XO, this alert looks like we finally have something to do besides sit on our asses," he said. "The OPORD calls for us to head west for the space port in Daarben. I want the recon mech companies moving in ten minutes and the main battle mechs and the infantry moving ten minutes after that."

"Ten minutes? Sir, it's an exercise."

"I saw that. I also saw where MAC-M said we are under imminent threat of an invasion, and this exercise will be full mission profile. In other words, train like we fight. If this was a real threat warning, I'd tell you to have all the lads on the road in five minutes. Since it is an exercise, and I know most of them were up late last night getting drunk, I'm giving them an additional five minutes."

Van der Cruyff was an old-school Space Marine who had clawed his way up through the ranks from private to major. Along the way, he had earned a reputation as an ass kicker who didn't suffer fools lightly. The major held his officers and NCOs to a higher standard, and he wasn't shy about telling them when they failed to measure up. He was tough on his Space Marines because he loved them and knew that their sweat was cheaper than their blood, and they returned the affection two-fold.

Ten minutes later, van der Cruyff stood by the compound gate and nodded with satisfaction as his two companies of recon mechs rolled out. Several of the drivers and gunners scowled as they passed, but he smiled and waved them on. Sore heads and sour stomachs were a small price to pay for combat readiness, and he knew that when they sobered up in a few hours, they'd be happy to be in the field.

When the last recon mech was gone, the major went in search of Captain Sheila Madison, Second Mech Logistics Officer and Major Moon's not-so-secret love interest.

"Captain, make sure we load extra hydration packs," he said when he found her. Captain Madison looked like she'd been up most of the night drinking with the battalion—which she had—and her gaze was unsteady.

"Hydration, sir?"

"Yeah. Hydration packs. There are a lot of hungover Space Marines headed into battle, and we can't afford heat casualties. I want them to be well hydrated, and supplying water is your job, remember?"

"Oh, uh, yes sir," the captain said. "I'll make sure we have plenty of water."

"Great, thanks. And don't forget rations, either."

Van der Cruyff returned to the gate and checked the time. Nineteen minutes and four seconds after he gave Moon the order to deploy, the first main battle mechs rumbled through the gate, followed by the armored personnel carriers (APCs) full of infantry. He didn't envy the Space Marines in the APCs. The vehicles were stifling when fully loaded, and all it would take was one Marine getting sick to make it unbearable.

The battalion command mech was the last vehicle in line. Van der Cruyff clambered aboard and squeezed through the hatch. He slipped into his seat and put on his headset.

"Here we go, Two-Mech-Eye!" he announced on the battalion-wide circuit, using the nickname they all despised for the Second Mechanized Infantry Battalion. He heard desultory groans and curses in return, which made him smile. He looked over at Sergeant Major Fessler, his command sergeant major, in the seat next to him.

"They sound like a bunch of fire-breathers today, Top."

Fessler returned the look with bleary, bloodshot eyes. "Yes sir. Fire breathers."

Van der Cruyff chuckled and keyed his mic. "DINLI!"

* * *

"*'m sorry, sir. The colonel isn't available to take any calls right now,"* the MAC-M communications watch officer told Deland.

Deland struggled to control his temper. "Did you hear what I said? This is Commander Deland, calling on behalf of Commodore Allard. We are under attack, and the commodore has an urgent message for Colonel Wisniewski."

"Commander, I heard you the first two times you said that, but the colonel is in the field observing our exercise. He's not available for exercise inputs. If you tell me what it is, I'll be sure to pass it on the next time I talk to the colonel."

"This isn't a goddamned exercise!" Deland shouted. "We are under actual attack! Do you understand that?"

"Sir, I—wait a second. This isn't an exercise?"

"No, you fucking moron. This is real. We've already lost one ship, and we are preparing to engage the enemy. Put me through to the colonel. Now!"

"Stand by, sir. I'll see what I can do."

Allard heard Deland shouting over the circuit and gave him an inquiring look. He threw up his hands and scowled.

"MAC-M decided to use our warning to run their own exercise, but nobody thought it would be a good idea to stay in contact with Colonel Wisniewski. The colonel is in the field observing their exercise."

"Are they getting him?"

Deland scoffed in frustration. "I think so, but I'm not a hundred percent sure. They didn't set up an exercise comms plan, so we don't have direct contact with him. I think he'll have to initiate contact with us via satellite link from his end."

"Give that to someone else to worry about. We need to focus on the approaching threat."

When Commodore Allard ordered Alert Condition Alpha, the spacecraft in the fleet had deployed from their peacetime orbit assignments to pre-planned wartime positions to maximize their tactical advantages. The destroyers *Marquis de Lafayette* and *Marquis de Choisy,* sister ships of *Comte de Grasse*, had taken up flank positions to the right and left of the threat bearing, while the smaller frigates *Tireless* and *Relentless* hovered close to *Giant*. The unexpected loss of *Comte de Grasse* and the departure of the Maltaani fleet had revealed the stark reality of their situation.

The five-ship formation was a far cry from the enormous fleet that had crowded the space around Maltaan during the invasion. *Giant*, although she was equipped with long-range rail guns and other weapons, was a flagship built to provide orbit-to-surface logistic support to Space Marine operations. Even though she carried rail guns, her shields and armor were not designed to fight fleet engagements. The destroyers were capable vessels for their size, but *Comte de Grasse* showed they were vulnerable to the unknown weapons they faced. The frigates might have been the workhorses of the fleet, but they were jokingly referred to as "missile sumps" by those familiar with their tactical limitations.

"Tell the frigates to launch reconnaissance drones to investigate the hostiles," Allard ordered. "Two each, but don't send them on intercept courses. I want the drones to pass close enough to get a look at what we're facing without looking like a threat."

"Yes ma'am," Deland said.

They watched as reconnaissance drone symbols detached from *Tireless* and *Relentless* and sped off toward the hostile contacts, which continued to close the fleet.

"Ops, I want you to send a report to Fleet Command detailing everything that has occurred thus far, including our current tactical dispositions. Start with the report from the asteroid miner and include the recording of *Comte de Grasse*. Ensure you include the slow-speed playback. Request that they send additional assets, too. Even though they're too far away to provide immediate support, it won't hurt to see what they think about all this."

When Deland was gone, Allard stared at the strategic display and willed time to slow down.

* * *

"Colonel, Daarben Flight Control just reported you've got a high priority call from Commodore Allard on the flagship," the hovercopter pilot told Toro. "I can't configure satellite comms in flight, so they requested we set down at the space port."

Toro frowned at Anchrum, who shrugged.

"Okay. Set us down at the space port, but be ready to launch when I'm done," the colonel said. "Do you have time to configure a satcom link on the tarmac while I'm on the horn with the commodore?"

"Yes sir. It only takes a minute, but we have to reset the system to do it. That shuts down flight controls, which is why we can't do it in flight."

"Major Anchrum, while I'm on this call, make sure battalion commanders and above know how to reach me aboard this thing," Toro told her. "We should have thought of this before we took off."

Anchrum winced at the reproach.

A few minutes later, the pilot landed the hovercopter, and a command mech raced out to meet Colonel Wisniewski. He climbed aboard and slid behind one of the consoles while he donned a headset.

"The flagship is standing by on Channel Seven," a crewman advised.

"*Giant*, this is MAC-M Actual, calling for Commodore Allard," Toro said into his mic.

After a brief pause, Allard answered.

"Toro, it's Eloise. We've got a situation you need to know about."

"I heard. We saw your threat warning and decided to use it to start our own security exercise. How's it going up there?"

"It's not an exercise anymore, Toro." Allard recounted everything that had occurred.

Wisniewski gave a low whistle. "You lost *Comte de Grasse*? She's destroyed?"

"It looks that way, yes. We analyzed the playback and she disappeared in three scans, with no debris."

"And these five contacts are responsible?"

"I don't know that for certain, but if not, it's one hell of a coincidence. I've put the Fleet in Alert Condition Alpha and launched reconnaissance probes to get a look at these contacts. I don't know what's going to happen, but I wanted to make sure you knew that we are facing a real-life crisis up here, and you should act accordingly."

"Okay, Eloise, I appreciate the head's up. Good luck, and good hunting. I have this channel in my hovercopter now, so there won't be any more delays. Let me know what we can do to help."

"Thanks, Toro. Giant, out."

When the colonel got back to the hovercopter, he saw ground crew rolling up a refueling hose. Anchrum met him at the door.

"Everything okay, sir?"

"Yeah. This exercise isn't an exercise anymore. Commodore Allard has unknowns inbound." He climbed aboard and slipped on his headset. He twirled a finger in the air. "Let's go."

"We've got the satcom circuit up," Anchrum told him as the hovercopter climbed into the sky.

"Where to, Colonel?" the pilot asked when they were airborne. "We've got a full bag of gas and clear weather in all directions."

"Let's head east to Ulvaan. We'll see how the mechs are making out."

* * * * *

Chapter Five

"Commodore, one of *Lafayette's* recon probes has sent back imagery of the hostiles," the BWC reported. "Screen Three."

The images were small and indistinct because of the extreme range. The display system operator zoomed in and processed the images for maximum resolution, and Allard and the watch got their first glimpse of the approaching ships.

"Not much to look at," Deland said. "Big, though."

As the probe neared the closest point of approach on its roundabout flight path, the image sharpened, and Allard could make out the boxy shape and configuration of the engines. There were no external weapons or markings.

"An initial scan shows the lead ship is twelve hundred meters long and six hundred meters high," the BWC said.

"Wow. That's big. Really big. Bigger than *Giant*," Deland said unnecessarily. "No question these are the ships the miners reported."

Allard frowned. The commander had a bad habit of talking too much when he was under pressure. She made a mental note to mention it to him later, in private.

If we survive.

"Their size indicates a high level of technological skill on the part of the builders." Deland kept talking to no one in particular. "They built those ships in zero-G, because the thrust required to get something that large into orbit would be enormous."

Allard threw a dirty look at him that shouted *Shut up!* and Deland blushed.

"The probes have passed their closest points of approach, and *Lafayette* and *Choisy* have requested further instructions," the battle watch captain said.

Allard thought for a second. "Bring the probes around to parallel the hostiles and report when they are in position."

"Aye aye, ma'am."

"I should have thought about that sooner," she said to herself.

"Thought about what?" Deland asked.

"Turning the probes around. At that speed, they'll be hard-pressed to complete the maneuver before the hostiles reach our rail gun range."

"The probes are unarmed, ma'am."

"I know that, thank you," she snapped. "They don't know that. I don't intend to attack with the drones, but there's a tactical advantage to having eyes on them. At least a distraction."

Chastened, Deland said nothing.

"Commander, follow up our initial report to Fleet Command with the probe imagery. Perhaps they know something we don't about who these contacts are and what their intentions might be. Battle Watch, how long until we're in rail gun range?"

"Just under two hours, ma'am," the BWC said. Allard turned to Deland.

"Hurry."

* * *

Major van der Cruyff called a rest stop, and Second Mech ground to a halt. Space Marines stumbled from their mechs and APCs and flaked out on the ground, while others leaned over and retched.

"What the fuck's going on?" van der Cruyff demanded over the command circuit. "Where's our perimeter? Why are there Space Marines wandering around like a bunch of love-sick monkeys?"

Officers and NCOs pushed and prodded their troops to form a defensive perimeter, while they set others to cleaning out the mechs and APCs where Space Marines had deposited the remnants of their hangovers.

"Top, pass the word that if I see that bullshit again, every company officer and NCO will walk the rest of the way to Daarben."

"Yes sir."

The major dismounted his command mech and walked the length of the convoy, pausing to trade a few words or pat the backs of the Space Marines. He found Major Moon and Captain Madison deep in conversation behind one of the supply trucks.

"XO, What's our status?"

Moon and Madison jumped at the sound of his voice, like little kids caught in the midst of misbehaving.

"I was just, uh, talking with the captain…" Moon said, but his voice trailed away.

"I hope you were talking about hydration, because there are a lot of thirsty Space Marines out there," van der Cruyff said. "Captain Madison, get your people organized and let's get some of those hydration packs issued. Two per Space Marine should be enough."

Madison turned bright red. "Yes sir. Two per man." She hurried away and van der Cruyff heard her shouting for the assistant logistics officer.

Van der Cruyff looked at Moon. "Major, I understand there is no stopping natural urges that occur between consenting adults. I was willing to turn a blind eye in garrison because you were discreet, and it didn't seem to affect your performance.

"It's a far different story here in the field. This might only be an exercise, but that means we must be extra vigilant when it comes to the troops. They're looking to us for leadership, and there are eyes on you all the time, even when you can't see them. When they see the executive officer cavorting with the logistics officer, they might be tempted to take a more casual approach to their own duties."

"Yes sir."

"Now, go do your fucking job, and if we have this conversation again, you'll jog behind the column with your pulse rifle over your head until you die or we get to Daarben, whichever happens first. Got it?"

When van der Cruyff emerged from behind the supply truck, nearby Space Marines turned away and became interested in anything besides the conversation they had eavesdropped on. The major smiled inwardly.

Good.

Van der Cruyff knew he had fucked up when he first turned a blind eye to the relationship between the two officers. ISMC regulations prohibited Space Marines in the same chain of command from engaging in personal relationships, but it had seemed harmless. Lately, it had begun to interfere with their duties. Worst of all, the other Space Marines had begun to take notice.

A hovercopter zoomed by overhead.

"Major!" Captain Funk, the battalion operations officer, trotted up. "Major, MAC-M is on that bird. They're putting down on the road ahead of the column, and Toro wants to talk to you."

Shit.

Van der Cruyff raced to the front of the column just in time to see the hovercopter touch down and Colonel Wisniewski climb out, accompanied by one of his staffers. The colonel waved at the officer to wait and moved away from the noisy bird. The major approached and saluted.

"Major van der Cruyff, reporting as ordered, sir."

Toro returned the salute. "This your battalion, son?"

"Yes sir. Second Mech."

The major got a knot in his stomach. Van der Cruyff was a hard ass, but the colonel wasn't nicknamed "Toro" for nothing. Van der Cruyff hadn't personally witnessed one of his outbursts, but he'd heard enough stories to know he didn't want to.

The colonel put a hand on van der Cruyff's shoulder, and the pair walked away from the hovercopter. The perimeter of Space Marines that had formed around the hovercopter moved with them but stayed out of earshot.

"Where were you when you got the order to move, Major?"

Van der Cruyff winced at the question.

Did we miss an order? Should we have been in the field?

"In garrison, sir. In Ulvaan."

Toro nodded. "Well, Second Mech should be proud of themselves. I've been flying around checking up on things, and so far, you are the only sonsofbitches doing what you're supposed to be doing."

The major felt pride swell in his chest. "Second Mech is always ready to fight, sir."

Just then, one of the Space Marines in the perimeter guard leaned over and vomited, which caused one of his comrades to vomit as well.

"I can see that," Toro said.

Van der Cruyff chuckled. "We had a birthday bash last night, sir, and some of the lads got carried away. But don't worry, Colonel. They fight better hung over than most Space Marines do clean and sober."

"Let's hope we don't have to find out."

"DINLI, sir."

The two officers began to walk back to the hovercopter.

"Major, instead of going all the way to the space port, I want you and your battalion to stop and hole up before you come out of the mountains."

"Sir?"

"Yeah. Scout ahead, find a suitable spot, and take cover. Twenty klicks before you hit the tree line ought to do it. There's something happening with the Fleet up there." Toro pointed in the air. "This fucking thing has changed from an exercise to an attack on the fleet, and I want to hold some troops in reserve until we figure out what's going on. Since you're head and shoulders above the other battalions, you're it. Make sure you give us a call and let us know where you're at when you get settled in."

"Roger that, sir."

"Keep up the good work, Major."

Toro climbed aboard the hovercopter and van der Cruyff stepped back and ducked away as the engines wound up, and the craft shot into the sky.

"What was that all about, sir?" Major Moon asked when the major rejoined the company.

"Change of plans, XO. Let's get the lads mounted up and moving. We're going camping."

* * *

As the seconds ticked away, it became clear to Allard that the recon probes would intercept the hostiles before they entered *Giant's* rail gun range. Instead of forcing the drones to make sharp turns which would have necessitated the craft slowing down and then racing to catch up, the drone operators guided them through wide turns. The wide turns covered more distance and positioned the drones on opposite sides of the hostiles, but the maneuver enabled the drones to maintain speed and overtake them faster.

Allard's statement to Deland about not attacking the hostiles was deceptive. In her mind, the destruction of *Comte de Grasse* was all she needed to justify an attack on the unknowns. When she designated them hostile, that was all the fleet needed to engage. Her plan had been to use the drones as a distraction while she engaged the hostiles. Deland had correctly pointed out that the drones were unarmed, but the enemy didn't know that. It was a long shot, but she didn't have many other options. Waiting to attack—

Why wait?

"BWC, order *Giant* to make best speed to intercept the hostiles," she ordered. Deland looked up from his console in surprise. "Tell all ships in company to conform to our movements and stand by to engage when they are in range."

"We're attacking?" Deland asked.

"We're seizing the initiative," Allard said. "We've been sitting here wondering what they're up to. I think it's time we let them worry about what we're going to do."

"But you'll attack?"

"Affirmative. I believe the destruction of *Comte de Grasse* was a deliberate hostile act, and if the hostiles don't alter course away from the fleet and Maltaan, I intend to respond."

Allard spoke in a clear, measured tone to ensure everyone listening knew she had made her decision after careful deliberation.

"All ships have acknowledged your orders, Commodore," the BWC reported.

"Very well. Bring up shields and place the rail guns in ready standby," Allard said.

The two fleets raced toward each other. The recon drones looked like sheepdogs herding a flock as they closed in from both sides. *Bringing sheep to a wolf,* Allard thought. The rail gun range ring touched the first hostile contact.

"Hostile One is in rail gun range," the BWC announced.

"Kill Hostile One with rail guns," Allard ordered.

Two bright weapon symbols appeared on the display and raced toward the hostile fleet.

"Slow to one-third and turn right ninety degrees," Allard ordered.

"Surveillance drones have visual contact," the BWC reported. One of the bulkhead-mounted screens flickered. Allard saw five white specks in the distance. Suddenly, the plasma projectiles from the rail guns appeared in the frame and intercepted Hostile One. There was a brilliant flash, and the screen went blank.

Cheers erupted as Hostile One disappeared from the strategic display, and the other four split off and turned away.

"Hostile One has been destroyed," the BWC shouted over the noise. "We lost contact on the surveillance drones."

"Silence!" Allard bellowed. The FOC fell silent. "Battle Watch Captain, report."

"Hostile One has been destroyed, ma'am. We lost contact with the surveillance drones."

"Very well. What is the status of our shields?"

"One hundred percent."

"And the rail guns?"

"Recharge complete, standing by to engage."

Allard looked at the strategic display. The remaining unknowns had split into two flights of two and headed off in opposite directions at high speed.

"Order *Tireless* and *Relentless* to maintain contact on the hostiles for one hour," Allard said. "Tell them to remain within sensor range of *Giant.*"

Allard watched as the frigates followed the enemy to the edge of the strategic display.

"Ma'am, *Relentless* reported the two hostiles have begun to orbit just beyond our sensor range," the BWC announced. Before she could respond, he continued, "*Tireless* reported the same."

"They still have contact?"

"Yes ma'am."

"Do you think they're baiting the frigates to follow?" Deland asked, putting a voice to Allard's thoughts.

"It could be. They may have figured out our maximum effective sensor range," she said. "BWC, instruct *Tireless* and *Relentless* to withdraw this way at slow speed but maintain sensor contact on the enemy. Let's see what their next move is."

* * * * *

Chapter Six

A red three.

Chief Warrant Officer Red Brumley looked at his hole cards and then at the pile of Maltaani currency in the middle of the table. His hand had started with such promise, and he had bet aggressively to capture the small pile of antes in the pot. Red wasn't bluffing; he didn't have a made hand yet, but his odds were improving as the cards continued to peel off the deck. The other players must have sensed it, because they folded as the action went around the table and the bets increased.

All but Haarkad.

Finally, the last card fell, and Red forced himself to remain still. A red three did nothing to improve his hand, which meant he was now bluffing with a whole lot of nothing.

Haarkad had pushed in piles of bills to match Red's bets every round, even as the pilot tested him by ratcheting up the size of the wager. Now, the question was, what did Haarkad have, and how much would Red have to bet to scare him away from the pot?

Playing poker against the Maltaani could be frustrating. They didn't have the same facial tics as their human cousins, and it was impossible to read their eyes because they didn't have any sclera. Haarkad played like an automaton, and he was impossible to read, too. Red might as well have been playing Solitaire.

When the Space Marines had first taught the Maltaani how to play poker, the Maltaani had been easy pickings. Gambling didn't come naturally to them; they were slow to understand how the changing odds increased or decreased the value of an outcome. There was no official exchange rate between Terran and Maltaani currency, and there wasn't anything to spend Maltaani currency on, but there was no substitute for the feeling of satisfaction of stuffing a wad of bills— even worthless bills—into one's pocket after a night of cards.

With his mind made up, Red opened his mouth just as the hangar door slammed open, and a ground crewman stuck her head in.

"Hovercopter on final for refuel. MAC-M is onboard!" she called.

"Crap!" Red dropped his cards and scrambled to his feet. "Sorry guys, I gotta go. I'm the duty air boss today."

The players and spectators clustered around the table groaned as Red trotted for the door. He barely got his flight suit zipped and his sunglasses on before he stepped outside and saw Colonel Wisniewski striding toward him with a couple other officers in tow.

"Welcome to Romeo-Nine, sir," Red said as he came to attention and threw up his best salute.

Wisniewski looked him up and down with a scowl on his face before he returned the salute. "Who's in charge here, Warrant?"

"I'm the duty air boss, sir."

"Not the duty guy. Who's in command here, son?"

"I have the duty as air boss today."

"You told me that already. Where's your commanding officer?"

At that moment, Red understood why Wisniewski was nicknamed "Toro." Red was unflappable as a pilot, and as a warrant officer he didn't worry too much about the games regular officers played. Still, something about Toro's demeanor gave him a nervous twinge deep in his gut.

"Sir, we don't have a CO here. We get our tasking from Daarben Flight Control, so I guess the major there would be our CO."

Toro shot an annoyed look at the female major who stood behind him, and she shrugged.

"I don't know how air ops runs their operation," she said by way of apology.

Toro turned his attention back to Red.

"So, you don't know what the fuck's been going on?"

Red shook his head. "We haven't heard anything, Colonel. What's going on?"

Toro pointed a finger at the sky. "Fleet might be getting into a shooting match with some unknowns. You know there's a security exercise in progress, right? That includes you."

"We haven't received anything about a security exercise, either. I'll call Daarben and verify."

The major cut in. "You don't need to verify it, Warrant. The colonel just told you there's an exercise in progress. He set Alert Condition Alpha. What you *need* to do is get where you're supposed to be in accordance with the OPORD. You're familiar with the OPORD?"

"I've read it, ma'am."

"And where are you supposed to deploy?"

Red gestured at the tarmac around him. "Romeo-Nine." He pointed to the three hovercopters chocked and chained near the hangars. "My bird, plus another attack hovercopter and a logistics bird, sir."

"Colonel, we're fueled up," the colonel's pilot called.

Toro had watched the exchange between Red and the major in silence. He looked at Red and nodded. "At least you're where you're supposed to be, even if you don't know why. Keep up the good work, Warrant. And get in touch with Daarben to ask them what the hell is going on. Tell them the colonel wants to know."

Red smiled as he saluted Toro. "Will do, sir."

The warrant watched as Toro's hovercopter climbed into the Maltaan sky and headed east.

"What was that all about?" asked Warrant Officer Johnson, Red's copilot, as he and several other flight crewmen sidled up behind Red.

"I have no idea." Red started for the tiny admin building. "I gotta call Daarben. Get Fender 454 and one of the other birds spotted for launch and start preflight checks. There's a security exercise in progress, so I want two birds at Alert 10."

A lieutenant named Eldryk answered Red's call.

"Yeah, Warrant, Toro stopped here, too, but he didn't tell us much. The support fleet is investigating some unknowns, I guess. MAC-M is running a security exercise, too."

"What do you want us to do? Do you have any orders?"

"Uh, no. No orders. You're at Romeo-Nine, right?"

"Affirmative. Fender 454, Blackjack 293, and a log bird."

"Okay, well, stay there and stand by for tasking, and we'll get back to you."

"Roger that."

The call ended and Red pinched the bridge of his nose between his thumb and forefinger and squeezed his eyes shut.

"You okay, Warrant?" the communications watch asked.

"Yeah, I'm fine. If you hear anything from MAC-M or Daarben Flight Control, let me know."

"What's the word?" Johnson asked when Red returned to the flight line.

"Beats me," Red said with a chuckle. "Daarben said there's some kind of security exercise going on, and we're to stand by here for tasking."

"Stand by to stand by, aye," Johnson said, and the pilots laughed. Both men were veterans of seemingly endless hours of flight alerts, and the phrase was the pilots' version of the infantry's "Hurry up and wait."

* * *

"R*elentless* is under attack!"

Allard saw four hostile missile symbols streak at the frigate as the vessel turned and sped back toward *Giant*. The first two missiles disappeared, but the second two intercepted her. *Relentless* didn't disappear, but her speed dropped to almost zero, and she veered off course, away from *Giant*.

"Send *de Choisy* to assist," Allard commanded. "Order *Tireless* to fall back before she is targeted."

"Too late, ma'am," the BWC announced. On the screen, four more hostile missiles headed for *Tireless*. When she saw what had happened to her sister ship, *Tireless* had turned away from Hostiles Four and Five. The maneuver had given her enough time to engage all four incoming missiles, and they disappeared from the strategic display.

"*Relentless* reports loss of propulsion," the BWC said. "Weapons are operational, shields at fifty-seven percent."

"Very well." Allard willed *de Choisy* to speed up as she closed the range to the stricken ship. Hostiles Two and Three disappeared from the strategic display.

"What happened to the enemy ships that fired on *Relentless*?" Allard demanded.

"They dropped out of the system when she was hit," Deland said. "She must have lost sensors."

Hostiles Two and Three reappeared as *de Choisy* approached, and her sensors picked them up. They were almost abreast of *Relentless*.

"Lost communications with *Relentless*," the BWC reported. "She said she was taking fire and then comms cut out."

"What are they doing?" Deland asked. "Do they mean to board her?"

"Order *de Choisy* to engage as soon as the hostiles are in range," Allard ordered. She looked for *Tireless* and saw that the other frigate was inside *Giant's* rail gun range. The two craft on her side of the formation had followed but hadn't reengaged. "Battle Watch, order *de Lafayette* to join *de Choisy* and kill the hostiles near *Relentless*. Turn *Giant* toward Hostiles Four and Five, and let's take them ourselves."

With a rough battle plan sorted out, Allard sat back to watch the fleet execute her orders. She winced when *Relentless* vanished from the display. *De Choisy* was still a few minutes from weapons range, with *de Lafayette* close behind. *Tireless* continued to close on *Giant*, with her pursuers still outside rail gun range.

Deland leaned close to her. "Commodore, we're not a dreadnought," he said. "We don't have the weapons or shields for fleet action like this."

"What choice do we have? The enemy is vulnerable to our rail guns, so we have to close the range. The sooner we do that, the sooner we can assist the destroyers."

"I'm just saying that it might be safer if we withdraw and let the ships that are built to fight do the fighting."

Allard stared at Deland for a long moment. "Commander, you are perilously close to displaying cowardice in the face of the enemy. Our fleet is under attack, and we're going to respond to that attack as best we can. That doesn't include withdrawing." She stopped short before her anger got the best of her. "Send an update to Fleet Command. Tell them we have engaged the enemy."

"*Marquis de Choisy* has fired," the BWC called out.

A full salvo of six missiles raced at Hostiles Two and Three, but they disappeared mid-flight.

"*De Choisy* reports some kind of energy weapon is draining her shields, she is at twenty percent and falling. She's turning to open the range."

A few seconds later, *de Choisy* vanished.

"Damn it! Pull *de Lafayette* back!" Allard ordered. "How long until we're in range of Four and Five?"

"Four minutes."

Two reconnaissance drone symbols launched from *Tireless* and headed for her pursuers.

"What are they doing?" Deland asked.

"Distraction, sir," the BWC said. "She's trying to buy some time."

Allard realized this was the first real fleet action the UNT had ever been in. There had been a few single-ship engagements with the Maltaani before the invasion, but they were mostly long-range and inconsequential. Thus far, the only weapons that had had any success against the enemy were *Giant's* rail guns, and their shields were ineffective against the energy weapons. Win or lose, Fleet Command needed that information.

"Commander Deland, make certain you inform Fleet Command that the hostiles appear to possess an energy weapon which can defeat our shields, and the only weapons we have that are effective against their ships are our rail guns."

"Yes ma'am."

"Battle Watch, turn *Giant* toward *de Lafayette* and direct *Relentless* to conform to our movement. I want to engage Hostiles Four and Five at maximum range and then close on Two and Three. Make certain Engineering knows we must have full power available for weapons and propulsion."

The closure rate between the flagship and Hostiles Four and Five slowed as the ship turned away. The enemy ships brushed away the drones from *Tireless* and continued to creep closer to *Giant's* rail gun range ring.

"BWC, what is the rail gun probability of kill for a target outside the maximum effective range?" Allard asked.

"Fifty percent for the first twenty kilometers, then it drops to zero at thirty kilometers," BWC said. "The projectile's plasma dissipates quickly."

"Thank you."

"Commodore, we received a response to our first report to Fleet Command," Deland said. "'Investigate and report.'"

Allard laughed at the inadequacy of their response and the desperation of her situation.

I hope they learn something from our sacrifice.

"All hostile contacts have increased speed! *De Lafayette* is under attack!"

On the strategic display, the destroyer had stopped, and the two hostiles were closing in on her. Then she disappeared.

"Turn back toward *Tireless*," Allard ordered. "Go to full speed and stand by to engage with rail guns."

The instant Hostiles Four and Five crossed the rail gun range ring, Allard ordered a full salvo, followed immediately by a hard turn toward

Two and Three. As soon as *Giant* fired, the targeted vessels split and raced out of range. Four and Five made a similar maneuver, and the four enemy ships encircled *Giant* and hovered just outside rail gun range.

"It looks like they figured out our rail gun range, ma'am," Deland said. "Now what?"

"Hostile Three is closing at a high rate of speed!" the BWC announced.

"Kill Hostile Three with rail guns," Allard ordered.

As soon as the flagship fired, Three made a hard turn and raced away, while Four and Five charged *Giant* from the other side of the formation. Eight missiles appeared on the strategic display and hurtled inbound.

"Shields at one hundred percent, point defense weapons in auto," the BWC said.

"Kill Four and Five with rail guns."

"Four seconds to rail gun recharge," the BWC advised.

As soon as the weapon system finished charging, plasma projectiles launched toward the enemy ships, which had already begun to turn away.

They're much bigger than we are, but they're also nimbler.

As *Giant* maneuvered to unmask as many defensive batteries as possible against the incoming missiles, it became apparent that she was not the intended target. *Tireless* twisted and turned, but the weapons continued to home in on her. The flagship was too far away to offer mutual defensive support, and Allard watched helplessly as the frigate engaged three of the missiles before the other five hit her.

"My God," Deland gasped as the frigate disappeared.

"Battle Watch, make best speed for the Maduro Jump Gate," Allard ordered. She turned to Deland. "Notify MAC-M and Fleet Command of the fleet status and inform them we are retiring."

"We're heading home?" Deland asked.

Allard shook her head. "Negative. We can't take the chance of leading them to Terra Earth, but I don't want to sit here and wait for them to attack."

The enemy craft maintained their relative positions around *Giant* as they raced toward the jump gate. Allard glanced at the clock, and it shocked her to see the engagement had only been ongoing for three hours.

It feels like forever.

Their situation reminded her of a wildlife documentary she had seen many years earlier. A pack of dogs had cornered a bear and surrounded it. The dogs had taken turns rushing in and snapping at the bear. The more powerful beast had been too slow to swat its tormenters. A few of the dogs were killed or injured, but they had worn out the much larger bear with a series of nipping attacks that sapped its strength and left it panting with exhaustion. At that point, as if by invisible signal, the dogs attacked from every direction, and the bear had gone down without a fight.

"Hostile Two has turned inbound," the BWC reported.

Two, which had taken a position ahead of *Giant*, had indeed turned back toward the flagship, and the rail gun range ring crept tantalizingly close.

"Do you want me to engage?" the BWC asked.

"No," Allard said. "Turn hard and head back to Maltaan. Let's see if we can brush some of them off by maneuvering around the planet."

The hostiles didn't anticipate the turn and scattered as *Giant* came about, but when she steadied up on her new course, they resumed their relative positions around her. They were quick to react, and Allard knew they would be difficult to engage. Perhaps she could use Maltaan as sort of an anvil to her hammer and trap one or more within range.

"Have we heard anything more from Fleet Command?" Allard asked Deland.

"No ma'am, there's been nothing in the message queue since they ordered us to investigate," he said.

"Send your last update to my console. I want to add some commodore's perspective and resend it. Has MAC-M acknowledged our update?"

"They acknowledged receipt but didn't respond."

"Hmm. Well, there's nothing they can do to help us out anyway." A sudden thought came to her. "Where's the *Sao Paolo*?"

"The *Sao Paolo*? Uh, she had a generator fire, remember?" Deland asked.

"Yes, I remember. That's not what I asked. She's not on the strategic display. Where is she?"

Deland entered a series of commands and read from his monitor. "She dropped out of the link to conserve power, but her last position was in orbit around Maltaan effecting repairs. ETA eight hours, and that was two hours ago."

"Do we have comms with her?"

"Let me verify that, ma'am." A minute later, Deland replied, "Yes ma'am, we have comms. They've restored power to some parts of the ship, but their estimated time of repair remains the same."

"Very well."

Allard stared at the strategic display while the update for Fleet Command sat open on her console screen, forgotten. An idea began to form in her mind.

The destroyer *Sao Paolo* was a generation older than *de Choisy* and her sister ships. She should have been decommissioned ten years ago, but the South American delegation to the UNT protested that she was the only Fleet vessel that bore the name of any place or person in their hemisphere. Her weapons and propulsion were obsolete by modern standards, but politics was king, and the Fleet kept her on the active roll. Now, she might represent their last, best hope to prevail against the hostiles.

"Commander, ask *Sao Paolo* if she has control over her weapons systems," Allard told Deland. "And their tactical data system."

"Aye aye, ma'am."

After a brief conversation on the net, Deland reported.

"*Sao Paolo* has local control of her missiles, and her tactical data system is operational. She can't generate enough power for shields or point defense at this time."

"Hmm. Very well."

Sao Paolo's missiles were of an antiquated fire-and-forget design. The firing platform programmed an aimpoint and an activation time for the terminal seeker. The weapon required no additional input after it launched, but the firing platform had no control, either. Modern systems included inflight guidance and self-destruction options.

"Commander Deland, have *Sao Paolo* report her position and orbit in the data link. I think we can use her to even the odds a little."

A few seconds later, *Sao Paolo's* symbol appeared close to Maltaan, along with her orbital track. After a quick analysis, Allard chuckled.

"Battle Watch Captain, adjust our speed so *Giant* passes Maltaan while *Sao Paolo* is on the back side of the planet," she ordered. "It's time we give the enemy a surprise."

* * * * *

Chapter Seven

Aboard *Fortuna*, Ogre sat in her control room seat and read through the data file Shade had left for her to read. In addition to being a magician with *Fortuna's* aging engineering plant, Shade was one of those weird genius types that knew a lot about a few things and little about everything else. He would get interested in something, learn as much as he could find about it, then move on to the next topic that got his attention. His career as a university student had ended when they tried to require him to declare a major field of study, and he became the engineer aboard *Fortuna* instead.

Shade's latest interest was orbital dynamics, specifically, the asteroid belt *Fortuna* was currently investigating, and he insisted Ogre review the results of his research.

Ogre skimmed the first page, a freshman-level introduction to asteroid belts, their formation, and orbit. The interesting stuff started halfway down the second page. Based on some rough calculations, Shade had determined the orbital period of the asteroid belt they were prospecting was about eighty years. This was crucial information to have in case DeeDee and his guys struck it big because then they would have a way to return to the same spot on the asteroid belt without using navigation aids that could tip off potential competitors.

The information on the third page stunned Ogre. According to Shade, the unmapped warp gate was located *inside* the asteroid belt, not on the edge as she had assumed. A gap in the outer edge of the belt had uncovered the warp, but the rotation of the belt would soon cover it back up. Shade included a short video file which illustrated his findings.

A blue circle indicated the position of the warp, and black Xs showed the approximate positions of the asteroids within *Fortuna's* sensor range. *Fortuna* appeared as a cartoonish rocket ship hovering near the gate. When Ogre hit "play," the asteroids began to orbit at 5X speed. The gap in the belt rotated past the warp which was soon covered by asteroids, and it remained covered as far as Shade could project asteroid belt movement.

On the final page, Shade had included a list of his findings.

1. The unmapped warp was located inside the orbiting asteroid belt.

2. A gap in the asteroid belt would uncover the warp for approximately thirty days.

3. When the gap orbited past, the gap would close, and asteroids would again foul the jump gate. He predicted this would occur within the next fourteen days.

4. Once the gap in the belt orbited past the warp, the warp would be impassable for about eighty years unless there was another as yet undetected gap in the belt further out.

Ogre reread the report from the beginning and watched the video file twice more. It was an impressive bit of analysis, doubly so because of *Fortuna's* rudimentary sensors and Shade's lack of formal education or training in orbital dynamics.

She attached the report to a message for the GRC. They would certainly be interested in the orbital period of the belt and the location of the unmapped warp gate. A warp gate this close to a resource-rich asteroid belt would be priceless if it were made safe for jumping. Ogre couldn't remember the last time someone had discovered a new warp, but she knew it took a long time and a great deal of study before the UNT would post a jump gate beacon and declare it safe for travel. Until then, the GRC could use it exclusively.

As an afterthought, Ogre added UNT Fleet Command as an addressee. They had a stake in this discovery, considering the alien craft that had jumped through the warp. She didn't know who the aliens were or where they were going, but she knew Fleet would be interested. If those unknowns were planning on going back the way they came, it had to be soon.

* * *

Allard watched the seconds tick off the clock and shook her head at the irony of wishing time would speed up after having so recently wished it would slow down. Time crawled by as *Giant* approached Maltaan and their last-ditch ambush, followed at a respectful distance by their enemies.

Her plan was simple. *Giant* would lead the hostiles past Maltaan as close as she dared while *Sao Paolo* orbited on the far side of the planet. When the flagship emerged on the other side, she would make a hard turn and engage whichever of the hostiles were within rail gun range. At the same time, *Sao Paolo* would emerge from the sensor shadow created by the planet and fire every weapon she had at *Giant's* pursuers. With luck, Allard figured they could destroy at least two and possibly three of their attackers and repel the fourth.

With luck.

Thus far, Allard hadn't had much luck during the engagement. The destruction of Hostile One could have been considered good luck, but the opportunity cost of destroying that lone ship might prove fatal to the rest. By engaging when she did, Allard had revealed her maximum rail gun range. It would have been much better to hold fire until she had multiple targets within range. The hostiles appeared to have determined the range and remained outside of it for the rest of the action. They also seemed to have recognized that *Giant* was the only human ship armed with rail guns, because they maneuvered to pick off the other ships in Allard's fleet without fear of counterfire.

As *Giant* approached Maltaan, Allard feinted at her pursuers whenever they got within rail gun range, but the flagship held fire. The commodore had been clear: no engagements until they were past Maltaan, ready to spring their trap. With several minutes remaining before they passed the planet, Allard turned her attention to the updated SITREP still open on her console.

She read through Deland's summary of the action so far. It was a recitation of events as they had occurred, but she wanted to include more than a barebones timeline. Doing so would give Fleet Command context for the engagement and allow them to apply lessons learned.

And stop them from second-guessing my decisions.

She began to type.

"Commodore's Insights: The hostiles are quite maneuverable for their size," she wrote. "Their reactions to our maneuvers are almost prescient, which indicates a high level of sensor performance. They are vulnerable to our rail guns, but they realized early in the engagement that *Giant* is the only ship armed with them.

"The hostiles have an energy weapon of some type that drains power from our shields, and it appears to outrange the missiles aboard our destroyers and frigates, but not *Giant's* rail guns. This may be the same weapon that destroyed our ships without a visible projectile.

"Only *Giant* and *Sao Paolo* remain. *Sao Paolo* is not fully operational due to a generator fire which left her without main propulsion or combat systems. She has restored some systems, and I intend to use them to full effect. My plan is to lead the enemy past Maltaan at close range to give *Sao Paolo* a chance to ambush them as they emerge from around the planet. At the same time, *Giant* will turn to engage their remaining forces. I'll send an update when we know whether this tactic succeeded.—Allard sends."

"Commodore, we're passing Maltaan," the BWC said. Allard looked up in surprise.

Already?

She hit "send."

"What is *Sao Paolo's* status?"

"She's standing by to engage, ma'am."

On the strategic display, Allard saw three of the hostiles were abreast of the planet.

"I only see three enemy ships."

"We lost contact on Five when we passed Maltaan," Deland said. "It's in the sensor shadow."

"Hard turn," Allard ordered. "Reverse engines."

The hostiles didn't react to *Giant's* maneuver right away, and two of them drove deep into rail gun range.

"Kill Hostiles Two and Three with rail guns."

Before Allard finished her command, projectiles left the rails and raced toward their targets. At the same time, *Sao Paolo* fired a full salvo of missiles at Hostile Four.

"Flank speed," Allard ordered. "Don't let them escape."

Giant vibrated as the engines responded to her rapid-fire orders. They were built for power and efficiency, not combat maneuvering, and the sudden changes in speed and direction induced stresses they weren't designed for.

"Main Engine Number One offline!" the engineering systems monitor announced.

"Hostile Number Five reacquired," the BWC reported. "She popped out from the other side of Maltaan!"

Sao Paolo didn't stand a chance against Five. The enemy craft appeared at close range from behind Maltaan, and the aged destroyer vanished without firing a shot in defense.

To make matters worse, *Sao Paolo's* missiles disappeared before they impacted Hostile Four. Two and Three turned hard and raced away from *Giant*, and the rail gun projectiles passed harmlessly behind them.

"Main Engine Number One back online!"

"Full power, head straight for Maltaan," Allard commanded.

"You're going to deorbit?" Deland asked in an incredulous voice.

"Negative. I'm trying to keep the planet at our back, Commander. We can't fight if we're surrounded."

Hostile Five had been lost amid all the confusion surrounding the destruction of *Sao Paolo* and the propulsion casualty, and it was suddenly close aboard *Giant*. The flagship bounced as she skipped along the outer edge of Maltaan's atmosphere, and Allard knew the friction was taking a toll on her shields.

"Rail gun recharge complete," the BWC announced.

"Kill Five with rail guns," Allard ordered. After a two-second delay, she repeated the order.

"Rail guns are inoperative," the BWC answered. "Propulsion offline. Shields at zero."

"They're using the energy weapon!" Deland shouted unnecessarily. "What do we do?"

Allard had known their fate the instant Five appeared behind *Sao Paolo*, and she gave Deland a serene smile.

"We've done all we can, Commander. Now, we die with dignity."

* * *

"Hey Major, check it out!"

Van der Cruyff poked his head through the top hatch of the command mech and looked up where the Space Marine pointed. He saw a brilliant ball of fire streaking across the sky. It was many times brighter than the Maltaani primary star, and it bathed the clouds with ethereal whiteness as it soared westward until it disappeared behind the mountains in the direction of Daarben.

"What the hell was that?" an anonymous voice asked over the circuit.

"It looked like a meteor entering the atmosphere," the major said.

Or a ship burning up on reentry.

"Whatever it was, it's not our problem."

At least, not yet.

* * *

Toro Wisniewski scowled as he paced the MAC-M command center at the defunct botanical gardens west of the Daarben space port. The heavy perfume of the surviving flowering plants played hell on his sinuses and left him in a foul mood.

"What kind of Space Marine puts their headquarters in a flower garden?" he had demanded when he assumed command of MAC-M. He wanted to move his headquarters to the space port, but his request had been denied with a curt message about unnecessary expenditures. There was no interest in spending any more on the Maltaan mission and doing so would call down an army of government cost cutters and auditors in search of a credit to pinch.

"Colonel, the strategic plot is available," Major Anchrum said.

Toro looked around. "Where?"

Anchrum pointed to a small monitor perched on the command table. "Right there, sir. Screen One."

Toro shook his head as he slipped into a chair and squinted at the screen. Four battalion symbols blinked back at him, along with a few scattered company symbols.

Pathetic.

When the mission on Maltaan had shifted from occupation to reconstruction and administration, the UNT reduced the Space Marine presence to bare bones. An army of civilian specialists led by a political appointee named Abel Hyatt, known as the Administrator, had set about remaking Maltaan in Terra Earth's image. The war was over, and there was no need for so many troops. Peaceful restoration of the agrarian Maltaani society was the order of the day.

General Boudreaux, MAC-M at the time, had submitted what he referred to as a "no-shit budget" that sent shock waves through the UNT government. He had requested Second Division, the force that made up MAC-M, be restored to pre-invasion manning levels. Anti-military members of the Grand Council had howled in protest and subjected the budget to intense scrutiny. They hadn't found much waste, but they used the political firestorm to get Boudreaux relieved, nonetheless. They also forced the ISMC to downgrade the MAC-M billet from a one-star general to a colonel and reduced troop strength to four battalions: two mechs, one infantry, and one aviation.

"These positions are accurate?" Toro asked.

"Those are the last reported positions of all four battalions," Anchrum replied. She used a pointer to highlight the various symbols on the screen. "As we saw earlier, First and Second Mech are deployed along the Daarben-Ulvaan road. A company of infantry from Third Battalion is here at headquarters, another is at the space port, and the third is in Ulvaan. Fourth Battalion logistics birds are split between here and Ulvaan, as are the attack birds. We've got one bird on the pad here, plus the birds we saw at Romeo-Nine."

"Pretty fucking thin. Do we have comms with everyone?"

"Yes sir."

"What about *Giant*? What have we heard from her?"

Anchrum shook her head. "Nothing heard since you spoke to the commodore. We've hailed them on encrypted and clear circuits, but they haven't responded."

"Damn it."

A flustered-looking lieutenant raced into the command center. "Pardon the interruption, Colonel, but we just observed a ship burn into the atmosphere."

"A ship? Are you sure?"

"Hmm. Not a hundred percent, but it was bigger and brighter than any meteorite I've ever seen. It went down to the west, over the water."

Toro stood. "Ops, set Alert Condition Alpha for all ground forces. Threat is unknown, threat axis is three hundred and sixty degrees. Weapons are tight; engage hostiles only. Notify the Administrator that the Fleet engaged an unknown enemy, we no longer have communications with the flagship, and I believe an attack is imminent. I recommend he activate whatever procedures they have in place to protect the civilians then send a message to Fleet Command and let them know what we're doing."

* * *

Van der Cruyff wiggled his hips and tried to ease the throbbing pain in his left ass cheek. The seats in the command mech were padded, but something about his anatomy wouldn't let him sit for more than a couple hours without discomfort. He considered stopping and having the battalion continue the movement on foot, but it wasn't much further to the position he had selected for them to hole up and await orders from MAC-M.

His console beeped and a red warning banner flashed across the top of his screen.

High priority traffic from MAC-M.

Van der Cruyff clicked on the banner, and a message appeared.

Alert Condition Alpha set for all MAC-M forces. Threat unknown, threat axis is three hundred and sixty degrees. Weapons are tight.

Major Moon's voice sounded in his ear. *"Skipper, did you see the message from MAC-M?"*

"I just read it, XO."

"What should we do, sir?"

"Keep going. We're almost at our layup position. When we get there, I'll report in and see if there are further orders."

Twenty minutes later, the recon mechs reached their spot, and the column stopped. Van der Cruyff and Fessler did a quick survey of the area and decided it was suitable as a layup position. The major was relieved to be out of the mech and moving around on foot, and he relished the walk from one end of their position to the other as he inspected the battalion. Satisfied with their disposition, he returned to the command mech and slipped on his comms headset.

"MAC-M, this is Second Mech. We have arrived at our layup position and are standing by for tasking, over."

"This is MAC-M, roger out."

Van der Cruyff slipped off his headset and stared at the console for a second. He had expected something more than a simple acknowledgement of his arrival report, like an updated SITREP to explain the increase in force readiness and maybe some follow-on orders.

What the fuck is going on?

* * * * *

Chapter Eight

"Who the hell is Commodore Allard?" one of the ISMC generals gathered in the UNT military General Staff conference room asked. "You're not trying to sneak a flag billet in on us somewhere, are you Brad?"

Admiral Bradley Knight, Chief of Staff of the UNT military, shook his head. "Of course not."

"How is he a commodore, then?"

"Admiral, I can answer that one." General Ellis Boudreaux's voice boomed throughout the room.

Knight nodded.

"Commodore Eloise Allard is the senior captain of the Maltaan support fleet," Boudreaux said. "She's also the daughter of Grand Councilor Allard, who sits on the Grand Council committee that oversees the Ministry of Defense. Therefore, Eloise Allard is a commodore because Allard says she's a commodore. She started calling herself that when I was MAC-M, but it doesn't mean anything. It's just Fleet pomp and circumstance bullshit to me."

The officers gathered around the table chuckled.

"You know her. What do you make of her message, Ellis?" Knight asked.

"Despite her inflated self-worth, Eloise is a capable officer, sir. I think we have to accept it at face value until we get some conflicting information."

Admiral Knight nodded. "I agree." He turned to his aide, Fleet Captain Phipps. "Captain, go find General Anders and ask him to join us. I have some questions for him. And tell him to bring The Brief, too."

* * *

General Anders walked down a passageway at Fleet headquarters, deep in thought.

"General Anders!"

A voice behind him brought Anders out of his reverie, and he blinked in surprise.

"I'm General Anders," he said, before he recognized Fleet Captain Phipps.

"Admiral Knight wants you in the conference room, sir," Phipps said.

"Right now?"

"Right now. He said to bring The Brief, too."

"I'll go grab it and be there as soon as possible. Please tell the admiral I'm on my way."

The two officers went in different directions: Phipps back toward the flag conference room, and Anders to his office to retrieve The Brief.

"The Brief" was a brief in name only. It was a long-term research project begun by General Boudreaux to capture the entire history of human and Maltaani interaction. He had started with the first encounter between the UNT frigate *Nelson* and an unidentified Maltaani ship and had continued through the Battle of Balfan-48, the rescue of Maltaani hostages on Menard-Kev and the subsequent détente, the failed first attempt at diplomacy between the races, and the ISMC invasion and occupation of Maltaan. When Boudreaux returned to Terra Earth, then-Colonel Anders had inherited the project.

Anders continued the project for three main reasons. First, he considered the discovery of the Maltaani, another sentient life form, one of the most important events in human history, made even more remarkable by the revelation that humans and Maltaani were cousins separated by a quirk of evolution and an unknown twist of fate.

Second, interest in the Maltaani was fading on Terra Earth, both in the public and in the UNT military. Most humans had begun to view Maltaan and the Maltaani as just another Terran colony. Anders attributed the attitudinal shift to unfulfilled expectations. Terrans had always assumed any sentient life forms they encountered would be more advanced than them and hold the keys to unlock the mysteries of the universe. An entire fiction genre was built on that assumption, and when they discovered the Maltaani were a less-developed branch on the human evolutionary tree and, thereby, had little to offer, the disappointment made them indifferent.

Third, Anders was bored. When General Boudreaux had relinquished his post as MAC-M and reported to the UNT General Staff, he had brought Anders with him. The ISMC promoted Boudreaux to major general and assigned him as Director of Operations. They had promoted Anders to brigadier general, and Boudreaux had created the Deputy Director for Operations and Intelligence position for him. Boudreaux had left Anders to create his own job responsibilities, but there was little for him to do. The network of agents and sources Anders had developed while he commanded the now-defunct

Intelligence, Surveillance, and Reconnaissance (ISR) branch had vanished. The only ongoing military operations were routine patrols throughout known space and the limited support provided to the UNT administrator on Maltaan. Operations on Maltaan were focused on reconstruction and administration, not military intelligence.

After a week watching other officers scurry around Fleet headquarters, clutching files and looking important, Anders had decided to resurrect what had since become known as The Brief. Now, he was considered the subject matter expert on the Maltaani and gave infrequent lectures on his work. Most officers had little interest in Maltaan, and the summons from Admiral Knight was unexpected.

Anders retrieved a data stick and a thick binder he used during his lectures and raced back down the passageway to the General Staff conference room. He paused at the door to take a deep breath and check his uniform, and the Space Marine sentry posted outside waved him in.

Admiral Knight stood at the head of the conference table. "It's critical that we—ah, Nils, good. Come on up here. We have some questions you might be able to answer."

"We" turned out to be every senior admiral and general in the UNT military, and a hard knot formed in Anders' throat as he joined Knight. He recognized General Boudreaux, and the general nodded at him.

"Gentlemen, this is General Nils Anders, the brains behind The Brief and our foremost expert on the Maltaani."

Anders blushed at the praise as heads nodded around the table. He was cautious but confident by nature, but in the presence of so many senior officers, he felt tiny.

"We've got a situation developing on Maltaan, and we need your help with some of it, Nils," Knight said. "Does the word 'badaax' mean anything to you?"

Anders thought for a moment. "Not off the top of my head, sir. It's Maltaani for 'harvest,' but—oh, wait a second. Let me check something." He set his binder down and flipped through the pages. "Yes sir, here it is. 'Badaax' is the Maltaani word for harvest, and they also use it to refer to another race they claim to have encountered before us. Let me show you."

Anders inserted the data stick into a computer on the side of the room and searched through the files until he found the one he was looking for. A blue holograph appeared and hovered over the conference table.

It was a skeleton, with a vague human shape, with one exception. It had a bulbous skull and rows of fangs in place of teeth. The bottom jaw jutted forward and gave it a menacing look.

"What the hell is that?" one of the generals blurted.

"That is what the Maltaani call a badaax," Anders said. "This skeleton was discovered in a mountain cave near the Daarben-Ulvaan railway right after the invasion." He entered a few more keystrokes, and a human skeleton appeared next to the badaax. "This is a nominal two-meter human skeleton for comparison."

The admirals and generals gasped. The badaax dwarfed the human by four meters.

"That thing is huge," said Knight. "This is real?"

"Yes sir, it's real. We showed the skeleton to the Maltaani scientists who were here as part of the Interspecies Scientific Congress, and that's when they told us about the badaax."

"Where do they come from? Are they on Maltaan now?" asked an angry-faced general Anders recognized as the ISMC chief medical officer.

"Sir, there have been no reports of a live sighting or evidence of their existence. Just these bones." Anders cleared his throat. "One of the Maltaani scientists told us the badaax exist somewhere else in the universe and appear once every generation for a short time. They allegedly kidnap, or harvest, as many Maltaan as possible in that time and then presumably return to where they came from."

"Why the hell would they do that?"

"Nobody knows, sir."

"Why haven't we been told about this?" Knight demanded.

"Admiral, there's not much to tell. We have a single skeleton, coupled with theories based on hearsay and legend," Anders said. "The scientist had no direct knowledge of anything he told us; he was repeating what he'd been told by his parents." He cleared his throat. "Frankly, the Maltaani have been less than forthcoming about many things, and we didn't know whether to believe it or not. The bones were sent back here for analysis, and it sounds like the story died there."

The generals and admirals traded looks around the table.

Anders cleared his throat. "Sir, may I ask why badaax is a topic of discussion for this group?"

"Commodore Allard, commander of our Maltaan support squadron, forwarded a report from a mining outfit stating that five unknown ships, larger than Fleet flagships, had emerged from an unmapped space warp somewhere out past Maltaan. Two days later, her fleet detected five unknown contacts approaching Maltaan from that direction. She sent a warning to MAC-M, her squadron, and the Maltaani ships in orbit. The Maltaani fleet responded with a one-word message and then turned tail and ran. Care to guess what that word was?"

Anders thought for a second. "Badaax."

"Exactly. Badaax. Commodore Allard ordered the frigate *Comte de Grasse* to investigate the contacts. The ship disappeared."

"Disappeared, sir? Through the warp?"

"No. When the event recording was slowed down, it appeared the ship was destroyed in the space of three scans by an unidentified weapon."

"My God."

"Allard sent imagery of the unknowns from surveillance drones deployed by her frigates. Have a look." The drone video appeared on the screen. "There's nothing to show scale, but Allard reported her scans revealed the craft are twelve hundred meters long and six hundred meters tall."

"That's enormous."

"And now we know why."

"If they're carrying Badaax."

"Since this started, Allard and her fleet have engaged the unknowns and suffered heavy casualties. Her last SITREP indicated she had two ships remaining, *Giant* and *Sao Paolo,* and she was maneuvering to attack. We've received nothing from the commodore since. Colonel Wisniewski, MAC-M, reported that ground forces are on high alert, and then he also ceased reporting. *That's* why badaax is a topic of conversation in this group."

"Do you think they're headed this way, through the Maduro Gate, sir?"

"It's possible. Just in case, we've positioned the destroyer *Duc de Mayenne* inside rail gun range of the warp with orders to destroy everything coming through they can't positively identify as human. What we don't have is visibility of events in the Maduro Sector."

"I'm sorry I can't offer you more information," Anders told Knight.

"No apologies are necessary, Nils," Knight said. He consulted the time and then looked around at the admirals and generals. "I'm due to brief the Minister in twenty minutes, and probably the President after that, so I want a recommendation. How should we respond?"

Anders tried to remain unobtrusive as the group debated suggestions from around the table. Their final recommendation involved an emergency sortie by Fourth Fleet and a recall of ISMC Sixth Division in preparation for deployment. Fourth Fleet would proceed directly to Maltaan, while the Space Marines would surge to a readiness position on the near side of the Maduro Jump Gate in case they were needed for ground operations on Maltaan. Finally, they would raise the readiness level across both the Fleet and ISMC in the event more forces were required.

"That's it, then," Admiral Knight said as he stood. "Thank you all for your attention." The rest of the officers stood when Knight did, and the admiral nodded at Anders as he passed.

When Knight and Phipps were gone, there was a collective sigh of relief around the room. By all accounts, Knight was an easy man to work for, but he was the most senior officer in the Terran military, and his presence added a layer of tension to every room he entered.

As the officers filed out the door, Boudreaux signaled Anders to join him at the table.

"Good job on your brief, Nils," the general said.

"I'm sorry I didn't offer much, sir."

"Don't be too sure about that. If you hadn't shown Admiral Knight what little we know about these Badaax, this meeting would have broken up without any decisions or recommendations 'pending further research.'" Boudreaux made air quotes to punctuate his sentence. "We'd be back here in a couple days having the same conversation, only we'd be even further behind events around Maltaan."

"What do you think is happening out there, sir?"

"I don't think we know enough to make any guesses right now. What do we have for intel assets in the Maduro Sector?"

"Nothing active, sir. There are a couple deep-space survey missions out there, but they're of no use for this."

"Huh. What do we have available here?"

"The reconnaissance vessel *Eclipse Wonder* is available for tasking. She just completed refit and reload of her drones and is now in lunar orbit."

"Any ground forces?"

Anders shook his head. "Just the recon companies that will deploy with Sixth Division." Before he could stop himself, he blurted, "Captain Fortis is available."

"Fortis? What's he doing these days?"

"Abner Fortis commands the Space Marine company involved in tactical development and evaluation for the IEBS program."

"Then he works for you?"

"Indirectly, yes sir. I just returned from Kinshasa where I observed a full-mission profile exercise with the IEBS company yesterday."

"Good. If you think Fortis will be useful, get him and his company aboard *Eclipse Wonder* and get going. My funny bone tells me we're in a shooting match with an unknown enemy, and I don't like it. We don't know a damn thing about what's happening out there, and that makes my balls itch. Understand?"

"Yes sir, but what about the Fleet? As soon as they get the order, they'll emergency sortie. It could be a matter of hours."

Boudreaux chuckled. "Let's talk turkey here, General. Right now, Admiral Knight is cooling his heels outside the Minister's office. An hour from now, he'll finish briefing the Minister, who will then spend an hour or two with his advisors before he briefs the President. After that brief, the President will spend several hours with *his* advisors before deciding what to do, and that's only if neither the Minister nor the President have questions. The Grand Council will want their say, which could add weeks to the process.

"With all due respect to our elected leadership, it's my experience that when politicians are confronted with matters they don't understand, a decision deferred is a decision made. Especially military matters.

"Now, we *might* get a decision in eight hours or so, but I have my doubts. Until we do, Admiral Knight can't even issue a warning order to the Fleet so they can prepare. Alarm bells would go off all over the government. As soon as they hear about it, the peaceniks would turn out in force and make things a helluva lot more complicated. They might even demand that we don't respond.

"No, I'd bet my next paycheck we won't get a decision until tomorrow at the earliest, which means the soonest Fourth Fleet will sortie will be the day after tomorrow. When Sixth Division would join them is anybody's guess.

"The good news is, I don't need anybody's authorization to deploy you and Fortis aboard *Eclipse Wonder* today, and you'll have at least a two-day head start on the Fleet."

"Me?"

Boudreaux nodded. "Yes, you Nils. It's apparent to me that Commodore Allard and her fleet have been destroyed, and we are blind to what's happening on and around Maltaan. I want someone senior on the scene to make sure Fleet doesn't fuck this up. I can't go, so that leaves you."

"I see your point, sir."

"I'm sending another officer with you, Nils. A Fleet major named Rho. She comes to us from the Joint Operations Center. Supposed to be a sharp cookie, but she lacks operational experience."

"Is this the right time for that, sir?"

"How is she going to get operational experience if she doesn't go on operations?"

Anders stared at Boudreaux. "She's related to someone, or you owe someone a favor."

Boudreaux smiled. "Your tasking is to observe and report. Prepare the battlespace for the arrival of Fourth Fleet and Sixth Division. You weren't made a general for no reason, Nils. Get it done."

* * * * *

Chapter Nine

"**C**ommand, Recon Two. Mechanized column approaching from the east."

Van der Cruyff keyed his mike. "Roger, it's First Mech. Let them come, I'll talk to them."

The major stepped out of the trees along the Daarben-Ulvaan road where his battalion was concealed and flagged down the lead mech of the approaching column. He recognized the Jolly Roger pennant streaming from the antenna. Alpha Company, First Mechanized Infantry Battalion. The column braked to a stop. A hatch on the lead recon mech popped open, and a female lieutenant poked her head out.

"I'm Major Van der Cruyff, Second Mech," he called to her. "I'm looking for your battalion commander, Major Southwick."

The lieutenant ducked back into the mech. After a couple minutes, van der Cruyff began to wonder if she had forgotten about him, but a command mech approached from somewhere in the middle of the column and stopped in front of him.

"Hi, Jan." Major Twila Southwick, commander of First Mech, climbed down from her mount, and the battalion commanders shook hands. "What the hell are you doing out here in the middle of nowhere?"

"We were on our way to Daarben when Toro caught up with us. He told me to hole up twenty klicks inside the tree line. Did you see him?"

"Yeah, he caught up with us back in Ulvaan and kicked my ass earlier," Southwick said with a wry smile. "He was mad because we got off to a slow start."

Van der Cruyff didn't mention Toro's compliments of Second Mech. "Are you headed for the space port?" he asked Southwick.

"That's what the OPORD calls for, and I haven't received orders not to," she said. "Do you think I should call for an update?"

Van der Cruyff shrugged. "I honestly don't know what to think. Toro ordered me to hole up, and then we got the Alert Condition Alpha order. When I reported where we stopped for the night, MAC-M acknowledged the transmission but didn't give me any orders. Have you heard anything?"

"Not a peep, not since he chewed my ass."

"Huh. I suppose you could report that you encountered Second Mech and see if that prompts the staff to update your orders. Otherwise, keep heading west, I guess."

"Yeah, let me give that a try. I'm sick of riding in this fucking box anyway." Southwick climbed back into her command mech and van der Cruyff stepped back into the cover of the trees. It was all he could do not to shake his head in disgust. Southwick represented everything he hated about the ISMC. She had been promoted well beyond what her knowledge and experience merited, her leadership style was slack, and she allowed her emotions to guide her actions.

"What do the clowns from First Mech want, sir?" Sergeant Major Fessler asked from their position in the undergrowth.

"The same thing we want, Top. Answers. All of our guys are south of the road?"

"Yes sir. We sent two patrols north, but the rest of the battalion is dug in over here."

"Okay, good. If MAC-M orders First Mech to link up with us here, they can have the north side. We don't want to get mixed up with them."

"Damn right we don't. Those dumbasses didn't even dismount their infantry and set a perimeter when they stopped. I don't want that shit rubbing off on our guys."

Van der Cruyff didn't mention their own dismal performance during their first stop.

Southwick climbed back out of her mech. "MAC-M ordered me to hole up here with you. Where do you want us?"

Fessler chuckled.

"We're deployed on the south side of the road, so why don't you take the north?" van der Cruyff asked. "I've got a couple patrols out on that side, but otherwise, it's all yours."

"Roger that," Southwick said. She spoke into her communicator, and troops emerged from their mechs all along her column. Some of them moved to take cover on the south side of the road and van der Cruyff heard angry shouts as they stumbled into Second Mech positions.

"Tell those fucking idiots the *north* side of the road!" Southwick shouted at nobody in particular. "Their military north." She turned to van der Cruyff and threw her hands in the air. "Sorry."

Van der Cruyff just waved.

"Major, I don't suppose I could convince you to issue a shoot to kill order for the next First Mech jackass that crosses the road, could I?" Fessler asked.

The major laughed and slapped Fessler on the shoulder as they started for their command post.

"That's our sister battalion you're talking about, Top."

"Sister my ass. Red-headed stepchild, you mean."

"Maybe so, but they're not as bad as Third Battalion."

"Don't tell me we have to bunk with the infantry, too."

"DINLI, Top."

* * *

Major Catalina Palacio, the MAC-M air boss, sat with her feet propped up and sipped cold juice from a tin mug as a holographic episode of her favorite show projected above the desk. The juice was from the same local fruit the Space Marines used to brew DINLI, but it was smooth and sweet, unlike its high-octane cousin. As a Space Marine, Palacio had enjoyed DINLI throughout her career, but after some drunken ground crew stole two hovercopters and drag raced them down the runway, she banned the brew at the space port. There was public grumbling, but Palacio knew they continued to distill it. The senior NCOs kept a lid on the hijinks, and she didn't feel the need to pursue the issue any further.

Her assignment as the MAC-M air boss automatically made her Daarben Flight Control, whose job it was to coordinate flight operations across Maltaan as well as the shuttle traffic to and from orbit, but she didn't technically command any aircraft. The ISMC logistics and attack birds stationed in Daarben and Ulvaan belonged to Fourth Battalion. The hovercopters contracted to the civilian administrator answered to their home companies and barely acknowledged Daarben Flight Control's existence unless one of them went down and required rescue. The daily flight schedule was viewed by all as a recommendation rather than something for flight crews to adhere to.

Palacio expected her tour as MAC-M air boss to be a career en-hancer, but MAC-M had drawn down so far that there were few flight operations to coordinate. A competent sergeant could have done her job with time to spare, and she came to view her time on Maltaan as treading water while her fellow officers continued to climb the ranks in the ISMC. Resigned to her fate, Palacio contented herself by binge-watching holo shows brought to Maltaan on monthly logistic runs and sleeping with a sergeant from the medical detachment posted at the space port.

When Wisniewski set Alert Condition Alpha, Palacio didn't know what that meant to her organization. The OPORD listed a series of actions expected of the air boss, but the directive hadn't been updated to reflect reduced force levels or change in mission. She notified her staff and the Daarben-based aircrews, and then she went and spoke to Abel Hyatt, the civilian administrator in charge of Maltaani reconstruc-tion. Hyatt, who was also headquartered at the space port, had pep-pered her with questions about the alert condition which she couldn't answer. When he determined he wouldn't get any useful information from her, he had dismissed her with a wave.

After Colonel Wisniewski ordered the security exercise, he had ap-peared at the space port. Following a quick satcom conversation with Commodore Allard on the flagship, he had taken off again without a word to Palacio or her staff. The whole episode left Palacio mystified, so she returned to her holo.

The deep-throated roar of engines brought Palacio to her feet. She could tell the engines were far more powerful than those of a hover-copter or shuttle, and she had a sudden thought.

Drop ship.

She dismissed the idea as soon as it came to her. There were no drop ships in the support fleet and no reason for one to be arriving, either.

"Cat, what the fuck is that?" First Lieutenant Shek Eldryk, Palacio's assistant, asked as he joined her in a dash for the door. "Are we expecting Marines?"

"No idea," she said. "Maybe we should ask the people that schedule air operations."

Eldryk's response was lost in the blast of noise that hammered Palacio when she ran outside. She stopped dead, Eldryk ran into her back, and they stood side by side and gaped at the sight.

An enormous black spacecraft with a strange boxy shape hovered over the tarmac. The engines howled as the craft descended until it touched down, but Palacio was too stunned by the sight to cover her ears. Three more of the strange craft landed in a neat line down the runway. All four cut their engines at the same time, and the sudden silence was like a slap across the face.

The craft landed vertically, but they began to tip over. Palacio held her breath as she waited for them to slam down, but they landed horizontally on skids that extended from the body. The entire evolution was completed without a sound.

"Who the hell are those guys?" Eldryk asked. Palacio could only shake her head.

Palacio estimated the four craft were three hundred meters long, bigger than some small interplanetary cargo ships. They were matte black, and their flat sides, sharp corners, and flight characteristics seemed to defy the principles of aerodynamics.

Ramps in the bellies of the craft opened. Two smaller craft rolled free of each and lined up next to their mother ships. The smaller craft were approximately one hundred meters long, and they had the same boxy lines as their mother ships. All eight zoomed down the runway in a neat formation and climbed into the Maltaani sky.

By then, scores of civilians and Space Marines had joined Palacio and Eldryk at the edge of the tarmac.

"Are those ours, Major?" Hyatt asked.

"I don't know," she said. "I've never seen anything like them before."

Captain Blaylock, commander of the Space Marine infantry company assigned as space port security, trotted up to her and saluted. "Major Palacio, I don't know who those guys are, but I don't think it's safe to remain here until we find out."

Palacio returned the salute. "I wouldn't be surprised to find out they are experimental craft being tested by Fleet Command."

"Ma'am, MAC-M is at Alert Condition Alpha. According to the order, the threat is unknown, and the threat axis is three hundred and sixty degrees."

"I read the same message, Captain. I appreciate your caution, but I've seen nothing to indicate these ships pose any threat."

Blaylock stared at Palacio for a long moment and then shifted his gaze to Hyatt, who shrugged. He shook his head briefly as if he couldn't believe what he was hearing and then came to attention and saluted.

"Request permission to carry on, ma'am."

"Carry on."

Meanwhile, a pair of the smaller craft began to orbit the space port. Palacio heard a low buzzing noise when they passed overhead, but they were otherwise silent.

Over by the hangars, the engines on a pair of attack hovercopters wound up as they prepared to launch.

"Who authorized that?" Palacio asked Eldryk.

"I don't know, but I'll find out." The lieutenant ran toward the hovercopters, but they were airborne before he got there. After an animated conversation with the ground crew, Eldryk ran back and rejoined Palacio.

"Captain Blaylock ordered the launch," he said, panting. "He put the hovercopters in Alert Ten when MAC-M set Alpha and gave the launch order a short while ago."

Anger surged in Palacio's chest, and she felt her face grow hot. "Blaylock ordered it? An infantry captain controls flight operations now?"

Eldryk threw up his hands. "I don't know, ma'am. He told the ground crew it was in accordance with the OPORD, so they did it."

Palacio whirled around, but all she saw were a few of her people and a gaggle of civilians.

"Where's Blaylock? Find him and tell him to report to me right now!"

"Look!"

Palacio stared in disbelief as dozens of figures emerged from the large craft. The creatures were bipedal and had a human-like body shape, but that's where the similarities ended. They stood at least four meters tall and had enormous heads, and their skin was pale blue. After they debarked the landing craft, they gathered and then headed for the crowd of humans.

Some of the civilians around Palacio and Hyatt began to run for the domes, while others stood rooted in their spots. Icy fingers of fear squeezed Palacio's chest, and she fought to draw a breath.

"What do we do, greet them?" Hyatt asked.

"Major, come on! We need to go!" Eldryk pulled at her sleeve, and she turned to follow him, but her legs refused to work and she fell to her knees on the tarmac.

The blue creatures charged the crowd, and the humans screamed in terror as they fled. Palacio struggled to her feet and followed on wooden legs.

One of the smaller craft that had been orbiting the space port hovered in the sky over the crowd. The people shrieked and tried to evade it as shafts of blue light shined down from the underside of the craft. The humans who were caught in the blue light beams stopped running and stood with their heads down and their hands by their sides.

Palacio looked back and saw that the blue giants had caught up with the slowest humans. Each of them carried a tall staff or a long whip, which they cracked over the heads of the panicked humans. Orbs atop the staffs emitted narrow beams of the same blue light as the flying craft, and it had the same effect on the humans.

The hovercopters zoomed by overhead and engaged the alien craft flying around the space port. Nose mounted automatic cannons and rockets tore into one of them, and it jinked back and forth before it rolled over and crashed behind the tree line along the eastern space port border. After the initial surprise attack, the second alien craft went into a steep climb before it nosed over and dove down to engage the hovercopters. The hovercopters were clumsy and slow compared to the boxy alien craft. Palacio watched in horror as they both slammed into the ground and exploded.

A whip cracked across Palacio's back, and the heavy blow slammed her to the ground. She lost all feeling in her lower body, and she scrabbled to get back to her feet but couldn't. Her blue-skinned attacker towered over her and prodded her with a massive foot until she rolled over onto her back. She bit back a scream when she saw the rows of sharp fangs in its gaping mouth.

Seemingly satisfied, the giant moved off in pursuit of the other fleeing humans. Palacio managed to prop herself up on an elbow, and she surveyed the horrific scene unfolding around her. Humans stood in ones and twos with their heads down as if mesmerized by the blue light. Bodies marked the path of the panicked humans like a macabre trail of breadcrumbs.

The unmistakable sound of pulse rifles drew Palacio's attention to the flight control building, and she watched a volley of energy bolts tear into one of the massive blue aliens. The creature stumbled but remained upright, and the Space Marines continued to fire. One of the alien craft swooped in and then paused in the sky over the Space Marine firing positions. A beam of blue light flashed down from the belly of the craft. The flight control building exploded, and the firing stopped.

Palacio cried out when pain lanced up her back as she regained the feeling in her legs. She rolled over and pushed herself up to her hands and knees and stopped there, exhausted from the effort.

"C'mon, Cat, you've got this," she said through gritted teeth. "Get up, bitch."

She dragged one foot forward and got it underneath herself as she pushed with her arms, and she managed to get up on her hands and feet in the bear crawl position. Her back spasmed with the effort, and she nearly gave up and flopped down on her belly, but an inner voice drove her to stand. With a final scream of agony and triumph, Palacio stood. Her legs were unsteady, and her lower body throbbed, but she was up.

The salty taste of blood filled her mouth, and the major realized she had chewed her bottom lip raw as she struggled to her feet. Palacio spat and then began to shamble toward the southern perimeter of the space port, away from the alien craft and the fighting among the buildings and hangars.

A shadow loomed over her, and she realized one of the colossal blue aliens had caught her from behind. She tried to increase her pace, but the alien took one step for every ten of hers, and it became a weird slow-motion chase. Palacio staggered and went down on one knee, but she forced herself to stand and continue.

Exhausted, the major was forced to stop. Her breath came in huge gasps, and the throbbing in her hips turned to white-hot agony. She turned to look at her pursuer, who stood in silence and stared at her.

"Fuck you, *puta*!" Palacio bellowed. "Fuck you and the ship you rode in on!"

The alien raised its staff, and blue light glowed from the tip. Palacio tried to shield her eyes with her arm, but she was too late. Her mind went blank, and she had one final thought.

Blue.

* * * * *

Chapter Ten

Toro Wisniewski had grown more nervous with each minute that had passed since the last report from Commodore Allard aboard *Giant*. His anxiety had peaked when he received a report of the ship burning into the atmosphere, and he forced himself to remain calm. After all units acknowledged his order to set Alert Condition Alpha, the communications circuits had grown quiet, and the resulting silence only served to intensify his feeling of dread.

"Colonel, Charlie Company, Third Battalion at the space port just reported four unknown spacecraft have touched down on the runway, sir," Anchrum told him.

"Unknowns? What are they doing?"

Anchrum put the circuit on an overhead speaker.

"…ramp opened. Second Platoon engaged, but there are too many." The Space Marine on the circuit sounded like he was on the verge of panic. "They're all over the fucking place. Watch out!" Toro heard pulse rifles firing. "Don't look at the light—"

The circuit went dead.

"What the fuck happened?" Toro demanded. Anchrum could only throw up her hands.

After repeated attempts on all channels to raise the space port went unanswered, Toro grew tired of waiting.

"Send the hovercopter to the space port and find out what's going on over there," Toro said.

A loud explosion shook the command center, and then the power went out. Headquarters personnel scrambled through the darkness for the doors. When Toro got outside, he saw thick smoke belching into the sky from the remains of the armory and ammunition storage magazine. An unfamiliar craft passed low over the compound. Shafts of blue light shone down from the belly of the craft, and the logistics Quonset burst into flames. Toro looked across the open field in front of the compound and froze.

A handful of blue aliens strode toward him. They were at least four meters tall, with oversized heads and blue skin, and Toro realized they were identical to the skeleton he'd seen before he took command. Some of the aliens wielded tall staffs with a glowing blue orb at the end.

They're real, and they're here!

Toro snapped out of his shock and shouted at nearby Space Marines who stared at their attackers.

"Open fire, goddammit! Shoot!"

Space Marines all over the MAC-M compound opened up. Blue-white plasma bolts sprayed the approaching alien hoard, but they had little effect. One of the aliens stumbled, but it rejoined the others, and they continued to advance. The aliens slammed their staffs on the ground, and rays of blue light shot from the glowing orbs. Whenever a ray hit a Space Marine in the face, he immediately stopped, dropped his pulse rifle, and stood still.

An errant pulse rifle bolt ricocheted off the ground and hit Anchrum low in the stomach, and she screamed as she went down, clutching a terrible wound.

"What the fuck?" Toro shouted. He fumbled to draw his pulse pistol as one of the aliens approached. He squeezed off two shots that seemed to bend around the alien's chest before the creature planted its staff, and the blue light flashed in Toro's eyes. He lowered his pistol, and it slid from his grasp as his mind went blank.

Blue.

* * *

"Command, this is Recon One. There's a convoy approaching from the west, about half a klick out. Several trucks and a bunch of Maltaani walking behind. Lots of women and kids in the group, and they appear unarmed. Looks like refugees."*

Van der Cruyff keyed his mic. "This is Second Mech Actual. Let them pass, observe and report."

"Roger, out."

"Notify First Mech about the refugees and tell them to let them pass."

The major crouched in the underbrush and watched as the column trudged by his position. The trucks were crammed with Maltaani, mostly women and children, and a hundred more followed on foot. Although they had very different features than their human cousins, van der Cruyff recognized their familiar body language.

Refugees. But from what?

"Sorry looking bunch," Fessler remarked in a low voice.

"Yeah." The major stood and handed Fessler his pulse rifle. "We need to find out what they're running from."

When he stepped into the road, his sudden appearance caused a minor panic among the refugees until they recognized him as human.

"Hello," van der Cruyff said in Maltaani as he raised a hand in the traditional   greeting. "Hello."

Although he'd had a cochlear translator implant for over a year, the major hadn't had a lot of practice with the Maltaani language. A Maltaani liaison officer had been assigned to the battalion when van der Cruyff took command, but the officer had failed to show up for duty one day and never came back. When van der Cruyff queried MAC-M about a replacement, the staff had told him it wasn't unusual for the Maltaani to simply quit, and they would arrange for a replacement. After six months of waiting, the major stood in the middle of a dusty road and hoped he wouldn't offend anyone with his rudimentary language skills.

One of the Maltaani, a stoop-shouldered old male, returned his wave but kept walking.

"Where are you going, Father?" van der Cruyff asked, using the honorific traditionally reserved for elders. "Why do you leave?"

"Badaax." The old Maltaani gestured back toward Daarben. "Badaax."

Van der Cruyff stared after the column as they continued east, and Fessler joined him in the road.

"Where are they going?" Fessler asked.

"He didn't say. The old timer just said, 'Badaax.'"

"What's that mean?"

The major shook his head. "I'm not sure, but I think it means 'harvest.' I think that's what the Maltaani fleet told the flagship before they hauled ass, too."

"Wrong season for a harvest," Fessler said.

"Yeah." Van der Cruyff tossed his head. "C'mon, let's go take a look at the troops."

* * *

It was dark when van der Cruyff and Fessler returned to the command mech from their inspection of Second Mech positions. They heard pulse rifle fire off to the west, followed by the *crump* of grenades. Confused and angry voices clobbered the inter-battalion tactical circuit.

"What the hell's going on?" the major demanded when he got inside the command mech.

"The First Battalion guys on the western flank reported heavy movement behind them, and then all hell broke loose," the comms watch told him. "I don't think they know who they're shooting at."

"All our patrols are south of the road, right?"

"Affirmative, sir."

An angry voice restored circuit discipline and demanded answers from the Space Marines involved in the firing.

"We heard a lot of movement behind us and then a herd of elephants charged through our position," a nervous-sounding platoon commander reported. *"They ran right through us and took off down the road toward Daarben."*

Fessler laughed aloud. "Those dumb bastards are shooting grenades at elephants?"

"Elephants" was the nickname the Space Marines had given the massive six-legged mammals that lived in the thick forests of the central region of Maltaan. The elephants were shy creatures that avoided contact with humans, but when they were spooked, they charged pell-mell like a runaway locomotive, smashing everything in their path. At least two Space Marine convoys had fallen victim to stampeding elephants along the Daarben-Ulvaan road since the invasion.

"I wonder what spooked them?" van der Cruyff asked.

"Nervous Space Marines with no trigger discipline is my guess," said Fessler.

"Have we heard anything from MAC-M?" the major asked the comms watch.

"Negative, sir. It's been real quiet since they ordered Alert Condition Alpha."

"Huh. Okay, I'll be out and about. Call me if you need me."

"Roger that, sir."

Van der Cruyff grabbed a pig square and a hydration pack before he climbed out of the mech. Fessler did the same, and the two men squatted in the darkness beside the mech and munched their meals.

"Something about this doesn't feel right," Fessler said. "Usually, we can't get the staff to shut up."

Van der Cruyff drained the last of his hydration pack. "I know what you mean. Makes me wonder what they're up to."

"What are we going to do?"

The major stood. "I'm going across the road to tell First Mech we're sending a recon element to the edge of the tree line ahead of us and launching a drone to look around the space port. Here's hoping they don't shoot grenades at them."

Ten minutes later, two Second Mech recon mechs headed west in search of answers.

* * * * *

Chapter Eleven

Fortis was sound asleep when hammering on his door woke him with a start. A training command orderly poked his head inside.

"Captain Fortis, Colonel Moultrie wants you in her office right now, sir. There's a general waiting for you."

"A general?" He swung his feet off his bunk and gasped when they hit the cold floor. "Okay. Gimme a second to get dressed."

"Any idea who the general is?" Fortis asked the orderly as they jogged across the compound to the training command administrative building.

"No sir, sorry. The colonel called me to her office and sent me to find you, and that's when I saw him. I'm just a corporal, so I don't keep up with all the generals."

Fortis laughed and slapped him on the shoulder as they jogged up the steps. "Thanks, Corporal."

When Fortis entered Moultrie's office, it surprised him to see General Anders and an unfamiliar female Fleet major seated in front of her desk.

"What can I do for you, General?" Fortis looked at Moultrie and then back at Anders.

Maybe I haven't been grounded after all.

"You're being deployed," Moultrie interjected. "You and the entire company."

"Deployed? Where?"

"Through the Maduro Jump Gate," Anders said.

"Maltaan."

"Possibly. Maltaani space, certainly. Your operational designator is India Company, First Battle Mech Battalion."

"What's going on, General?"

Anders stood. "We don't have a lot of time right now, Abner. Get your Space Marines over to Hangar Nine as soon as possible for gear issue. There are two shuttles waiting to load at the space port to transport us to *Eclipse Wonder,* which will carry us to the Maduro Gate. I'll explain everything once we're on our way. You've got one hour."

By the time Fortis got outside, it was obvious the word was already out. Some of the company had already packed duffels and headed for the hangars. LT Penny caught up with him as he trotted for the barracks.

"Hey, Captain, I sent Gunny Ystremski to his house last night since he didn't have any of his stuff here. I just called him, and he said he'd be here in thirty minutes. I hope that's okay."

"That's fine," Fortis said as the pair mounted the steps of their quarters. "You got the word to everyone?"

"Yes sir. The orderly called with a heads up, and the lads did the rest."

"Good. Any problems?"

"None reported. Master Sergeant Brooks isn't making the trip."

Fortis stopped and looked at Penny. "Why not?"

The LT shrugged. "He said the colonel was pulling him back to her staff now that we have a new senior NCO."

"Okay. Grab your stuff and let's get moving. Ystremski will catch up with us at the hangar."

* * *

Ystremski stuffed clean socks and skivvies into his duffel on top of the pig squares and hydration packs he stored in the bag for just such a contingency. He looked up and saw his wife standing in the doorway with her arms crossed.

"Tanya, I'm sorry—"

She shook her head. "There's no need, Petr. I've been a Space Marine's wife too long to need an apology."

He stood and took her in his arms and marveled at how someone so strong could feel so small. "I'm sorry all the same."

They held the embrace for several long seconds. She put her hands on his chest.

"Petr Ystremski, we've been lucky to have you here as long as we have, but I knew that as soon as you cleared medical, you'd be itching to go. Just promise me that you'll be safe out there, and no more sword fighting with Maltaani generals."

Ystremski chuckled. "I'll meet you halfway. I'll be safe." He consulted the time and looked at her with one eyebrow cocked. "You know, I have a few minutes before I have to leave."

Tanya gave him a coquettish look. "Why, Gunnery Sergeant Ystremski. You're not suggesting we squeeze in a quickie before you go, are you?"

The gunny swept his duffel off the bed and laid her down. "That's exactly what I'm suggesting."

* * *

Ystremski ran up to the hangar with a minute to spare and joined Fortis in front of the formation.

"You're late," Fortis said with a sly smile.

"I was unavoidably detained by a minor domestic disturbance," the gunny said. "It was all I could do to keep her from killing me for deploying on short notice."

"By blaming me, no doubt."

"The only time your name came up was when I was on my way out the door. She told me to tell you to get your ass back here in one piece. What's our status, sir?"

"We're ready to go, now that you're here."

A small army of program technicians loaded rows of IEBS into cargo boxes that they placed aboard the shuttles to transport to the waiting ship. A second shuttle was parked nearby, waiting for the troops.

General Anders arrived, accompanied by Moultrie, Wright, the female major, and Doctor Dunker.

"Fall in!" Ystremski ordered, and the Space Marines fell into ranks by platoon.

"All present and accounted for, sir," Fortis reported to Anders with a salute.

"Listen up!" Anders called. "You've been activated as India Company, First Battle Mech Battalion. There's trouble brewing, and you're the Space Marines we've selected to go downrange and take care of business. Colonel Moultrie and Major Wright have done an outstanding job training you and testing the IEBS, and now, it's up to Captain Fortis to lead you into action." He turned to Fortis. "Captain, take charge of your company and get aboard the shuttle. The doctor and several of his technicians will ride up with you, and the pack-up kit will ride on the other shuttle."

Fortis saluted. "Aye aye, sir. India Company, you heard the general. Move out!"

While the Space Marines lined up to board the shuttle, Fortis looked at Anders. "Doctor Dunker is coming with us?"

"He insisted. None of his technicians know the IEBS as well as he does, and he requested to go in case there are any technical issues."

Colonel Moultrie stepped forward. "General, are you sure you don't want Major Wright to command India Company? This seems like too important a mission to trust to a mere captain."

Anders smiled. "Abner Fortis is much more than a mere captain, Colonel." He looked at Wright. "Major, how much training have you had on the IEBS?"

"I've been with the program since testing began, sir," Wright said.

"That's not what I asked. How much training have you had on the IEBS? How many hours have you spent on the range? Have you had a chassis fitted for you?"

"No, sir, but—"

"Captain Fortis will lead India Company."

It surprised Fortis when the general followed him to the shuttle ramp.

"You're coming with us too, sir?"

"Affirmative. I'll explain everything later, but General Boudreaux's balls are itching."

The two officers laughed as they climbed the ramp into the shuttle.

* * *

Once they were in orbit, India Company waited aboard their shuttle while the cargo shuttle transferred the IEBS to *Eclipse Wonder*. When the equipment was secured in the cargo bay, the first shuttle returned to Terra Earth, and *Eclipse Wonder* recovered the personnel transport into her shuttle bay.

The Space Marines debarked, and Penny, Young, and Ystremski approached Fortis.

"Captain, we were talking on the way up here, and this is how we think the company should be organized," Penny said as he passed Fortis a hand-drawn diagram. "Two forty-five-Marine platoons and a ten-man command element. Four equal squads of riflemen, sappers, and grenadiers, and five scout-snipers per platoon."

Fortis rubbed his chin as he looked over their plan. "What about corpsmen?"

"We're a little thin there," Young said. "I guess nobody expected us to go operational, because we've only got one corpsmen in the entire company, Doc Velez. We'll leave him with the headquarters element. There are a dozen or so others who have received advanced first aid, so we'll spread them across the platoons."

"You're good with this?" Fortis asked Ystremski.

"Yes sir. Right now, the company is organized alphabetically. That makes administrative sense, but we're operational now, so we need to reorganize. I don't know the men personally, but if the platoon commanders are good with it, then I am, too."

Young cut in. "Sir, we can always flex if there's an operational need to mix and match, but right now we need to break the company down by squads and platoons so the lads know who they're with, and we can get the comms straight."

"Okay then, it's fine by me," Fortis said as he passed the diagram back. "When you make final assignments, give me a smooth copy."

"Don't you want to show it to the general?" Penny asked.

"Why? He doesn't command this company."

"But I thought—well, hell, I'm not paid to think," the lieutenant said.

The group laughed as General Anders and the female major walked up.

"I get nervous when I see Captain Fortis and his leadership laughing," the general said. "It makes me think you're plotting something."

"No sir, no plotting here. Just getting the company organized."

"Good. This is Major Kylie Rho. She's my assistant for this mission. Captain Fortis, when you get some time, we need to talk."

"I'm available now if you'd like."

Anders tossed his head toward one of the hatches. "Follow me."

As Fortis followed Anders and Rho through the passageways, the general talked about the ship.

"*Eclipse Wonder* was built to haul big loads and large crews to distant mining colonies. We claimed her from salvage orbit, replaced her powerplant, and equipped her to operate reconnaissance drones."

"And a company of IEBS," Fortis added.

"I hate to break it to you, but India Company was an afterthought." Anders stopped and opened a door. "This is me."

The cabin was spartan by civilian fleet standards, with plain faux wood paneling on the bulkheads, a narrow bunk on one side, and a small computer workstation on the other. Two large monitors hung above the bunk. One displayed *Eclipse Wonder's* navigation status, and the other was blank.

Anders waved Fortis into one of the chairs as he pulled a data stick out of his tunic. "Let me plug this in, and we'll get started." Rho took a position by the door.

The general walked Fortis through the timeline of events that had occurred around Maltaan. When he was finished, he gave a grim summary.

"Allard's last report was that she had two ships remaining, *Giant* and *Sao Paolo*, and it was her intention to attack. We've heard nothing since."

"What about MAC-M, sir?"

"We haven't heard anything from either Colonel Wisniewski or the forces assigned to him since he ordered Alert Condition Alpha. The commodore's SITREPs indicate she apprised MAC-M of the situation in orbit, but we don't know how those events have impacted the ground forces on Maltaan.

"*Eclipse Wonder's* primary mission is to conduct all-sensor surveillance in preparation for the arrival of Fourth Fleet, which General Boudreaux expects to sortie no earlier than the day after tomorrow. Sixth Division will follow at some later date.

"We will begin by launching a pair of recon drones to operate in and around Maltaan. Based on what we find, Fleet Command will determine the next course of action. We are to remain on this side of the Maduro Jump Gate until Fourth Fleet deploys and then jump, with instructions not to approach Maltaan."

"What's your plan for India Company, sir?"

"Right now, there isn't one. In fact, as of the minute we lifted off, no deployment decisions had been made for a Fleet battle group or an ISMC division. That's why we're holding on this side of the jump gate."

"Hurry up and wait."

Anders smiled. "It sounds bad when you put it that way. How does 'prepositioned in preparation for future action' sound?"

Fortis returned the smile. "It sounds a lot like hurry up and wait to me."

"Despite his position as Director of Operations on the General Staff, General Boudreaux has no operational control of conventional Fleet or ISMC forces without specific orders from Admiral Knight, and Knight is forced to wait for a decision from our civilian leadership before he can issue orders."

"Since we're R&D, we're not conventional, so Boudreaux can send us without anyone's permission," Fortis said.

"I asked General Boudreaux if I could bring you along, but you're correct. This move is being made under the purview of the general."

"Huh."

Anders seemed to sense Fortis's skepticism. "Abner, this is a time-critical situation. The general ordered us to deploy because we can get there days ahead of any fleet or division they can send. There's an information gap we need to fill. I asked to bring you and India Company along because decisive action by a small force *right now* can do more to create the conditions for victory than an entire division that arrives next week. Everything depends on what we find when we get to Maltaan."

"Can I brief India on what you've given me so far?"

"Of course. They need to know what's going on. Make sure you explain that I don't know what your tasking will be."

"Roger that, sir. You know we'll do our best to carry out whatever orders you give us, even if it means hurrying up to wait. DINLI."

"I know you will, Abner, and so does General Boudreaux. If an opportunity to insert India Company presents itself, with a chance to impact our chances for success, I'll get you into the action. We'll just have to wait and see."

* * * * *

Chapter Twelve

"Captain Fortis, a moment please."

Fortis turned and saw Dr. Dunker in the passageway behind him.

"Hiya, Doc."

"Whew." Dunker stopped and took several deep breaths. "You're a hard man to catch up with, Captain. Your men said you were with General Anders, but when I got to his quarters, he said you had just left."

"What can I do for you?"

"I have some information for you about Sergeant Connelly's IEBS and also your company organization plan."

"Let's grab some coffee, Doc."

Dunker waited until they were seated in the crew's mess to begin talking.

"My technicians began to assess and repair Unit Eight as soon as we returned to the lab after Sergeant Connelly's incident. I oversaw the work on the retro rocket fuel system, but we did not find a leak or obvious malfunction. The system held pressure, and the monitoring system functioned properly for eight operational tests in a row. I had planned on a series of fifty tests, but General Anders returned."

"The cause of the failure is unknown then," Fortis said.

"No. Well, not exactly. I know what failed, but I have not yet duplicated the failure to prove it. As you know, RRFL is a pre-drop check. Our maintenance logs proved all checks were completed and satisfactory on Unit Eight before the drop, as they were on every other IEBS. Our challenge became figuring out what component could abruptly malfunction and allow the fuel to bleed away." Dunker smiled. "We failed to do that."

"Doc, you lost me. You're happy because you can't figure out what failed?"

"My apologies, Captain. Allow me to explain. In early designs of the IEBS, we measured the actual fuel level in the retro rocket system. We abandoned this approach in favor of measuring system pressure after we built the first prototype and tested it in a zero-gravity environment. When the IEBS is operational, a series of check valves in the system prevent fuel from leaking or being wasted, and sensors monitor pressure at various points throughout. When the fuel system is being refilled, the pressure is measured at the fill system check valve only.

"What I believe happened was the check valve on the fuel fill system failed shut, and the sensor erroneously read full pressure during pre-drop checks. As soon as the system was activated and Sergeant Connelly fired his rockets, the faulty valve began to operate properly, and the system pressure sensors read the accurate pressure.

"That sequence of events is the only one that makes sense, given what we know about the incident. When I programmed a failure of that check valve into the IEBS simulator, it performed exactly as I described. What we haven't been able to do is reproduce the failure in the actual system."

"How do we solve it, then?" Fortis asked. "Airborne assault without a chute is an important advantage we get from the IEBS."

"It's quite simple. I've added a step in the pre-drop checklist to activate the retro rocket system. This new step will test all the system sensors, the check valves, and the system levels. We should have thought of this before, frankly."

"You want us to fire the retro rockets before we drop? Inside the launch platform?"

"No, not fire the rockets. When the wearer switches the system from Combat Mode to Maintenance, the retro rocket system goes into recirculation. No fuel is sent to the rockets, but all the valves and sensors are flexed. When the check is complete and satisfactory, the wearer switches back to Combat Mode."

Fortis nodded his understanding. "I see now. The lads will be glad to hear this."

"Please know that we won't consider this problem solved until we figure out why the valve failed in the first place. Until we do, this added step will ensure the system is fully operational. I came along on this deployment specifically to handle any IEBS issues personally."

"You're always welcome, Doc."

Dunker nodded. "Before I forget, I am building a new IEBS for Connelly instead of repairing his old one. Until I am one hundred percent certain the check valve is the culprit, I won't deploy a suspect system."

"Great. That will make Connelly happy." There was a moment of silence as they sipped from their mugs. "What about the company organization plan?"

"Ah, yes. I received a copy of your plan from the platoon commanders, and I wanted to inform you that I brought more than enough equipment to provide them with the requested number of baseline units for each platoon, as well as snipers, sappers, and grenadiers. What I need from you is how you want the ten-man command element configured."

"Doc, I saw the plan for about thirty seconds in the shuttle bay right after we got here before General Anders pulled me aside. Give me a couple hours to talk it over with Gunny Ystremski, and I'll get something to you."

"Very good, Captain." Dunker stood. "Speaking of the gunny, my techs are building his chassis as we speak."

"Make it a little tight in the crotch if you don't mind, Doc."

Dunker laughed. "Thank you for your time, Captain."

The two men shook hands and then walked toward the shuttle bay. Dunker turned and headed for the cargo bay where his pack-up kit was located, while Fortis turned for the shuttle bay.

"If you're looking for your men, they're in the cargo bay," Dunker said. "They're assisting my technicians with the configuration changes to their IEBS."

Fortis stopped inside the cargo bay hatch and watched the activity taking place around the cargo bay. The Space Marines and Dunker's technicians had arranged the IEBS in ranks, and teams of two or three were working together to configure the IEBS.

Ystremski noticed Fortis watching and joined him.

"Have I told you how much I hate Maltaan?" Fortis asked.

The gunny snorted. "Only every fucking day. How's the general, sir?"

"He's good. He plans to brief the company before we get to the gate. How are things going here?"

"Once we got organized, things started moving right along. We're almost finished with First Platoon's configurations. When we're done, we'll stow the IEBS and break for chow, then reconfigure Second Platoon."

"Good. Doc Dunker asked me how I want the command element configured. What do you think?"

Ystremski thought for a second. "Six grenadiers and four sappers ought to do it."

"I can understand the grenadiers. The dual forty-millimeter launcher is pretty awesome, but four sappers? Do you think we'll need breaching charges and anti-personnel mines?"

"No sir, but the flame generating units are a good piece of kit."

Fortis nodded. "I forgot about the FGU. What about snipers? Do we want a couple of them with us?"

"We've only got a few long-range shooters in the company, so we assigned them to the platoons. If we get into a long-range gunfight, I'd rather throw frags downrange than try and snipe our way out of trouble."

"Okay, let's do that. I'll take one of the grenadier setups, and you can figure out who else gets what. Give me a heads up when we start work on the command element."

"Roger that, sir."

Fortis watched as Ystremski went back to overseeing the Space Marines while they assembled the IEBS. The mood in the cargo bay was light but not frivolous; in typical Space Marine fashion, they happily went about their deadly serious work.

It pleased him that Gunny Ystremski had joined the company, and he was also pleased that Moultrie had reassigned Brooks. The master sergeant was close to retirement, and he took the billet with the IEBS program as a way of getting an inside track on a civilian career in the program when he left the Corps. Brooks had performed his duties as the senior NCO of the company in exemplary fashion while they tested the IEBS, but there was a world of difference between administering the company on the training grounds in Kinshasa and leading them into harm's way. There was no other Space Marine in the Corps Fortis would rather go downrange with than Petr Ystremski.

"Something wrong, Skipper?" LT Penny had approached Fortis while he was lost in thought. "You were shaking your head."

"Was I? No, there's nothing wrong. I was just thinking. How's it going with First Platoon?"

"We just finished, and the boys are stowing our IEBS. After chow, we'll get back at it and work on Second Platoon. We should be done soon."

"Excellent. General Anders is going to brief the company on the current situation on Maltaan sometime soon."

By then, LT Young had joined them.

"The lads are anxious to get back in action," Penny said. "Honestly, I am, too."

Young nodded in agreement.

"We don't have a good grasp on what's happening on Maltaan right now," Fortis told them. "I think we need to keep a lid on talk of getting back in action. There's a good chance we'll spend our time drilling circles in space waiting on Sixth Division, so don't let the company get too excited."

True to their word, India Company got back to work on Second Platoon's IEBS after chow, and they were restowing the last of the reconfigured units when *Eclipse Wonder* passed the word for lights out. After the platoon commanders detailed plans to work on the command element IEBS in the morning, they dismissed their men. Fortis decided to check on the status of the drones before he turned in.

When he poked his head into the drone control room, Anders waved to him from a row of consoles in the back.

"We're just about to launch," the general said when Fortis slid into the empty seat next to him.

"Don't we have to slow down?" Fortis asked.

"No. *Eclipse Wonder* has a purpose-built drone launching system that allows her to launch drones at speed," Anders said. "Unlike the systems you've seen on the flagships, there are no rails to extend. Everything is internal to the ship. Each drone is carried in its own cell, and when the launch order is given, the cell door opens, and the drone rockets fire."

"Sounds like a big improvement over what we were using."

"It is. It's funny, really. We used to launch missiles like this all the time, but with the advent of rail gun technology, someone decided to use rails for everything. Now, we've circled back to using cells again, and some people talk about it like it's a major innovation."

"General, we're ready to launch," one of the control room personnel reported.

"Launch," Anders commanded.

Fortis didn't hear or feel anything, but he saw two drone symbols separate from the ship on the tactical display and speed away.

"They'll arrive at the gate tomorrow, and by the time we get to the gate the day after, they'll be on their way to Maltaan and hopefully have some answers for us."

"It would be good to know more about what we're facing," Fortis said. "For your information, we have completed reconfigurations on First and Second Platoon IEBS. We'll work on the command element in the morning and should be finished no later than midday."

"That was quick work," Anders said.

"I was told the company is anxious to get back into action." Fortis grinned. "I can't say I blame them, but I told the platoon commanders to temper their excitement."

"Has the equipment casualty to Sergeant Connelly's IEBS been resolved?"

"Not resolved, but Doctor Dunker came up with a workaround to make sure it doesn't happen again. He believes it was a faulty valve and sensor in the retro rocket fuel system, so he added a step to the pre-drop checklist to fully test the system in Maintenance Mode. He also built Connelly a new chassis rather than use a suspect one, at least until he knows for certain the fault has been corrected."

"Good. Dunker is a brilliant man, and the IEBS program has been his sole focus for a long time." Anders stood. "I'd love to talk some more, but it's been a long day. Do you have anything else for me?"

Fortis followed Anders into the passageway. "No sir."

"Good night."

* * * * *

Chapter Thirteen

The Second Mech command comms watch stander sat up and fumbled for her headset when the circuit came to life.

"Command, this is Recon One. We're in position at the edge of the forest, but there's nothing here. Standing by for tasking."

"This is Command, roger, wait." She poked her head up through the hatch and looked down at Major van der Cruyff who was snoozing on the ground next to the mech. "Major. Major! Recon One is on the horn."

Van der Cruyff sat up, wide awake. "Okay, thanks." He stood, stretched out the kinks in his back, and climbed inside.

"They said they're in position," the comms watch said as the major slid into his seat.

"Recon One, this is Second Mech Actual. What's your status?"

"Sir, we're on the edge of the forest, but there's nothing here. The road is empty, and the fields are deserted."

"Roger that. Launch a drone to recon the space port. While you're at it, scout around for a new position for the battalion."

"This is Recon One, roger."

The major took off his headset and stood. "Find the XO and the company commanders and ask them to join me down here for a quick huddle-mumble," he told the comms watch stander before he climbed out.

"Are we moving out, sir?" Fessler asked when van der Cruyff's boots hit the ground.

"I don't know. Probably. We can't stay here."

Van der Cruyff loathed meetings, and he considered the authority to call meetings one of the most dangerous powers ever given to officers. Nevertheless, the current situation merited a face-to-face with his commanders. He didn't lead by committee, but he wanted their input before he made his final decision. The major could have ordered the battalion to mount up and head west and they would have obeyed, but that style of leadership bred uncertainty and stifled initiative.

A short while later, the Second Mech leadership cadre gathered in the muted glow of an orange chem light.

"We're one short," van der Cruyff said. "Who's missing?"

"Gunny Vinn went with Recon One," Gunny Perkins, commander of Recon Two said. "I'll fill her in when we're done."

Van der Cruyff nodded. "Before I start, does anyone have any issues?"

Chief Warrant Officer Heinz, commander of Main Battle Mech Company Yankee raised a finger. "Skipper, Yankee Two Six has a major fault in the main pulse cannon power generator that we can't clear. It's the same thing as last time, and it will be inoperative until we get the replacement part. *If* we get the part." He cast a look at Captain Madison, who flushed red in the dim orange light.

"It's on order, Chief. What do you want me to do, fly back to Terra Earth and pick it up in person?"

Van der Cruyff held up his hand. "Enough already. We don't have time to get into that now. Can Two Six still roll?"

Heinz nodded. "Yes sir. Everything else works just fine. Mini guns and grenade launchers are all good. I'd send her home, but we might need a rolling hangar queen to cannibalize."

The major pointed at Madison. "How about you, Captain? Are we good on bullets and beans?"

"We have two days' food and water," Madison said. "We haven't received any requisitions for ammunition or pulse rifle batteries."

"Two days? That's not much."

"The OPORD calls for all units to deploy with three days' worth," she said in a matter-of-fact tone. "Resupply will be organized by the logistics companies after final deployments are made."

"The OPORD was written when there were still logistics companies to resupply us," van der Cruyff replied. "They're all gone, so we need to be a little more self-sufficient these days." He looked around the group. "Anybody else?"

They all shook their heads.

"All right then. I brought you together to tell you that we're going to move west to a position closer to Daarben. I haven't received any orders to move, but we can't stay strung out along the road waiting for orders that might not come. I sent Recon One ahead to reconnoiter Daarben with drones and maybe get some answers to what the fuck's going on. Does anyone have any questions?"

"What about First Mech?" the XO asked.

"I'll let Major Southwick know what we're doing. If she wants to move First Mech with us, that's her decision. We'll coordinate with them as necessary."

"Sir, what time do you expect to move out?" Madison asked. "I'd like to send a couple trucks back to Ulvaan to load up more rations and water."

"It won't be for a couple hours, at least. We need to give Recon One time to find a place for us to move to. When I—"

A call on the command circuit interrupted him.

"Command, Recon Two. That Maltaani convoy is coming back, but there's something strange going on. There's a shuttle flying overhead, and it's shining a blue light on them."

Recon Two was the second recon mech company in the battalion, positioned at the eastern end of their position.

"Stand by," van der Cruyff told the battalion officers and NCOs. He climbed into the command mech and grabbed his headset. "Recon Two, this is Second Mech Actual. Say again, over."

"Sir, this is Recon Two. It looks like the Maltaani are headed back to Daarben, but it's weird. They're all on foot, and there's a ship with a blue spotlight flying over them. It's like they're lighting the way."

"This is Command, roger. All stations, stay under cover. Out."

The major grabbed his helmet from where he'd left it in the mech and climbed out. "There's something happening on the road back toward Ulvaan. Get back to your posts."

The group broke up, and Fessler and Moon joined van der Cruyff in the road. They looked east, where an eerie blue glow grew visible in the distance.

"What's that?" Fessler asked.

"I don't know." The major put his helmet on and dialed up the command frequency. "Recon Two, Command. Report your status."

"This is Recon Two. The blue light...it's...I can't describe it. Don't look at it without your visor. The Maltaani are walking, but it's like they're asleep or something. It's hard to see, but the ship with the light is bigger than a cargo hovercopter. It's quiet, though. Just a low buzz."

"All stations, this is Command. Stay in your positions with visors down. Do not fire unless fired upon." He switched to the inter-battalion net. "First Mech, this is Second Mech Actual, looking for your CO."

After a brief pause, he heard Southwick's voice. *This is Southwick, go ahead.*

"My eastern recon reports the Maltaani refugees are headed back this way, escorted by a ship with a blue light. Are your folks seeing that?"

"Affirmative. We've received a couple reports about it so far."

"Be advised, my recon warned us not to look at the blue light without visors. I don't know what's going on with the light, but that might be worth passing on to your troops."

"This is First Mech Actual, roger, thanks for the heads up."

By then, van der Cruyff could see the shadowy shapes of the Maltaani trudging along, bathed in the blue glow.

"Let's get off the road," he told Fessler and Moon. They ducked back under cover and waited for the Maltaani to pass.

As the procession approached, van der Cruyff saw that Recon Two was right; the ship hovering over the Maltaani was much bigger than a cargo hovercopter, and quiet, too. The refugees slogged along in eerie blue silence, heads down, arms loose.

"Are they prisoners?" Moon muttered.

"It sure as hell looks like it."

"It's gonna take a while for the road west to clear," said Fessler.

After the group of refugees was well down the road, van der Cruyff crossed and found Major Southwick.

"Hey, Twila. I came over to tell you I'm moving Second Mech closer to Daarben as soon as those refugees are clear of the road. You're welcome to come with us."

"Have you heard from MAC-M? What did they say?"

"I haven't heard a word from them."

"Then why are you moving? Shouldn't we wait for guidance?"

"I don't think Toro intended us to stay here for long," van der Cruyff said. "When he told me to hole up, I took it to mean for a few hours, maybe overnight. That was before we lost contact, and the blue light parade went by. Now, I don't know what the hell is going on, but I know our position sucks and we need to move."

"I don't like it, Jan. Moving without orders, I mean."

Van der Cruyff shrugged. "You don't have to come. It's up to you."

"Who's senior, you or me?" Southwick asked.

"This isn't a matter of seniority," van der Cruyff said. "It's a matter of force readiness. If I'm senior, I'm not ordering you to follow, and if I'm junior, I'm moving anyway. None of this feels right, and I don't like our tactical disposition. I sent my Recon One ahead to the edge of the forest to conduct drone surveillance of the space port and scout around for a good position for Second Mech. Do you want me to task them with finding a good spot for First Mech?"

"Hmm." Southwick rubbed her chin. "I don't think so. What if Toro orders us back to Ulvaan?"

"I guess he'll chew my ass," van der Cruyff said with a smile. "In the meantime, Second Mech is moving out. How are you fixed for food and water?"

"I'm not sure. I guess we're okay. My logistics officer hasn't said anything."

Van der Cruyff stifled the urge to laugh in her face. "We've got two days left, so I'm sending a convoy back to load up on pig squares and water. Tell your folks to find Captain Madison if you want to get in on it."

"Sounds good, thanks. Say, Jan, what do you make of all this? I mean, you were in on the invasion, so you know a lot more about this place than I do. What's going on?"

"I wish I could tell you," he said. "When I talked to the colonel, he told me the exercise had turned into an attack, but he didn't give any details. Who's attacking, the Maltaani? What are they attacking with? Then we saw those refugees and that ship with the blue light. Who was that?" Van der Cruyff stopped himself when he realized he was giving voice to his uncertainty. "The short answer is, I don't know, but I know we won't get any answers sitting here. Maybe holding First Mech here is the best move. If we're ordered to move on Daarben, you'll be in position to support, and if we move on Ulvaan, we'll support you."

Van der Cruyff agreed to share any intel gathered by Recon One, and the officers returned to their battalions.

"Major, Gunny Vinn called while you were talking with Major Southwick," the comms watch stander told him when he climbed back in the command mech. "She requested that you contact her as soon as you returned."

"Is there a problem?" Van der Cruyff asked as he donned his headset and sat at his console.

"She didn't say, sir."

"Recon One, this is Second Mech Actual. I'm looking for Gunny Vinn."

"This is Vinn. We found a new position for the battalion and got our first dump from the drone. There are a bunch of unfamiliar craft at the space port, but we haven't observed other activity. I can't get a lock on a satellite circuit to send you the video, but there's not much to look at."

"Huh. Okay, Gunny. Be advised, the same foot convoy that passed us heading east just passed us headed west, but this time, they have an escort. Some kind of ship with a blue light. We don't know what it is, but don't look at the light without your visor."

"Roger that, thanks for the heads up, sir. Do you have any further instructions for the drones?"

"Not right now. Shut down and let your guys get some rest. Let us know when those refugees are clear so we can get on the road. Maybe we can get some answers tomorrow."

* * * * *

Chapter Fourteen

After Recon One reported the refugees had passed them heading west, Major van der Cruyff ordered Second Mech to mount up. He repeated his offer to Major Southwick, but she demurred again. He waved as Second Mech pulled out.

When Second Mech arrived at their new position, he directed the command mech driver to pull over, and he stood in the open hatch and watched as the rest of the battalion rolled past and followed Recon One's directions into the forest. Gunny Vinn climbed onto the mech and joined him.

"It's been quiet since we talked, Major. The group of Maltaani went past and kept going down the hill toward the space port. That blue light is kind of spooky," she said with a self-conscious chuckle.

"I don't know what it is," he said. "I'm hoping to get some answers from MAC-M when we get comms with them."

A low rumble in the distance drew their attention. Vinn cupped her hand to her ear and swiveled to identify which direction the sound came from.

"East," Vinn said as she pointed back the way Second Mech had come. Van der Cruyff stared up the road and caught a faint blue flash on the horizon.

"Did you see that?"

"Yes sir, I saw it."

He ducked into the mech. "Call First Mech and request their status," he ordered the comms watch.

After several unsuccessful attempts to raise First Mech, van der Cruyff made up his mind.

"I'm going to send Recon Two to check it out." He put on his headset. "Recon Two, this is Command. I just detected some blue lights flashing in the sky behind us and what sounded like explosions. Send one of your mechs back to investigate and report. Don't get too close and watch out for unidentified craft."

"Roger that."

Van der Cruyff emerged from the mech in time to see the last vehicle in the column, a recon mech, peel off and speed back up the road.

"They going to check it out, sir?" Sergeant Major Fessler, who had been assisting Major Moon in guiding the battalion to their positions, stood next to the command mech.

"Yeah. First Mech isn't answering, so I sent Recon Two to take a look." He motioned to the forest. "What's the status of the battalion?"

"They're all deployed. Gunny Vinn found us some good ground," Fester said as he nodded at the Recon One leader.

"Good. Any idea where the XO is?"

"I left him with the clerks and jerks when I heard those explosions."

"Huh."

Space Marine infantry referred to administrative and logistics personnel as "clerks and jerks," although they did so with grudging respect. Every Space Marine was a warrior first, but someone had to keep the regular infantry fed and watered. As battalion executive officer, Moon spent most of his time orchestrating the support the Space

Marines needed to fight but van der Cruyff knew Moon's interest wasn't out of concern for the infantry, it was for Captain Madison.

Van der Cruyff ducked into the mech. "Follow the column into the woods and park this thing," he told the driver. "I'm gonna stretch my legs and take a look around."

The major jumped down to the road next to Fessler and watched the command mech bump off the road and disappear into the trees. Even with his low light visor, he had a hard time spotting the Space Marines concealed in their new positions, and if it weren't for infrared, the few he could detect would have been invisible.

"Let's go find the XO," he told Fessler.

* * *

Lance Corporal Charity Will yawned and rubbed her eyes. As the command mech comms watch for First Mech, it was her job to monitor communications and keep the tactical plot current, and she was good at her job.

Too good.

Will had anticipated sleeping in the previous morning after a late night spent partying with the guys from Second Mech, but the security drill had torpedoed her plans. She'd been up all day as the battalion rumbled their way west toward Daarben, and after the convoy stopped, Sergeant Barksdale, the mech commander, had assigned her the night watch. She sighed and cracked another stim-pack, a jolt of chemical energy in capsule form. The stim-pack made her jittery, but it gave her plenty of energy to count the days she had remaining on her enlistment as she replayed the circus that had been First Mech's deployment so far.

From the moment Barksdale had shaken Will awake eighteen hours ago, everything had been a clusterfuck. Major Southwick was a nice person, but she was ill-suited to command a Space Marine battalion, and her incompetence created havoc despite the best efforts of the battalion staff and company commanders. Will had had to page through the OPORD to identify what actions the battalion should take when they received the first message from MAC-M, because Southwick hadn't known how to access it through the command mech electronic library. Even then, it had taken badgering from the company commanders and the sight of Second Mech moving out to convince Southwick it wasn't a command post exercise, and the battalion was supposed to deploy.

First Mech had barely begun to organize when MAC-M arrived via hovercopter and gave Major Southwick the most savage ass-chewing Will had ever witnessed. It worked, because the major snapped out of her torpor and began to issue orders. It took two hours, but First Mech finally got on the road. That's when Will's real troubles began. Her well-earned hangover had become a world class headache as First Mech moved west, and the command mech's stiff suspension turned every bump and rut in the road into a bone-jarring jolt. Barksdale had assigned the mech driver to stock the vehicle with hydration packs, which the driver had promptly failed to do. Will scrounged hydration packs from the rest of the convoy, and she hit up Doc Brumley for painkillers during one of their infrequent rest stops, but the pounding in her head persisted.

The symbols for the supply convoy began to flash on her map screen, which usually occurred when the vehicles stopped updating their position in the tactical data system. Just as Will keyed her mic to call the convoy, the symbols disappeared.

What the hell?

She switched to the internal comms circuit.

"Major, the supply convoy just dropped out of the system."

"Wha-what?" Southwick's voice was slurred, and Will knew she'd been sound asleep at her console in the next compartment.

"The supply convoy stopped updating and then dropped out of the tactical data system, ma'am." After a long moment of silence, Will repeated, "The supply convoy stopped updating in the system, and then they disappeared."

"Where are they?"

"Their last reported position was near Ulvaan."

"Maybe they shut down when they got there."

Will sighed and shook her head. "They're not supposed to do that when detached from the main force. Their last reported position should still be on the display until it's deleted by the system manager."

"Have you called the system manager? Maybe they deleted their position for some reason."

"I—you—are the system manager. I mean, the command mech runs the data system, not individual stations."

"So call them and tell them to get back up in the system. I don't understand why you're bothering me with this."

The major's voice had gone from sleepy to annoyed, and Will fought the urge to snap back.

"I was about to call them when they dropped out. I'm advising you, the tactical commander of the convoy, that some of your units have dropped out of the system."

"Fine. Fix it."

Will made several attempts to contact the supply convoy, but her hails went unanswered. She completed successful comm checks with other units in First Mech, and even the Second Mech command mech, but the supply convoy still wasn't answering. Finally, she had the First Mech XO's mech watch attempt to contact them, to no avail.

"Will, what's up?" Major Dabrowski, First Mech's executive officer, called her on a point-to-point channel from the other command mech. *"I hear you calling around."*

"Sir, the supply convoy dropped out of the system, and Major Southwick directed me to call and get them back up. They weren't answering me, so I asked your comms watch to try. I guess the problem is on their end, because I can talk to everyone but them."

"Huh. What do you think it is?"

"It's not the range, because we can talk to MAC-M from Ulvaan. If they didn't drop on purpose, my guess is it's an atmospheric thing. Maybe there are minerals in the mountains interfering with the signal."

"System fault, maybe?"

"I don't think so, sir. I ran a quick diagnostic routine and there were no faults. I guess I can reboot the system to see if it clears, but that means bringing the entire system down for a moment."

There was a moment of silence, and Will imagined Dabrowski rubbing his hands together like he always did while he contemplated a decision.

"Do it. Alert all units you're rebooting and then do it. It will be light in an hour or so, and we can't start a new day with a jacked-up system."

"Roger that, sir."

"And let me know when it's back up."

After she notified the battalion the system would be down for a moment, Will's fingers flew across her keyboard as she entered the commands to reboot her computer. She wasn't confident the reboot would resolve the supply convoy issue. The ISMC had the best computers lowest bidders could provide, and there was no telling where an undiagnosed fault might exist. She hit "enter" and waited for the login screen to appear. Instead of the familiar ISMC logo, she got the blue screen of death.

Fuck.

Will powered down her console and brought it back up, but the blue screen persisted. Panic set in as she tried everything she could think of to get her console operating again, to no avail. Exasperated, she slammed her hand on top of the console, and the login screen appeared.

"About fucking time," Will grumbled as she entered the boot-up commands. As soon as the system was restored, alarms began blaring and hostile symbols filled her screen.

"What's going on?" Major Southwick demanded over the circuit.

"I rebooted the system to clear the supply convoy errors, and now it thinks we're under attack."

A large explosion rocked the command mech.

"What the hell was that?"

"We're under attack!"

A second explosion slammed into the vehicle, and Will tumbled from her seat as the force of the blast rolled the mech onto its side. She heard a *pop* in her neck when she landed on her head in a heap of hydration packs, pig squares, and personal gear. While the mech rolled, unsecured hatches popped open, and Will clearly heard the sound of main battle mech pulse cannons. Her comms headset had stayed in place, and she found the push to talk button.

"This is First Mech." The effort it took to transmit was almost more than Will could bear. "Something's happening. The enemy are all over the fucking place. Who are they?"

Exhausted, Will slumped into the debris of the mech and closed her eyes.

* * *

Befor van der Cruyff and Fessler could leave the road in search of the XO, they heard more explosions and saw blue lights flashing in the distance.

"What the fuck is going on back there?" Fessler asked.

"Sir, First Mech just called," the command mech comms watch reported. *"The transmission was…well…weird. I tried calling back, but they're not responding. I've got it queued up at your console if you want to listen to it."*

"I'm on my way." The major looked at Fessler. "Keep an eye on things out here, would you?" He almost collided with a group of Space Marines that had begun to gather on the road and stare at the dark eastern sky. "Get where you're supposed to be!"

Van der Cruyff chuckled as he ducked into the forest and heard Fessler growl at the Space Marines. When he was a brand-new recruit, his drill instructor had often ordered his company to "Get where you're supposed to be!" Since nobody had known where they were supposed to be, the recruits scrambled in all directions and tried to look busy. He imagined the Space Marines scrambling to avoid Fessler's wrath.

"Whaddya got?" the major asked as he climbed into the command mech.

"Button Four, sir,"

Van der Cruyff donned his headset and dialed up the right channel.

"This is First Mech," an agonized voice groaned over the circuit. He heard pulse cannons firing in the background. *"Something's happening.*

The enemy—" the circuit cut out for a moment *"—all over the fucking place. Who are the—"* The circuit went dead.

"That's all of it, sir. I've been calling, but there's no answer."

"Those were pulse cannons in the background. Who are they fighting?"

"I don't know, sir. Nobody has reported Maltaani troop movements since we left Ulvaan."

"Fuck!" Van der Cruyff looked at his tactical display. The symbol for Recon Two was halfway between First and Second Mech.

"What about Recon Two? Have they reported?"

"No sir."

"Order them to hold where they're at. Get off the road and into cover. What about the supply convoy? Any word from them?"

"Negative. Captain Madison said she hasn't talked to them since they left. I can't raise them either."

"After you get ahold of Recon Two, try the supply convoy again and get their status. If they're in Ulvaan, tell them to stay there and wait for orders."

"Roger that, sir."

While the comms watch called Recon Two and the supply convoy, van der Cruyff dialed up the command channel to talk to his company commanders.

"This is Actual. Something is happening back east, around First Mech. We just received a broken transmission from them, and it sounded like there was fighting."

"Who are they fighting?" CWO Heinz asked.

"I don't know, Warrant. It's gotta be the unknowns Toro warned us about. The ships with the blue lights, maybe."

"This whole situation is FUBAR."

"Maybe so, but we're still at Alert Condition Alpha," van der Cruyff reminded his leaders. "It's almost full light, and we should get more information when the recon mech reports. Until then, maintain maximum readiness."

* * * * *

Chapter Fifteen

Private First Class Benny "CB" Brumley crouched in the undergrowth atop a small ridge on the mountain slope above the Daarben-Ulvaan road. All around him, the other members of the squad-sized patrol were also catching their breath and resting their tired legs.

When CB heard about the early morning foot patrol, he had surprised Sergeant Ferguson, the leader of First Squad, when he volunteered to go. As one of two corpsmen assigned to Alpha Company (Recon), CB normally didn't go on patrol with anything smaller than a platoon, but then again, CB was anything but normal. He had a habit of allowing his hair to grow within a millimeter of acceptable ISMC grooming standards and an irrepressible good nature that shone brightest when conditions were toughest. Most ISMC corpsmen answered to "Doc," but CB had earned his nickname from his favorite quip, "What's up, chicken butt?" CB came across as a screwball, but he was a skilled corpsman and became deadly serious when circumstances demanded it.

Ferguson had led the patrol a hundred meters up the mountain before they turned west along a rocky ridge that paralleled the road below. When the patrol set off, their movements had been slow and deliberate, but as the sky lightened, the pace picked up. The patrol had the feel of a lark. Nobody expected trouble, but the ongoing security alert had given the patrol an added sense of adventure. As CB had

150 | P.A. PIATT

moved among the Space Marines of First Mech dispensing pain killers and stim-packs the previous day, even battalion leadership had thought the whole thing was an exercise.

"Break's over," Ferguson said on the patrol channel. *"On your feet."*

When CB stood, his legs protested. A sudden cramp knotted his left calf, and he stumbled a half-step backward. Loose rocks gave way under his feet, and he tumbled over the back side of the ridge.

"Crap!"

CB rolled and slid to a stop at the bottom of a steep ravine. After a quick self-check revealed no injuries, he untangled himself from the bushes and stood.

"Brumley, what are you doing?" CB looked up and saw Ferguson and several other Space Marines peering over the edge of the ravine. *"Are you okay?"*

"I'm okay, Sergeant. I missed a step."

"Well, quit screwing around and get back up here. We're moving out."

"Roger that." CB adjusted his pulse rifle tactical sling and checked to make sure he still had his first aid kit.

Before he could begin the climb to rejoin the patrol, he heard a low growl from the dark underbrush and froze. Five meters away, a huge Maltaani dog stepped into view. The beast had thick, muscular shoulders and a wide, flat head. Drool leaked from its mouth, and CB watched its glistening nostrils quiver as it investigated the unfamiliar human scent. His mouth dried out, and his pulse quickened as he eased his hands down onto his pulse rifle. A strange calm settled over CB as a million thoughts raced through his mind, and his initial jolt of fear became a surge of joy at his good fortune.

Since the first encounter between the Space Marines and the Maltaani during the Battle of Balfan-48, the humans had developed a powerful hatred for the Maltaani dogs. The Maltaani trained the beasts to savage their enemies, especially prisoners, and the Space Marines destroyed the dogs every chance they got. A necklace made from Maltaani dog fangs was a much sought-after souvenir, made all the rarer since the nationalist insurgency ended, and the Maltaani had stopped breeding the hounds to use as weapons. The best chance a Space Marine had to kill one of the elusive creatures was in the wild. Like now.

What made this encounter especially important was that CB's older brother Red, a hovercopter pilot with Third Division, had a necklace with a single dog fang. One of the special operators Red worked with had presented it to the pilot as a thank you for a hairy mission, and the elder brother made sure to work it into the conversation whenever they met. If CB could kill the dog, he'd have a whole necklace to answer Reds taunts.

If.

"CB, what's the hold up?" Ferguson demanded.

"I've got a small problem, Sergeant." CB fought to keep his hands and voice steady as he raised his pulse rifle. "There's a dog down here."

The slobbering monster glared at CB. Its ears were laid back, and yellowed fangs protruded from under a curled top lip, but it didn't advance.

CB had his pulse rifle halfway to his shoulder when the dog perked up its ears and looked back over its shoulder. Before CB could react, it turned and disappeared into the underbrush in a single bound.

"Did you say a dog? I don't see a dog down there."

CB stared at the spot where the dog had disappeared and waited, alert to the possibility it would return and attack, but the beast was gone. He let out a ragged breath.

"It's gone, Sergeant." CB looked up at the near-vertical incline. "If it's okay with you, I'm going to follow this ravine for a little way and find a place that's not so steep to climb out."

"Make it quick. There's something going on back at the convoy, and we're headed that way. Give me a call when you're out."

In the background of Ferguson's transmission, CB heard what sounded like pulse cannons firing.

Who's shooting?

He considered making a quip about Space Marines leaving a comrade behind but decided against it.

"Roger that."

A tingle—fear? —went up his spine as CB started to follow the ravine in search of a place to climb out. He didn't want to turn his back on the place where the dog had disappeared, but he wasn't going to follow it into the dense underbrush. He stopped and looked around every few steps, but the forest was silent. CB was comfortable in the woods, having grown up exploring and hunting the wilderness around his boyhood home, but there were no murderous dogs or man-eating snakes there.

After fifteen minutes of snaking through the boulders and fallen logs that clogged the ravine, CB let out a sigh of relief when he saw the forest canopy begin to thin out ahead. He scrambled up to the ridge and stopped to catch his breath, and when he did, he heard the sounds of a distant battle.

What the heck?

He tried calling on the circuit, but his transmissions were met with silence. CB figured he was about five klicks from the convoy, well within range, but there was no answer. After a final glance into the chasm, CB began to pick his way through the forest back toward First Mech.

* * *

Sixty minutes later, CB stopped to assess the situation. He estimated he was five hundred meters from the convoy, but the sounds of battle had faded as he made his way through the forest, and everything was quiet.

"Any station this net, this is Brumley," he whispered into his mic. There was no response.

He continued to descend to the road, moving from tree to tree and stopping every few steps to listen for any signs of the battalion. For a brief second, he thought they might have left him behind, but he dispelled the notion with a shake of his head.

CB paused at the edge of the tree line and looked at the road below. What he saw shocked and scared him.

Mechs were scattered haphazardly along the road as if the drivers had all tried to go different directions and caused a massive traffic jam. Several of the main battle mechs were charred wrecks, and CB recognized two recon mechs amid the wreckage. Half a dozen APCs lined the middle of the road with their hatches open and ramps down as if waiting for Space Marines to load up. It was obvious there had been a desperate battle fought on this stretch of road, but something about the scene left CB especially distressed. He finally realized what it was.

Pulse rifles and other gear littered the ground, and bloody drag marks smeared the gravel. An entire battalion had fought and died on the road, but there were no Space Marines, dead or alive, among the vehicles.

Where is everybody?

* * *

Lance Corporal Will came to with a start.
How long was I out?

Her head ached, and her body tingled, and it took her a moment to remember where she was and how she ended up there. Her arms gave out when she tried to prop herself up, so she rolled over onto her belly and squirmed for the open hatch next to her. She flopped onto the road amid a pile of debris next to the upended mech and looked around.

Acrid smoke from an electrical fire stung her nose, overlaid by the burnt ozone smell of pulse cannons. Burning mechs dotted the road, and she saw dead Space Marines sprawled among the wrecks. She heard pulse rifles shooting near the head of the convoy, but the firing quickly died out.

A sudden thought seized her, and Will scrambled to get off the road and into the bushes. Whoever had destroyed First Mech would be back, and Will didn't want to be there to greet them. She felt clumsy, like her mind had occupied someone else's body, but she managed to stagger several meters into the forest before she lost control of her legs and slumped down behind a fallen tree.

A buzzing sound got her attention, and Will peered out from her hiding place. A large black craft, like the one that had overflown the mech battalions the previous night, hovered over the shattered remains of First Mech. A brilliant beam of blue light flashed down to the ground, and on instinct, Will rolled over and covered her eyes. Second Mech had warned against looking at the light without a visor, and Will's helmet was somewhere in the rubble of the command mech.

Along with my pulse rifle and battle armor.

The buzzing faded as the craft moved slowly to the west, and Will chanced a peek at the road. The wrecked vehicles were still there, but all the Space Marine casualties were gone. She crept forward and looked in the direction the craft had flown, and her stomach lurched.

Hundreds of Space Marines were trudging along with their heads down and arms loose at their sides, bathed in the blue light. Some were dragging their grievously wounded or dead comrades by an arm or leg, and long smears of blood on the gravel marked their passing. The scene was even more horrific because they shuffled along in complete silence.

Deep sobs wracked her body, and tears poured down her cheeks as she curled into a ball and hugged her knees to her chest. Will had seen no action in her two years of service in the ISMC, not even a bug hunt, but she'd had unshakeable confidence in their warfighting prowess. The horror of watching her fellow Space Marines so easily defeated and the sight of them marching away as prisoners shocked and frightened her. All her bravado vanished in an instant, and Will became the twenty-year-old young woman she was.

After she cried herself out, Will forced herself to sit up.

Stop feeling sorry for yourself, idiot.

She could push away self-pity, but the realization that she had survived the attack by running away sent a tidal wave of guilt breaking over her. She gasped and almost started crying aloud before she caught herself.

Stop it!

Will focused on her immediate problem, survival and rescue. She had regained the use of her arms and legs, but her neck still ached, and when she touched the sore spot, she discovered a knot just above the collar of her mech crew coveralls. She had skinned the knuckles on both hands somewhere between the upended mech and her hiding place in the woods, and one of her sleeves was ripped from shoulder to elbow, but Will was otherwise intact. She knew there was a first aid kit somewhere in the command mech, along with pig squares, stim-packs, and most importantly, hydration packs.

Will studied the scene on the road and searched the sky for more of the black ships. When she was confident she was alone, she left the cover of the trees and crossed to the command mech. She held her breath as she ducked inside, afraid of what she might find, but the mech was deserted.

The locker that held her hydration packs had sprung open, so Will slumped down next to it and sucked down two without stopping. Warm hydration packs had always had a faint metallic taste to Will, but those two tasted as sweet as the DINLI the Space Marines brewed from local Maltaani fruit. After she slaked her thirst, Will looked around and realized she was sitting next to her pulse rifle. She worked the action and checked the battery charge. Satisfied the weapon was battle ready, she dug around and found her battle armor and helmet in the pile. Pain exploded down her neck when she slipped the helmet on, so she stacked it on top of her armor next to the open hatch.

Will paused and considered her situation. Someone on- or off-planet knew what was going on and would dispatch a fleet to respond. Maybe a whole division. It might take a week or more for them to arrive, but they would be there. All she had to do was manage on her own until then with whatever rations she could find. Even on its side, the command mech was a better shelter than anything she could make in the forest. If the black ships returned, she might be caught in the open. Still, she didn't relish the thought of sleeping in the forest. She'd seen enough Maltaani dog fang necklaces and ten-meter snake skins during her short time on Maltaan to convince her the forest was a dangerous place to be.

Will cracked the hatch and peeked into the commander's compartment. She was terrified she would find Major Southwick's body, but it was empty. She checked the driver's compartment, but it was likewise vacant. Satisfied that she was alone, Will sorted out the mess in her compartment, then she clambered into the driver's compartment and gathered all the first aid gear and rations she could find. Southwick's compartment received the same treatment.

While she worked, Will pushed thoughts of Barksdale and Southwick out of her mind. The things she collected didn't belong to them anymore, they belonged to her, and this helped assuage the guilt she felt as she dug through their personal lockers and gear. She faltered when pictures of Barksdale and his family back on Terra Earth spilled out as she opened a drawer, and she hurriedly tucked them out of sight.

When she finished in the command mech, Will had a hundred hydration packs, twice as many pig squares, a big handful of stim-packs, and four first aid kits.

Not even three weeks. Not enough.

With a sigh, Will climbed out of the mech and surveyed the nearby vehicles on the road. After a long look around, she slung her pulse rifle over her shoulder and headed back to her hideout in the trees. There would be time enough for scavenging later. Right now, she just wanted to sleep. Her head ached, and when she closed her eyes, she saw a bright blue light behind her eyelids.

As she sank into unconsciousness, Will thought she heard hovercopter engines.

Just a dream.

* * * * *

Chapter Sixteen

Just after first light, Red entered the Romeo-Nine admin building. "Heard anything from Daarben or MAC-M?" he asked the Romeo-Nine comms watch.

The watch tapped his keyboard, and the holo of "Galaxy Command," a popular game among wannabe Fleet admirals, vanished. "Negative, Warrant. All the circuits are quiet. Just the way I like it."

"Yeah, I agree, but there are too many units moving for it to be this quiet. Do a comm check with Ulvaan and see if they're up."

The comms watch did as he was ordered, but there was no response.

"Try any station," Red said. "Somebody out there has to be listening."

The comms watch nodded and keyed his mic. "Any station this net, this is Romeo-Nine, radio check."

"This is Fender Four Five Four, I read you loud and clear."

"Fender 454? What the heck?" Red stuck his head out the door, and Johnson waved from the cockpit of their hovercopter. He shook a fist at his copilot and closed the door.

"Warrant Johnson, fooling around," he told the watch stander.

"At least we know the circuit's working," the watch told him.

"Keep trying," Red ordered as he left the space. When he got outside, he gathered the other pilots on the tarmac.

"There's something going on," he told the group. "We don't have comms with anyone, and nobody is talking on the net. There's a security exercise going on, and there should be all kinds of chatter. We've been sitting here for a whole day and heard nothing. Now, we can't talk to anybody."

"What do you want to do, Red?" Warrant Hull, lead pilot of Blackjack 293, asked.

"Go flying," Red answered. "454 and 293 will fly up the Daarben-Ulvaan road and see if we can find the mechs out of Ulvaan." He pointed to Warrant Officer Meeks, the other lead pilot. "Dane, after we're gone, spot Tacker 369 and put her in Alert 10."

"I don't know, Red," Meeks said. "Did Daarben Flight order it?"

Red shook his head. "Daarben Flight isn't answering."

"You think we should do this?"

Red looked up into the now bright Maltaani sky. "I'm sick of sitting around playing poker on such a beautiful day. I'd rather be flying."

"You don't need to worry about losing any more money to Haarkad," Hull said. "He's not around. In fact, none of the Maltaani are here. Weird."

"They're gone?"

"Yeah. Bugged out last night, I guess. Their barracks is empty."

Romeo-Nine was a joint human-Maltaani refueling base. The Administrator felt Romeo-Nine was a good way for the two species to cooperate, even though the Maltaani didn't have hovercopters of their own and generally didn't like to fly because they found human hovercopters too cramped. There wasn't much to do since the drawdown of MAC-M, but the air crews and ground personnel were happy to include their Maltaani counterparts.

"You don't think all this security stuff is because of the Maltaani, do you?" Johnson asked. He looked around at the undefended perimeter. "Our ass is in the breeze here."

"All the more reason why we should be flying," Red said. "The birds can't do much for us on the ground."

After some quick planning, the group broke up. Brumley and Hull would take their craft up and search the surrounding area for any signs of activity in the forest around Romeo-Nine. Meeks would spot his bird and be ready for launch. Gunny Pickens, the commander of the Romeo-Nine security platoon, would deploy his Space Marines and be ready to react if the hovercopters discovered anything. If they came up empty, Brumley and Hull would then follow the Daarben-Ulvaan road in hopes of locating other MAC-M forces.

As Brumley and Johnson trotted to their craft, they saw Sergeant Varney, their crew chief, had pinned the doors open and mounted door guns on both sides.

"You expecting trouble, Varney?" Red asked as they mounted their bird.

"We might get a chance to do some shooting, Red, and I want to be ready."

After twenty minutes of orbiting the area around Romeo-Nine with negative results, Red turned the flight north. They intersected the Daarben-Ulvaan road and turned west. Johnson worked the radio while Red flew.

"Romeo-Nine, this is Fender 454, we're turning west at the road, over."

Silence greeted the report. Johnson repeated it twice more, but there was no answer.

"What the hell's going on with comms?" he asked Red.

"I don't know. Call Blackjack and tell them to make the report."

They copied the Blackjack 293 transmission to Romeo Nine but didn't hear a response.

"No joy," Johnson said.

By pre-flight agreement, Blackjack took the low lead while Fender stayed high. Both craft had door guns and rocket pods hanging on stubby wings, and Blackjack also had a chain gun mounted on her nose which was controlled by sights mounted on the copilot's helmet. Fender was a former cargo hovercopter, slower but more heavily armored than Blackjack.

"Two o'clock low," Hull reported.

Red looked and saw the burned out remains of a vehicle in the middle of the road. More destroyed vehicles dotted the tree line, and he recognized the hulks of two supply mechs among the charred wreckage.

"What happened here?" Johnson asked.

The hovercopters slowed to get a good look at the scene, but there were no signs of life amid the burned-out vehicles.

"Those are supply mechs from a mechanized battalion," Hull said, giving voice to Red's thoughts.

"Since when do the Maltaani attack our supply convoys?" Red asked. "They can barely wipe their noses."

The carnage shocked Red, and there was stony silence as the hovercopters departed to the west, toward Daarben.

* * *

"What's that on the road, twelve o'clock low?" Red asked Hull.

"More burned up trucks. Wait, those are mechs."

"Bogeys six o'clock level!"

Red's eyes flicked to his tactical display at Johnson's warning. Two contacts had appeared on the screen, and when he looked back up, he saw flashes of blue that looked like weapons fire.

"Break high right!" Red ordered Hull in Blackjack 293. He threw Fender 454 into a sharp left turn and flew as close to the towering mountains as he dared. His pursuer hesitated for a second, and Red was able to bring his hovercopter around far enough to get the craft into his weapons envelope. Fender 454 shuddered as Johnson unleased a full spread of rockets and missiles from the underwing pods. Red shoved the controls to the right, but the contact had already maneuvered above and behind them.

Red twisted and turned as hard as he could to regain a firing position, but Fender 454 was slow and clumsy compared to the unknown. The cockpit lit up in brilliant blue light, and warning alarms blared in Red's ears as the dials on the instrument panel spun wildly, and the digital readouts showed errors. He pulled back on the controls as hard as he could, but the rocky mountain slope filled his windscreen.

"Red!" Johnson shouted just before the hovercopter slammed belly-first into the mountain.

The force of the impact jammed Red up against his five-point restraint harness and snapped his head forward and back. He felt the craft break in two and begin tumbling down the mountain, and a wave of orange heat flooded the cockpit.

"Fuckin' fire," Red said through gritted teeth.

The front half of the hovercopter slammed into some trees, and Red fought to stay conscious as the tumbling became a screeching slide. Finally, the wreckage came to rest against a large rock formation.

He struggled to punch the release button on his harness, but his vision narrowed to a bright dot, and a wave of darkness overtook him. Just before he passed out, Red had the sudden thought that his mother would be disappointed that he cursed with his last breath.

* * *

CB crept out of his hiding place and was almost on the road when he heard the distinct sound of hovercopter engines approaching from the east. Uncertain what to do, he dashed back into the trees and strained to catch a glimpse of the craft.

Two hovercopters roared past in a tandem formation, and CB saw two unfamiliar black aircraft close behind. The hovercopters suddenly split. The leader went into a steep climb and bright flares popped from the tail, while the second hovercopter banked hard up against the steep mountains. The black craft split up and followed without hesitation.

High in the sky, CB saw the first hovercopter twist and spin to escape its pursuer, to no avail. It seemed to stop in midair before it went into a steep dive and disappeared behind the distant mountains, and CB heard a hollow *boom* a second later.

By then, the second hovercopter had circled around and engaged the black craft with rockets. The strange craft shuddered from the impact, but it was too quick for the hovercopter, and it easily maneuvered behind the slower craft. The second hovercopter skipped off the rocky slope of a mountain and broke in two pieces. The rear of the craft exploded in a brilliant fireball as unexpended fuel and ordnance detonated. The forward piece slammed into the mountainside and skidded out of sight several klicks down the road.

CB stood and stared as the black craft formed up and flew off to the west, toward Daarben. The entire engagement had taken less than a minute, and the brutal efficiency with which the enemy had destroyed two hovercopters shook him to his core. Coupled with the destruction of First Mech, the shock was almost more than CB could process. He slumped onto a fallen log, took a long drink from a hydration pack, and pondered his next step.

He could hunker down in place and wait for friendlies to arrive, but he had no idea how long that might be. The supply convoy might come along at any minute, or it might be a heap of smoking wreckage like First Mech. He could hike back to Ulvaan, but the base had emptied in response to the security exercise. He might hump all the way there, find out he was alone, and have to turn around and walk all the way back. That would suck.

Although CB's knowledge of Maltaan geography was a little sketchy, he knew if he followed the road west, he would eventually find Second Mech. He didn't know how far it was, but he guessed they were probably closer than the base in Ulvaan. If he failed to find Second Mech, he could press on to the space port in Daarben or even MAC-M headquarters. The idea of traveling all the way to Daarben on foot was a little daunting, but he didn't have any other realistic option.

DINLI.

CB felt like a ghoul as he checked some of the wrecked vehicles for pig squares and hydration packs, but the missing and presumed dead Space Marines wouldn't need them anymore. He ignored the personal items strewn throughout the stricken vehicles; he knew if he focused on the family photos and other memorabilia, it would be too much to bear.

166 | P.A. PIATT

After thirty minutes of searching, CB had gathered a massive pile of rations and water. He separated enough for five days to carry with him and cached the rest in the trees above the road. He hoped he wouldn't need them, but it didn't hurt to be prepared.

After a last look around, CB shouldered his pack and started walking toward Daarben.

* * * * *

Chapter Seventeen

Fortis joined Anders and Rho in the back of the drone control room to observe the operations over Maltaan.

Drone operators were manning two consoles along the front of the space. The drone watch commander sat at a third console behind them. One of three large monitors in the front showed the curve of Maltaan from space. On a second monitor, Fortis recognized the Daarben space port from high overhead. The third monitor displayed mission statistics like time of flight and fuel remaining.

"We've got two birds up," Anders told him. "Alpha Bird is tasked with searching the space above Maltaan, and Bravo is focused on the surface."

"Alpha Bird has detected two ships in orbit at a range of forty-two kilometers," one of the drone operators announced. The view on the first monitor changed to the infinite blackness of space with two red rings superimposed on it. "We can't make them out yet, but that's where they're at."

"Hold Alpha in orbit at thirty kilometers," the watch commander ordered. "What's the status of Bravo Bird?"

"Bravo Bird is in geosynchronous orbit forty kilometers north of the spaceport," the second drone operator replied.

"Maintain orbit and conduct a long-range wide area all-sensor scan of the space port."

"Watch Commander, how much fuel does Bravo have for atmospheric operations?" Anders asked.

The watch commander turned to Anders. "General, I recommend against atmospheric operations while we're controlling from this side of the jump gate unless it's an emergency. Too much risk of losing control due to the time lag in comms."

The general nodded but said nothing.

On the Bravo Bird screen, Fortis saw rows of domes stretching for several kilometers north of the space port. "This place has changed a lot since I was here a year ago," he said. "That was all empty fields the last time I saw it."

"The Administrator brought in agricultural experts to solve the feast or famine cycle caused by the rainy season," Anders told him. "They determined agri-domes were the way to go and spared no expense to build them. If I recall correctly, your father's company was one of the bidders."

"Why are some of them blue?" Rho asked.

"We scrubbed the image and determined the blue is an internal light source reflecting on the opaque dome," the watch commander said. "There's nothing in the system to indicate why they're using blue lights. Maybe the analysts back at Fleet will know."

Anders gave Fortis an inquiring look. "Any ideas?"

Fortis shrugged. "My degree is in how to build them, sir. I don't know anything about agriculture. Maybe the lighting is crop specific."

"They're huge," the operator blurted.

"And where is everyone?" Anders asked.

"No ground activity visible," the Bravo drone operator announced. "Switching to thermal scan."

As soon as the Bravo drone display changed to infrared, the domes glowed with heat signatures. The blobs were indistinct, but it was obvious many of the domes were crowded with warm-blooded life forms. The controller guided the drone through two orbits over the domes, but there was nothing else to see.

"It looks like everyone is inside, General," the watch commander said.

"Alpha Bird has gained two more contacts," the Alpha operator announced.

Anders and Fortis turned their attention back to the Alpha display. Two additional red rings had appeared.

"Still can't make them out," the drone operator announced.

"Have we detected any emissions from the targets?" Anders asked. "Scanners, communications, anything?"

"No sir," the watch commander replied. "Nothing in any spectrum that we can detect."

"Hmm. Let's close the range and get a better look."

"Roger that, sir."

The watch commander ordered Alpha to close within twenty kilometers of the unidentified ships. As the drone got closer, the craft began to take shape. The view on the display zoomed in, and the image sharpened, but details were hidden in shadow.

"That's a combination of visual and scanner inputs," the drone operator announced.

"Maintain current range and reposition Alpha between the primary star and the targets," the watch commander ordered. "It's hard to make out any details when they're backlit like that."

As the operator maneuvered Alpha as ordered, Fortis turned his attention back to the Bravo monitor. He could make out the familiar layout of the Daarben space port. Boxy black vessels lined one side of the runway, and smaller craft lined the other. They dwarfed the Quonset huts the Space Marines had built at the space port years earlier. There were no human hovercopters or shuttles visible.

"What are those?"

"I don't think they're human," the watch commander said. "They don't look like any known Maltaani craft, either. They're big, though. The initial scan shows the smaller ones are one hundred and four meters long, and the larger ones are three hundred and eight meters in length."

"Looks like the Badaax beat us to the surface," Anders muttered to Fortis.

"Beat us *on* the surface, too, if they're parked out in the open like that. I don't see any of our stuff."

"We can't do anything about it right now." The general raised his voice. "Watch Commander, maintain Bravo orbit and let's finish with Alpha Bird."

The lighting angle had changed on the Alpha monitor. Fortis was able to make out more detail. He saw the engines under the fuselage and the stubby wings. The sides of the craft were smooth black surfaces.

"Just like *Fortuna* reported," Rho said.

The mission statistics monitor updated to reflect the information about the targets.

"Our scan confirms the target size. Each ship is twelve hundred meters long and six hundred meters high," the watch commander said.

"Can you make out any hatches or access ramps?" Anders asked.

"Not at this range, sir. We're at twenty kilometers now. Do you want to get closer?"

Anders shook his head. "No, I don't think so. They haven't reacted to the drone, so they might be unaware of it. If we get too close, we might alert them to our presence and provoke a response."

"Perhaps we should open the range back to thirty?" Fortis asked. "If there's nothing to be gained closer in and we can maintain contact at thirty kilometers, there's no reason to stay there."

"Good point. Watch Commander, pull Alpha back to thirty kilometers and maintain contact on the four unknowns. What's the status of Bravo?"

"Standing by for tasking, sir."

"Send Bravo over MAC-M headquarters and let's see what's happening down there."

"General, with your permission, I'd like to get Ystremski and the company commanders up here to observe the Bravo mission," Fortis said.

"Good idea."

Fortis passed the word for the trio of Space Marines as the Bravo Bird operator maneuvered her craft high above the western edge of the Maltaan landmass.

"The four unknowns are in orbit close to the space port," the watch commander told Anders. "We'll burn some mission time coming in from the west, but I think it's safer that way."

The delay gave Ystremski, Penny, and Young time to reach the drone control room and crowd into the back.

"Bravo Bird is just about over MAC-M headquarters," Fortis told them. "Coming in from the west to avoid the unknowns orbiting over the space port."

Fortis soon recognized Island Ten, where he and Tango Two Two had landed at the start of the ISMC invasion of Maltaan.

The MAC-M headquarters compound came into view. Located in a former botanical garden on the far western edge of the city, it was the spot where Second Division had landed during the invasion and that had later become the headquarters of MAC-M. The scars left by orbital strikes and mech battles had grown lush and green, and a casual observer wouldn't have known it had been the site of desperate fighting.

Fortis didn't see any activity in the MAC-M compound or the surrounding area. The only unusual detail was a hovercopter on its side on the launchpad. Scorch marks stained the tarmac around the craft, but it appeared undamaged. Otherwise, the compound looked like the occupants had just walked away.

"Where is everybody?" Young asked.

"Switch to infrared scan," the watch commander ordered. "Maybe they're inside or under cover."

The drone operator switched from black and white thermal to colorized heat map displays, but Fortis didn't see any discernable human-shaped signatures.

"It's like they just...left," Penny said.

"Go back to visual scan and zoom in on the hovercopter," the watch commander said.

The drone operator did as she was instructed, and a collective gasp swept through the room. They saw the top half of a human body sticking out from under the stricken craft and pulse rifles scattered on the ground around it.

"What the hell happened?" Anders demanded. "Where are the Space Marines who carried those weapons?"

The question hung in the air, unanswered, as the drone continued to orbit over the defunct botanical garden. The operator tried different sensor and data processor combinations, but she couldn't bring out additional details.

An *Eclipse Wonder* crewman entered the space and slipped General Fortis a note. After the general read it, he nodded.

"Acknowledge receipt and report we are proceeding as planned," he told her.

"Yes sir."

"Watch Commander, abort the mission and recall the drones. Fourth Fleet has deployed, and we're cleared to jump through the gate. I want those birds recovered before we do."

* * *

"What do you think? Are we going in?" Ystremski asked Fortis when they were back in the cargo bay.

"I don't know what to think right now. I know that's a bullshit answer, but there's a lot we still don't know about the situation on the surface," Fortis said.

"I'm not a fan of dropping in without knowing what the fuck is going on," the gunny said. "We're a long way from reinforcements."

"We should get more information when we send a drone into the atmosphere. Until then, we hurry up and wait some more. How are your IEBS lessons going?"

"I'm ready to go," Ystremski said. "As long as I don't have to manually operate the retro rockets, that is. I can't wait to engage with the mini pulse guns for real. They're a helluva lot of fun in the combat simulator."

Each IEBS had mini pulse weapons mounted on each shoulder that fired plasma bolts analogous to an eighteen-millimeter ballistic round. The sighting system was integrated into the helmet optics, and engagements were voice-activated. All the Space Marine had to do was acquire a target in the crosshairs and say the wearer-specific word to engage any target out to one hundred meters.

"They're fun, but they take some getting used to," Fortis said. "We had a bunch of friendly fire incidents in the simulators when we first started training with them. It's easy to forget your engagement order is active, and if you move or someone crosses your line of fire, it can get hairy."

Ystremski nodded. "Penny and Young warned me about that."

"What mode did you decide on, sapper or grenadier?"

"Sapper," the gunny said with a sheepish grin. "I'm a sucker for the FGU."

Fortis chuckled. "If we come across any bug holes on Maltaan, you're going first."

"Just don't tell Tanya."

"Now that you mention it, I haven't had a chance to ask. How did she take this? No-notice deployment and all that."

Fortis winced inside as soon as the question left his lips. Ystremski was a professional warrior with long experience compartmentalizing his thoughts of home and family to avoid any distraction that could be fatal. The gunny had every right to tell him to mind his own business, but they had been friends long enough that Ystremski forgave the faux pas.

"She's been a Space Marine wife for a long time," Ystremski said. "She's got her job, and I've got mine. She knows she doesn't have to like it."

"DINLI."

"Indeed."

* * * * *

Chapter Eighteen

CB made good time as he hiked along the shoulder of the road. He stopped frequently to look and listen, but the forest and skies were silent. He passed several sets of Space Marine remains along the way, but after the first two, he forced himself to look at them without seeing. They were in terrible shape after they'd been dragged this far, and the sight was sickening. CB knew most of the Space Marines in First Mech, at least by face, and he wasn't sure how he would react if he recognized one of them.

As he crested a low rise, CB looked up and saw a gash of broken trees on the opposite mountain slope. The breaks looked fresh, and he realized it was where the hovercopter had crashed. He looked closely and recognized a section of a hovercopter body. It didn't look too far up the slope, maybe five hundred meters, so he decided to investigate.

The climb was steeper than it looked from the road, but CB scrambled up on all fours. He came to a spot where fallen trees topped a large pile of boulders, and he was certain he was at the crash site. After he clambered around the jumbled obstacle, CB caught sight of the familiar olive drab hovercopter paint scheme under the rubble. When he got close enough, he could make out the number 454 painted on the side.

Red?

CB's heart quickened at the sight of his brother's hovercopter smashed on the mountainside, and he started to toss aside broken branches and boulders to uncover the craft. The wrecked hovercopter was on its side with its nose pointing downslope. The front half of the tandem cockpit was buried under dirt and rocks, and CB saw a helmeted figure slumped sideways in the rear seat. He released the canopy locks, heaved it aside, and gently tipped the unconscious pilot's head back.

Red!

* * *

Something brushed Red's lips, and he sputtered as water dribbled down his chin.

"Try a little more." a familiar voice said.

Red squinted at the blurry figure crouched next to him as he sucked on the hydration pack.

"Take it easy, brother." The face came into focus, and Red recognized the smiling face of his little brother. "What's up?" CB asked.

"Chicken Butt?"

"That's me." CB laughed.

"What are you doing here?" Red tried to sit up, and his skull exploded in pain. "What happened?"

"You were in a dogfight and got shot down. I was on the road and saw the crash, so I checked it out."

Red's memories flooded back. The fight, the crash… "Where's Lance?"

"Hm. He's your copilot, right?"

"Yeah. Lance Johnson."

"He, uh, he didn't make it, Red. Sorry."

Red took a deep breath and let it out slowly. He tried to sit up. "Unbuckle my harness and help me out of this thing."

"I tried," CB said. "I released the harness, but the instrument panel folded down onto your lap when you crashed. It's got your legs pinned, and I can't get it off."

Red felt a surge of panic. "What are we gonna do?"

"Calm down and let me think for a minute. I had just started lifting it when you woke up. I didn't see any blood when I checked you out. Do you feel any pain?"

Red took a quick inventory. "My head hurts, and my left ankle is throbbing. Other than that, I feel pretty good."

"Good. Here, drink some more of this while I look around for something to use as a lever. Take it slow, okay?"

Red accepted the hydration pack and sipped it while CB climbed around the wrecked hovercopter. The wiring and circuit boards that controlled the craft and its weapons lay exposed by the collapsed instrument panel, and he thought he could see an olive-colored helmet under the debris. He dug into the jumble of electronics and had a sizable hole cleared when CB returned.

"This wood is crap," CB reported. "It's all rotted or too soft to use—hey!" He pushed Red's hands away and shoved the electronic junk back into the hole. "You really don't want to do that, Red."

Red sat still for a long second and willed away the tight feeling in his gut.

"Okay, fine. What's this about the wood?"

"It's really spongy. I can wring the water out of it with my bare hands." CB held up a chunk of a splintered tree and squeezed, and water ran down his hands. "It's too soft to work as a lever."

"Straddle the cockpit and pull up, and I'll push from below. Maybe we can move it that way," Red said.

"Yeah, okay." CB did as Red instructed and grabbed the instrument panel. "Ready?"

Red counted down, and the brothers heaved on the instrument panel with all their strength. CB turned bright red, and veins stood out in his neck and forehead. Red groaned with the effort. The panel didn't move.

CB sank down next to Red. "That thing didn't budge an inch." He panted as he looked around the cockpit. "Anything left in that hydration pack?"

"Sorry, bro. I finished it."

"Figures. I'm doing all the hard work of rescuing you, and you're sitting around taking a little break."

"Dude, seriously? I'm trapped in this thing, and you're busting my chops?" Red scoffed. "What kind of Space Marine can't lift an instrument panel, anyway? Aren't you infantry types supposed to be strength-enhanced he-men?"

CB shook his head as he dug in his pack for another hydration pack. "I'm not infantry, I'm a corpsman. Besides, I've been in the Corps just over a year, so I'm only enhanced to Level Three. What about you? You've been in for years, but I don't see you moving this thing."

Red chuckled. "I'm not strength enhanced at all." He saw an incredulous look cross CB's face. "I'm a pilot. What do I need strength enhancement for?"

CB threw up his hands. "I don't know. Maybe someday, you'll be trapped in a crash, and you can rescue yourself if you're not as weak as a kitten."

"Huh. You might have a point, little brother."

After the brothers finished drinking, CB went in search of something to pry up the instrument panel.

"Maybe there's a piece of the hovercopter we can use further up," he told Red. "I'll climb up a hundred meters or so and see."

"Okay. Be safe up there. I'll wait here."

CB smiled and started to climb.

Gotta keep him smiling.

Red knew his brother better than anyone, and he knew he couldn't allow CB to get down. Red, himself, had been in tight spots before, but this was the direst situation by far. The instrument panel weighed heavily on his legs, and he could barely move his feet. Unless they came up with something to pry it up, Red would be stuck until they could get help.

Red had spent many hours maintaining and repairing Fender 454, and he was familiar with the tangled mass of wiring and circuit boards that lay open in front of him. The aircraft performance cluster was of no interest, but the weapons control circuitry was. He was certain the wing pods had still held rockets when he crashed.

Maybe we can burn through this thing using rocket propellant or use some of the explosive inside a warhead?

It sounded crazy, but they couldn't afford to take any options off the table. Neither he nor CB were electronics experts, but he'd done enough troubleshooting and replaced enough parts to know what fired the rockets and detonated the weapons.

Red couldn't twist around far enough to tell if the wings with their weapons pods slung underneath were intact. He also couldn't see if the engines were still there or, if they were, what condition they were in. If the auxiliary generator was functional, they'd have plenty of power; otherwise, they'd have to rely on whatever battery power remained in the reserve bank in a compartment under his feet.

He pulled out a couple components he recognized from the launch circuit and set them aside. As he wiggled a stubborn switch to pry it free, Red accidentally touched two wires together. A brilliant spark flashed, and he caught a whiff of burning electronics. A moment of panic crossed his mind as he imagined being trapped in the burning cockpit, but he pushed it away.

Idiot. But at least I know there's voltage available.

The primary weapon controls were in front with the copilot in the tandem configuration, but the pilot had switches on the instrument panel to arm and fire weapons in secondary. Red thought about where everything was located on the panel and then stuck his hands underneath. He traced the familiar switches and knobs with his fingertips until he located a star-shaped switch. It was the rocket arming switch, and it was shaped like a star to allow the pilot to identify it by touch, even in the dark. He clicked it while he watched for a reaction, but there was nothing.

Dead.

Red located the corresponding electronic cluster on the back of the instrument panel. If he could pull the components from the firing circuit, they would have a means of...what? They couldn't blow the instrument panel apart with a rocket. The more he thought about it, the less he liked the idea of using a weapon for anything.

CB returned with a thick metal bar. "This is all I could find. It's a little short, but it might work."

The brothers worked together to wedge the bar under the instrument panel, and they used the edge of the cockpit as a fulcrum. Red was skeptical whether it would work, but CB's enthusiasm was infectious. On three, Red heaved up with all his might while CB pulled down on the end of the bar. Nothing happened at first, but Red thought he saw a small shift.

"Pull!" he said through gritted teeth.

CB swung a leg over the lever and started to bounce, and tiny bits of dirt shifted around the edges of the panel.

"Harder!"

CB threw his entire body into the effort, and the instrument panel surged with every bounce. Without warning, the metal bar bent in half and CB slammed face-first onto the rocky ground next to the hover-copter.

"Damn it!" the brothers shouted in unison.

CB rolled over and sat up, clutching his injured face. "What do we do now?" he asked through his gloves.

"I guess we wait."

* * * * *

Chapter Nineteen

Ogre dozed in her chair in *Fortuna's* control room where she'd been almost continuously since they first observed the unknown ships come through the warp. The fleet around Maltaan had acknowledged her first report, but she had heard nothing since. Something about the silence left her unsettled, and she struggled to shake off the feeling of impending doom.

The Galactic Resource Conglomerate (GRC), under whose contract *Fortuna* sailed, was displeased when they learned of her report to the fleet. The wildcatters operated in strict secrecy. The Maduro Sector had only recently become available for human exploration and exploitation, and the GRC was determined to get ahead of the competition. Their method was simple: send wildcatters like Ogre and DeeDee to the four corners of the sector to prospect as many sites as possible. Conglomerate scientists analyzed and evaluated samples, and if they judged them profitable, the GRC staked a claim and dispatched a full mining crew. The newly discovered asteroid belt presented a huge opportunity, and the conglomerate jealously guarded the discovery.

This far from Terra Earth, a claim was only as strong as the claimant. Claim jumping was not unheard of, and the GRC employed a small army of mercenaries to protect their claims. Other mining concerns had accused the GRC of using their mercenaries to jump claims, but the United Nations of Terra (UNT) had neither jurisdiction nor interest in investigating these accusations.

Despite the extreme hazards of wildcatting, the potential payoff made it worthwhile to the wildcatters. A medium-sized asteroid could yield upwards of a trillion credits worth of rare earth metals, and the standard one percent cut of profits for the wildcat crew might reach ten billion credits. It wasn't retirement on Easy Street money, but two or three such discoveries could set a wildcatter up for life.

A warning beep from the console brought Ogre fully awake, and she searched her display for the cause of the warning. The gap in the asteroid belt began to shimmer.

Here it comes.

Four more of the massive ships she had seen before emerged through the warp, formed up, and disappeared into the distant blackness of space.

Ogre struggled with what to do with the new information. The GRC had threatened to cancel her contract after her first report, and even though she thought they were bluffing, she didn't want to take the chance she was wrong. For all she knew, there was another wildcat crew on the way to replace *Fortuna* right now.

"Screw it," Ogre said, and the sound of her own voice in the otherwise deserted space surprised her. The fleet around Maltaan needed to know there were four more ships headed their way, and if the GRC got their panties in a twist, so be it.

She tapped out a quick note to the Maltaan fleet, and after a moment of contemplation, included GRC Fleet Command as an addressee. There was no point in trying to hide it, and if the conglomerate decided to get ugly about it, she might be able to find an ally among UNT Fleet Command. She hit "send" and sat back. An aphorism from a popular old holo ran through her mind.

It is what it is.

Shade stuck his head through the control room door.

"Still here," he said, more of an accusation than a question.

"You missed all the fun," Ogre replied. "Four more unknowns came through the warp."

"No kidding? You should have called me."

"For what? It was the same as last time. They came through, formed up, and flew away."

"Did you get a record?"

"We're too far for the cameras, but they were the same kind of ship as the last time, I think. I'll dump the event from the system into a file and send it to you, but there's nothing new."

"Did you report it?"

Ogre nodded. "Yeah. Sent it to the fleet and GRC. Let them fight over it."

"Naughty girl."

"What are they going to do, send me on a deep space mineral survey?"

Captain and mechanic shared a laugh.

* * *

After *Eclipse Wonder* completed her jump through the Maduro Gate, the India Company officers, along with Gunny Ystremski, gathered in the back row of the drone control room with General Anders and Major Rho.

"We've got another two-bird mission this time," Anders told them. "Alpha Bird is tasked for an atmospheric mission, and Bravo will be tasked as necessary. Alpha is entering the atmosphere over the ocean to the west right now. It's nighttime, so we'll be on low-light and IR."

"Alpha has entered the atmosphere. Flight checks are complete and satisfactory, standing by for tasking," the Alpha drone operator announced.

"Go feet dry over Island Ten and proceed to MAC-M headquarters," the watch commander ordered.

The surface of the ocean was cold and showed up as black with an occasional smear of a heat signature. Fortis saw the edge of the warmer land mass approach and pass under the drone.

"Feet dry," the operator reported.

"Welcome home," Ystremski muttered, and Fortis shook his head.

"I was hoping I'd never see this place again. Have I told you—"

"Every fucking day, sir."

"There's MAC-M headquarters," Anders said.

The headquarters compound appeared unchanged from the first time they had surveilled it from orbit. The hovercopter was still on its side on the launch pad, but the body they had seen before was gone.

"Damn dogs," Ystremski said, and Fortis shuddered as he touched his dog-tooth necklace through his utilities. Ystremski had saved him from being torn to pieces by one of the beasts on Balfan-48, and the Space Marines had made him the necklace as a memento.

"The pulse rifles are still there," LT Young said. The weapons they had seen from orbit were still scattered around the area. "It looks like they just dropped them."

"Let's head east," Anders said. "Follow the main road, and we'll take a look at the agri-domes before we get to the space port."

The display tilted as the operator banked the craft and headed east. When it steadied, Fortis watched the familiar streets flow past. It looked as though the Maltaani had repaired much of the damage caused by the civil war and subsequent human invasion.

Rho pointed. "There's the embassy."

The former embassy, a Maltaani monastery repurposed to host the Terran ambassador, still bore the scars of the hovercopter strikes that had saved Fortis when he and his men were trapped on the roof.

"I guess they're not interested in repairing that one," Fortis said wryly.

"I read somewhere that the foundation was damaged," Rho replied. "The government won't pay to fix it, and the religious order that controls it won't let them tear it down."

The drone overflew the fields north of the space port, and many blurry heat signatures appeared on the monitors. The drone operator entered a series of commands into her console, and the images sharpened. "IR only."

"Elephants," the watch commander said. "A whole herd of them."

The field was filled with the six-legged mammals, but there was no fence visible. The animals stood in docile stillness.

"They're not moving," LT Penny said. "Are they dead?"

"I don't think so," Anders replied. "If they were dead, they wouldn't have heat signatures."

A group of bipedal figures approached the field. Their body shape was similar to humans, but their heads were outsized glowing orbs of heat.

"What the fuck?" Ystremski blurted.

"Badaax," Anders said. "Watch Commander, make sure the system is recording this." He turned to Fortis. "Our first live sighting of a Badaax."

The Badaax entered the field and slipped ropes over the heads of three elephants. One of them held a staff high overhead and led a procession of Badaax and animals into an adjacent field.

"Look how tall they are," Rho said. "I've seen elephants that were three meters tall, and the Badaax are bigger."

Anders nodded. "We recovered a skeleton from a cave near the railroad that would have stood between four and five meters in height. Wait until you see their teeth."

More Badaax gathered near the field and formed a line. As the humans watched, a Badaax raised a large, bladed weapon overhead and slaughtered one of the elephants with a single stroke across the neck. The other beasts didn't react as the Badaax continued to hack the animal into pieces while another Badaax handed the pieces to those in line.

"Looks like feeding time at the zoo from your nightmare," Young said.

"Why aren't the other elephants reacting?" Fortis asked as the Badaax butchered the next elephant.

"Watch Commander, switch from IR to low-light," Anders ordered.

When the image shifted, they saw that the staff brandished by the lead Badaax was emitting a ray that bathed the area in light.

"Go to straight visual."

The image shifted again, and pale blue light from the staff shone over the passive elephants.

"That explains why the other elephants aren't resisting. Some sort of mind control," Anders said. "Let's go back to IR."

The drone orbited, and the slaughter continued in the field below. Fortis counted at least twelve fields filled with the familiar shapes of elephants, and all of them were bathed in the weird blue light.

"How many elephants do you think they had in that first field? Thirty?" he asked.

Anders shrugged. "That seems like a reasonable guess."

"I counted twelve fields with elephants, which means about three hundred and sixty animals."

Within a few minutes, the Badaax had consumed the three elephants and dispersed among the agri-domes.

"Head over to—wait a second. What's going on now?"

A long column of Maltaani appeared from the city, led by a Badaax with a tall staff. Others wielded similar staffs up and down the shuffling crowd.

"Where are they going?" Anders asked nobody in particular as the Badaax and their Maltaani captives trudged toward the agri domes next to space port.

The Maltaani reached one of the domes, and the Badaax ushered them straight in.

"Slaves," Fortis said. "They're capturing slaves."

"Or food," Ystremski said.

"'Harvest,'" Anders added.

An *Eclipse Wonder* crewmember entered the space and approached Anders. "General, Emergency priority message from Fleet Command."

"Emergency?" Anders took the message and read it. "Watch Commander," he snapped. "Priority tasking for Bravo Bird to surveil the Badaax fleet in orbit." He held up the message. "Four more Badaax ships have come through the warp and are headed toward Maltaan."

"Roger that, sir. Bravo, position your bird thirty kilometers from the Badaax fleet orbit station and stay backlit. General, what do you want to do with Alpha?"

"Continue the mission," Anders said. "We need to gather as much intel as we can."

The same crewmember that delivered the first message from Fleet Command appeared at Anders' elbow.

"Another Emergency message, sir."

Anders read the message and then slapped his hand on his console. "Damn it!"

His uncharacteristic outburst startled everyone in the space.

"Fleet Command has ordered us to use drones to surveil both the Badaax ships orbiting Maltaan and the Maduro Jump Gate in support of Fourth Fleet's pending jump. Apparently, more Badaax ships have come through the warp near the asteroid belt, and they don't want any surprises waiting for Fourth Fleet on this side of the gate."

"Don't they know we might need the second drone to support India Company on the surface?" Major Rho asked.

Anders shook his head. "No. In fact, they might be unaware India Company is here."

"Huh. That's a problem, sir."

The general scoffed. "Yeah, it is."

"What do you want us to do, sir?" Fortis asked.

"Stand by for further orders," Anders said. "We've got to get Alpha Bird back and refueled so we can send it to the gate. We'll link up after that and figure things out."

* * * * *

Chapter Twenty

Fleet Admiral Conor McTighe had to suppress a smile as he sat in the Flag Operations Center (FOC) aboard his flagship, *Invictus*. He was finally going to experience the real fleet action he'd waited 27 years for, and he would experience it in command of the most powerful battle group the UNT had ever assembled.

Invictus was a *Furrer*-class dreadnought, bristling with the most advanced weaponry available. She carried four long-range rail guns, sixteen intermediate-range missile launchers, and a cocoon of point defense systems. *Invictus* could deploy attack and reconnaissance drones, and she boasted two surface bombardment guns in case she was called upon to support Space Marine operations on Maltaan.

Accompanying *Invictus* were *Baron de Macau*, *Duc de Nemours*, and *Marquis du Bouchet*, three of the newest destroyers commissioned by Fleet Command. The fleet also included the frigates *Persistent*, *Remorseless*, *Tenacious*, and *Resolute*, along with a handful of logistics vessels and the hospital ship *Compassionate*. All the destroyers and frigates were armed with rail guns, which McTighe had insisted on when Fleet Command gave him command. He had read Allard's SITREPs, and it was obvious to him what his strategy had to be when he came to grips with the enemy fleet—keep them at range and overwhelm them with rail guns.

192 | P.A. PIATT

It was an awesome collection of firepower, and Fleet Command had seen fit to assign McTighe to lead it.

"Coffee, Skipper?"

Warrant Officer Aleki Ngotel, McTighe's Assistant Material Officer and long-time companion, offered the admiral a steaming cup.

"Great. Thanks, Boats."

Ngotel used the traditional term favored by fleet personnel when referring to their commanding officers, which McTighe had been to Ngotel, twice. McTighe replied with the traditional naval term for a boatswain's mate, which had followed the fleet into space and referred to cargo handlers and spacecraft hanger specialists. The pair were long-time companions; McTighe had first served with Ngotel when he was an ensign and the Pacific Islander had been a junior enlisted man. Their careers had intersected several times over the years as they climbed their respective rank ladders.

The two men could not have been more different. McTighe was of smallish stature, with a spare frame and narrow features, while Ngotel was massive, with a broad face that could break into a wide grin at any moment. Despite their differences in background and rank, the two had become fast friends, as friendly as fleet regulations permitted. Ngotel was a steadying presence, and McTighe strove to keep him close as the officer climbed through the ranks. It was McTighe who had convinced Ngotel to accept the warrant officer promotion and made room for him on his staff. When asked what his duties consisted of, Boats Ngotel would smile and say, "To keep the boss happy."

The pair sipped their coffee in silence while Ngotel surveyed the strategic display on the forward bulkhead of the FOC.

"That's a fine fleet," he said. "Biggest I've seen."

"Not as big as the invasion fleet."

"That wasn't a fleet, sir. That was a clusterfuck."

McTighe allowed himself to smile. During the UNT invasion of Maltaan, all nine ISMC division flagships and their escorts had surrounded the planet. Every division commanding general had urged their flagship captains to jockey for the optimum drop orbits, and the ensuing confusion had forced General Tsin-Hu, Supreme Commander of the invasion, to order five of the nine flagships and their escorts to take stations hundreds of kilometers from Maltaan.

McTighe had commanded *Colossus*, flagship of ISMC Eighth Division, during the invasion. He had resisted the urge to engage in the close-in maneuvering and posturing, and it had paid off when Tsin-Hu directed Eighth Division to return to Terra Earth first. Although *Colossus* and Eighth Division played no part in the swift victory over the Maltaani, they had gotten caught up in the swell of patriotism and hero-worship that swept Terra Earth as quickly as war fever had. The Space Marines and crew of *Colossus* had been treated to a schedule full of parades, fetes, and public adulation. By the time the Space Marines who had actually played an active role in the invasion returned home, the tide of public opinion had turned, and there were calls to reap the dividends of peace by slashing the Fleet and ISMC.

"Excuse me, Admiral." The FOC watch officer approached. "We just received another update on the Maltaan situation from Fleet Command. The surveillance ship *Eclipse Wonder* collected some drone footage of the unknowns in orbit and some activity on the surface. It's queued up at your console, or I can put it on one of the big screens, sir."

"My console is fine, thanks."

"Click the cursor, and it will play, sir."

Ngotel looked over McTighe's shoulder as the update played. When it ended, McTighe leaned back and folded his hands behind his head.

"No sign of Allard or our ships, and nothing new on the hostile fleet," the admiral said. "The activity on the surface is concerning. What are they up to?"

Ngotel didn't respond. He seemed to understand that the admiral wasn't looking for conversation, he was thinking aloud. The admiral continued.

"Now that *Eclipse Wonder* is through the gate, perhaps we'll get more detail."

McTighe looked at the countdown timer mounted on the starboard bulkhead. "Six hours to the gate, and forty-eight more after that." He shook his head. "I don't think we're going to get there in time to help Commodore Allard." The admiral stood and slapped Ngotel on the shoulder. "Come on, Warrant. Let's go up to the flag mess and grab something to eat."

* * *

Anders summoned Fortis to his quarters so they could talk in private.

"I'm not in favor of sending you in, Abner. Without the drones, we have zero visibility on what's going on down there."

"That's exactly why we should go, sir."

Anders leaned back in his chair and folded his hands behind his head. "And face what, exactly? We lost an entire fleet to the Badaax, and quite possibly all of MAC-M. Why should I risk India Company?"

"General, you brought us because you said a small force could have an outsized impact on events if employed in a timely manner.

The way things are playing out, now's the time to let us make that impact, or should we stay 'prepositioned in preparation for future action?'"

"Don't do that. You know it's more complicated than that."

"I disagree, sir. India Company is a tool, no different than one of your drones. You need to know what's happening down there, and we can find out."

Anders stared at him but said nothing.

"Let me come up with a plan on how to get in and gather the intel about what's really going on. I'll run it past you, and if it passes the sniff test, we'll go."

"Okay, fine. Come up with a plan, and I'll give it a look, but it better not be a one-way mission."

Fortis smiled. "We might be a little crazy, but we're not suicidal, General. I'll be back here as soon as I can."

* * *

Thirty minutes later, Fortis, Ystremski, and the platoon commanders met Anders in the drone control room. Both drones were up and in position to surveil the Badaax fleet and the jump gate, while the controllers fought to stave off boredom.

"Our insertion plan is simple," Fortis said. "*Eclipse Wonder* will launch her shuttle with us aboard. Just after dark, the shuttle will enter the atmosphere far to the north of Daarben, over the ocean, and make a low-level approach to the landmass. When we're feet dry, the shuttle will climb over the mountains and fly parallel to the Daarben-Ulvaan road, and we'll conduct a low-level powered drop onto the road.

"India Company will proceed west until we reach the space port and then take up concealed positions to observe and report. If conditions permit, a squad will continue west to investigate MAC-M headquarters in the old botanical garden."

"Comms?"

"I talked to the comms supervisor, and she said they've been unable to synch up with any of the MAC-M birds in orbit, so we'll have to use line of sight with *Eclipse Wonder*. She calculated an orbit that keeps the ship in the sensor shadow of Maltaan but maintains comms with the drones. The ship will pop up during predetermined comms windows to pass and receive traffic from India Company."

"Support?"

"If the mission goes sideways, we'll escape and evade and call in the shuttle for extraction. Fourth Fleet should be here in a couple days, and I'm sure they've got some surface bombardment capabilities. If I recall correctly, there was a Black Hole constellation when we were here last, too."

Black Hole was the code name for armed satellites that showered ground targets with five-centimeter metal rods plummeting at high speeds from orbit. The effect was comparable to an explosive weapon, without the explosion. Fleet had placed a constellation of Black Hole satellites in orbit around Maltaan in preparation for an earlier invasion and left them in place after the drawdown.

"You're determined to go, aren't you?" Anders asked as he surveyed the group. They all nodded in response. "How long until *Eclipse Wonder* is in position to launch the shuttle?"

"Fourteen hours," Fortis said. "We'll load up thirty minutes prior to launch and conduct checks with Doctor Dunker. The shuttle pilot told me we'll be over the road twelve minutes after we enter the atmosphere."

"It's a go," Anders said, and the India Company officers smiled and patted each other on the back. "Let me warn you, though. If I receive other orders from General Boudreaux that change your tasking, or the situation on the surface changes, I'm reserving the right to scrub the mission. Is that clear?"

"Yes sir."

* * *

Nine hours later, Gunny Ystremski caught up to Fortis in the shuttle bay.

"What's going on, sir? Did you get any sleep?"

Fortis scoffed. "You know I can't sleep before a mission. How about you?"

"Like a baby. Any word from the general?"

"No. I don't want to bother him."

"You think he'll get cold feet? Scrub the mission?"

"Hmm, he won't get cold feet. He's always been cautious, so his hesitation doesn't surprise me. I think there are a lot of pieces to this puzzle we don't have control of, and maybe he feels like he's being pushed into doing something unwise. As of now, we're still a go. That doesn't mean he won't pull the plug up until the moment we're heading down the ramp."

"Sir, if there's a way to find out what the fuck is going on down there without risking our lives, I'm all ears."

"I'm with you there. How are the lads? Are they ready?"

"They're good. Some nerves, but nothing too bad. They're happy we're making a low-level drop. Even though Doc Dunker says he figured out what happened to Connolly, some of them aren't convinced."

"So leave them here."

"Fuck that. Try it, and you'll have a fight on your hands. Don't worry about it, sir. Everyone will go down the ramp just like they're supposed to. DINLI." Ystremski nodded. "Are you good? Did you pack extra pig squares?"

"As many as I can carry, along with hydration packs and stim-packs. There's no telling how long we'll be down there without support."

"I've been looking over the IEBS, and I can't figure out how to carry a pack," Ystremski said. "You can't wear it on your back, or it gets tangled in the miniguns, and if you sling it across your chest, it interferes with the pulse rifle. I don't think the designers thought that through."

"Huh. That's a problem. We can't go in without rations."

"I talked to the doc, and the best we could come up with is to deactivate the miniguns until we know we'll need them. He said he'll look at workarounds, but he's not going to come up with anything before we drop."

"DINLI, I guess."

* * * * *

Chapter Twenty-One

Anders joined Fortis at the shuttle ramp as the Space Marines loaded for their drop. After the last one climbed aboard, Anders and Fortis shook hands.

"Any changes, sir?"

"No. Your mission is a go. Be safe out there, Abner."

"Will do, General."

The pair exchanged salutes, and Fortis climbed the ramp before it closed.

The shuttle ride over the mountains was bumpy, but it smoothed out as the ramp opened, and the pilot guided the craft over the highway. The drop lights changed from red to green, and Fortis led India Company on their first combat drop.

The drop altitude was ninety meters, and his retro rockets fired on schedule. Fortis barely had time to prepare for landing before his boots hit the gravel. The rest of the company was down in seconds, and it gratified him to see his advisory page remained alarm-free. India Company landed by squad, and the entire company was on the ground and clear of the road in less than a minute.

Penny reported first. *"First Platoon, clear."*

"Second Platoon, clear," White said.

"Command Element, clear," Ystremski said.

"All clear."

For five full minutes, India Company remained hidden as they watched and listened to the forest around them. The pause allowed the Space Marines time to acclimate to their surroundings, while Fortis tapped a status report into his burst transmitter. He put it in the transmission queue and resumed waiting.

When he was satisfied their insertion had gone unnoticed, Fortis keyed his mic.

"First Platoon, send out the point."

"Roger that."

A squad from First Platoon started west down the road toward Daarben. When they were fifty meters out, Fortis stood.

"India Company, move out."

All around him, Space Marines got to their feet, and First Platoon set off behind the point squad. Fortis and the command element were next, and Second Platoon brought up the rear. The squad leaders staggered their troops on either side of the road, and they moved at a rapid pace. Their mission objective was somewhere ahead in the darkness, and they seemed anxious to get there.

"Halt," the point squad leader said over the company circuit. *"Cover."*

The company took cover in the trees and waited. Fortis was tempted to switch to the First Platoon channel and listen in on the point squad, but he knew better. First Lieutenant Penny was an experienced platoon leader, and Fortis knew if he intruded as the company commander, Penny would chafe under the micromanagement. Instead, he waited.

"False alarm," Penny said. *"Something moved in the forest, but whatever it was is gone."*

Fortis looked at Ystremski, who shrugged.

"Let's go."

Just as the column moved out, a burst of pulse rifle fire sprayed the road around First Platoon. The Space Marines scrambled for cover and returned fire at the flashes. Some quickly suppressed the inaccurate fire while the rest crossed the road and flanked their attackers. Three quick explosions silenced the incoming fire as the Space Marines ended the attack with a salvo of grenades.

"Moving up," Penny told Fortis. Two minutes later, he came back on the circuit. *"Command, we found four dead Maltaani with one pulse rifle between them. There are no blood trails or drag marks, so I think this was all of them."*

"Any idea why they attacked?"

"Negative. They're dressed in shabby army uniforms, so they should have known better."

"Do we have casualties on our side?"

"No sir."

"All right then, let's move out."

* * *

India Company made rapid progress throughout the night. There were two more stops for movement in the forest, but Fortis was untroubled by them, because it was proof the point squad remained alert.

When the sky began to lighten, he called Ystremski.

"Hey, Gunny, let's take a break and give the lads a rest and a chance to hydrate."

"Roger that, sir. We're making good time."

Fortis walked up and down the column, exchanging nods or a quick word with the Space Marines. Their morale seemed high, and if any had second thoughts about their mission, they hid them well. He consulted Penny about moving Second Platoon forward to take point, but as Fortis expected, the lieutenant refused.

"My lads are fresh and ready," Penny said. "Besides, I feel safer with First Platoon in front."

Fortis chuckled at the good-natured rivalry between platoons. He was certain if he put the same question to LT Young, the response would have been the same.

When he was done, Fortis returned to the command element and climbed as far back into the undergrowth as he could. He fished out a pig square and a hydration pack. He wasn't especially hungry, but he didn't know when he would next have an uninterrupted moment to eat.

Gunny Ystremski found him, so he scooched over and made room.

"Hungry?" Fortis asked as he offered his half-eaten pig square.

"Thanks, but just finished one. I couldn't eat another bite."

"Every meal's a banquet."

"What's the plan, sir? You want to lay up until dark?"

"No. I don't think so. The sooner we can send intel up to the general, the sooner he'll get the fleet overhead. It's a risk, but if we keep to the shoulder under the trees and stay alert, we can manage it. What do you think?"

"I'm a gunnery sergeant. I'm not paid to think, but if I was, I would say the captain's plan is sensible."

Fortis shook his head. "You're a lot of help, Gunny."

* * *

Fleet Admiral McTigue took several deep breaths to calm his roiling stomach before he looked over at Boats Ngotel, seated at the console next to him, and smiled. The warrant officer's eyes were squeezed shut, and sweat droplets beaded his face.

"You can open your eyes, you big baby," he said in a teasing tone. "We're through."

Ngotel blinked and let out a big breath before he wiped his face with a massive hand. "I hate warp jumps." He slid out of his seat. "I gotta get something to drink."

The admiral was no fan of jumping, and it secretly pleased him to see his hulking friend was afraid of *something*.

He grunted with satisfaction as he watched the vessels of his fleet take their stations according to the attack plan he had ordered after they completed the warp gate jump.

The fleet was divided into two wings, with the flagship *Invictus* in the center, accompanied by the destroyer *Marquis du Bouchet*. The left wing was led by the destroyer *Baron de Macau*, in company with the frigates *Remorseless* and *Tenacious*. The destroyer *Duc de Nemours* led *Persistent* and *Resolute* on the right. The hospital ship *Compassionate* and the logistics ships would loiter near the jump gate until any potential action was over.

During their transit to the jump gate, McTigue held a series of meetings with his senior tacticians and Fleet captains to develop their plan of attack. Based on the reports from Commodore Allard, the Badaax had determined her fleet's sensor and weapons ranges early in the engagement. They had then used superior speed and firepower to strip away the layers of protection until *Giant* and *Sao Paolo* were all that remained, and they were easily destroyed.

Unlike Allard, McTigue's fleet boasted the most advanced sensors and weapons available, and he planned to use them to their maximum capabilities. All his ships carried sensors and rail guns that outranged those aboard *Giant*, and the frigates were faster and more maneuverable than any ship in Allard's fleet.

Also unlike Allard, McTigue would not hesitate to attack. She had done as well as anyone could have with outdated ships against an unknown enemy, but underneath all the analysis and reconstruction of the engagement, the hard truth was that her indecision to engage had cost her fleet dearly. When she finally did, it was too late. He would not repeat that mistake.

His plan was simple. The fleet would approach Maltaan and engage whatever Badaax responded to their appearance. All ships would respond as if their weapons and sensors were the equivalent of Allard's. When ordered, the frigates would dart forward and fire full salvos with their rail guns and then retreat under cover of their destroyer escorts to recharge and reposition. *Invictus* would maintain a mix of armed and unarmed drones on the periphery of the action until an opportunity to use them presented itself.

The captains protested when McTigue warned them that disabled ships would have to deal with their own damage until the engagement was over, but he stood firm. No vessel would attempt to engage the enemy alone or leave the collective protection of the fleet, and that included going to the aid of a stricken ship. Allard had allowed her ships to be drawn away in ones and twos, he explained, and they were destroyed piecemeal. He would attempt to position the fleet to give damaged ships some cover, but helping them would not be the primary reason for any maneuvers.

The big unknown in their planning was the Badaax energy weapons that had easily defeated the other ships. Shields had proved ineffective, and the best guess of the energy weapon range was the range of the missiles fired by *de Choisy*. In spite of this, McTigue was confident in their plan.

It has to work.

Warrant Officer Ngotel slid into the console next to the admiral and passed a steaming mug to him. McTigue blew on it and then sipped. To his surprise, the liquid was not the bitter coffee he had expected.

"This isn't coffee," he sputtered. "What the hell is it?"

"Too soon for coffee, Skipper. It's broth. Doc said it's good for the stomach." The massive Pacific Islander rubbed his midriff. "That fucking jump."

McTigue laughed. "A big strong lad like you lets a little thing like a warp gate jump bother him? What kind of warrant officers are we promoting these days?"

The FOC watch officer interrupted their conversation. "Admiral, Eyes Only Uniform priority message for you from Fleet Command. It's on your console."

Uniform priority? What the hell?

"Eyes Only," or EO, was assigned to communications intended only for McTigue. It was most often used to send sensitive information Fleet Command didn't want widely distributed. EO messages were double encrypted, decipherable only by senior officers who were privy to the proper decryption sequence.

The Uniform priority concerned McTigue. Fleet communicators prioritized messages due to limited bandwidth through the jump gate communications portals. Alpha was the lowest priority and was assigned to routine administrative message traffic. Zulu was the highest priority and was reserved for warning of imminent enemy attack. In 27 years, he'd never seen a higher priority than Quebec.

A page of unintelligible characters appeared on McTigue's console. He entered the correct decryption command, and the message appeared in plain language. It was from Admiral Bradley Knight, Commander of Fleet Command.

From: Fleet Command
To: Fleet Admiral McTigue
EYES ONLY
Conor, the Grand Council overrode the President's decision to deploy Sixth Division. They forced a vote of no confidence in the government, so the President and the Minister of Defense resigned. Don't expect any support from this end until a new government is formed. Stay safe.—Brad

McTigue read the message twice. He hoped it was an elaborate practical joke with a hidden punchline, but it was real.

"Those stupid bastards," he muttered. "Dumb, dumb bastards."

"Something wrong, Skipper?" Ngotel asked.

The admiral waved at his screen. "Lean over and read this."

Ngotel read the message and gave a low whistle. "What does that mean for us? Are we going back?"

"No, it's not a recall order. It's a warning to proceed very carefully, though."

"The Space Marines aren't coming?"

"It doesn't look that way, but I haven't seen anything to indicate there's a need for them, either."

"It would be nice to have them along, just in case, sir."

McTigue shook his head. "There's no appetite for nice-to-haves, and no budget, either. We fucked up during the invasion. We spent trillions of credits deploying nine divisions for the invasion, and four divisions defeated the Maltaani in three days, while the rest of us drilled holes in space. The peaceniks have been pounding the podium over that ever since, and now, it looks like they're getting their revenge."

"What are we going to do?"

"We're going to Maltaan. Very carefully."

* * * * *

Chapter Twenty-Two

India Company continued to push west. Their progress was slow because Fortis ordered frequent halts to ensure they weren't being observed. Moving in the open went against all of his training and instincts, but he had an overwhelming urge to get to the space port as soon as possible.

"Cover."

The company scrambled into the underbrush and waited for information from the front of the formation.

"Sir, it's Penny. The point man has sighted some vehicles on the road ahead. They look burned out, like they were attacked."

"Roger that. Investigate and report."

Twenty minutes crawled by, and Fortis was just about to request an update when Penny called back.

"It looks like the tail end of a mechanized convoy, sir. The mechs are definitely destroyed, and there's a bunch of Maltaani armed with pulse rifles crawling all over them."

"I'm on my way."

Fortis moved forward in a low crouch with Ystremski right behind him. When they reached Penny's position, they could clearly see the mechs.

"How many Maltaani?"

"I counted seven, sir," Penny said. "I haven't seen any coming or going into the woods, and they haven't set a perimeter, so I think that's all there are."

Just then, they heard a scream coming from the mech convoy. A female human scream.

* * *

Will jerked when a shadow crossed in front of the command mech hatch. She scrambled for her weapon but froze when a pulse rifle barrel was stuck in her face. A Maltaani soldier grabbed her by the legs, yanked her out of the mech, and dumped her on the ground. Pain radiated through her body, and she screamed as her initial shock at the sight of the Maltaani wore off.

A handful of Maltaani soldiers gathered around and loomed over her. One of them prodded her with a boot, and she tried to crab backward.

"Hey. Hey, guys. We're on the same side, remember?" Will searched her mind for the few Maltaani words she had learned during her brief tour on the planet, but she drew a blank. One of them crouched next to her and stroked her cheek with spindly fingers and stared at her with solid black eyes. The touch made her skin crawl, but it was the lack of sclera in his eyes that made her shudder. His hand went down to her breasts, and Will knew what was coming next.

"Fuck you, bug eyes!" She kicked and punched at the Maltaani, who toppled backward in surprise. His comrades broke into the half snarl, half grimace that passed for smiles among their race, and Will rolled over and tried to crawl away. One of them planted an oversized boot on her leg and pinned her to the road as her original attacker grabbed her by the back of her coveralls.

* * *

"They're attacking a Space Marine!" Penny said.

"Kill those fuckers," Fortis ordered.

Penny immediately leapt into action and charged onto the road with his platoon right behind him. A salvo of pulse rifle bolts tore through the Maltaani, and they all went down with precise headshots. The Maltaani who had grabbed the female Space Marine tried to scramble away, but Penny was on him in a second. He held up his hands as if begging for mercy, and Penny shot him in the face. The rest of First Platoon formed a perimeter, alert for more Maltaani. The forest remained silent.

"Clear!"

Fortis and Ystremski moved up along with Doc Velez, the company corpsman.

"Whaddya got, sir?" Ystremski asked Penny.

"Seven shots, seven kills," the lieutenant said.

"Nice shooting on that last one." Fortis stood over the headless Maltaani. "I should have told you to keep one alive. Maybe we could have gotten some answers from him."

"Fuck 'em," Penny said. "I don't speak that gibberish anyway."

"I do."

"Captain Fortis." Doc Velez waved Fortis over to where he knelt by the female Space Marine. "This is Lance Corporal Will, command mech crewman in First Mechanized Battalion. No external injuries, but she's complaining of a severe headache and tingling in her extremities."

212 | P.A. PIATT

"Thanks, Doc." Fortis kneeled next to Will. "How's it going, Marine?"

"Just great, sir. Who are you guys?"

"Space Marines, ma'am." Connelly, who had moved up with the command element, stood next to Fortis.

Ystremski glared at him. "Connelly, fuck off and go find somewhere else to be." He turned back to Will. "We are, in fact, Space Marines. Most of us, anyway."

"No shit, Space Marines. I mean, *who* are you? What outfit? And what's with that armor?"

"We're India Company, First Battle Mech Battalion," Fortis said. "We just dropped last night. This is an experimental battle chassis." He gestured to the destroyed vehicles that littered the road. "Who did this?"

"Blue bombers. Came out of nowhere. Marched them all away."

Before Fortis could ask another question, Ystremski cut in. "Captain, we need to get out of the open, sir. I redeployed First Platoon up front and brought Second in, but we can't sit here."

After Doc Velez and some of the others moved Will under cover on the side of the road, Fortis continued to ask her questions.

"I heard you were in the command mech. Driver?"

"No sir. Comms watch."

"Then you probably know more than the average infantryman about what's going on. Good. Let's start at the beginning, okay?"

Will talked him through the events of the first 24 hours. "It started as an exercise, and then it became real. Nobody knew what the fuck to do, because the OPORD hasn't been updated since before the drawdown. We got a late start, and Toro chewed Southwick—Major Southwick, the battalion commander—a new ass."

"Who's Toro?"

Will squeezed her eyes shut for a second. "Colonel what's-his-name. MAC-M."

"Wisniewski?"

"Yeah. Colonel Wisniewski. I guess things were pretty fouled up, because Major Southwick was almost in tears by the time he was done. Anyway, we followed Second Mech and linked up with them here. That's when we first saw the blue bombers."

"What are the blue bombers? Tell me about them."

"Ships. Big ships. They look like flying boxes, with blue rays that shine out of the bottom," Will said. "Second Mech warned us not to look at the rays without visors because something about the light makes you crazy. A group of Maltaani refugees went past us, headed for Ulvaan, and then they came back this way with the blue bombers over them."

"And the blue bombers did this?" Ystremski gestured to the wrecked vehicles.

"Second Mech pulled out and headed for Daarben, and Major Southwick decided to stay here to wait for our supply column. The tactical data system was acting weird, so I rebooted it," Will said. "When it came back up, the blue bombers attacked. An explosion blew my mech over, and I crawled into the woods." A sob caught in her chest and tears spilled down her cheeks. "I ran away and hid. I was scared, so I hid."

"Hey, hey. It's okay," Fortis said as he took one of her hands. "Your mech was destroyed, and you had a concussion."

"They're all gone. I should have fought."

214 | P.A. PIATT

Ystremski snorted. "With what, your pulse rifle? I see a bunch of main battle mechs smashed and burned, and you think you and your pulse rifle would have made a difference? Nah, not a chance."

Fortis weighed in. "I don't want to scare you, Will, but nobody knows what the hell is going on down here," he told her. "The Badaax—the aliens flying the blue bombers—showed up and destroyed the support fleet. Our mission is to collect intel to support Fourth Fleet and Sixth Division when they get here."

"They're not here yet?" Will's eyes widened. "Who is supporting your division?"

"We're operating on our own right now, but they'll be here soon," Fortis said.

They tried to get more information, but Will's answers became less coherent as her strength faded. She kept repeating "blue bombers," but gave them nothing useful. Doc Velez interrupted to give her another quick exam and then waved Fortis and Ystremski out of earshot.

"She's got a concussion for sure, and maybe a fractured vertebra in her neck. All I can do is immobilize it with an inflatable neck brace until I can get her to a proper medical facility. She's got a pretty big knot on the back of her head, too."

"Can she travel?"

"If we carry her on a litter. She's not going to like it, but she can travel."

"Get her ready; we need to get moving. Gunny, a word."

Ystremski followed the captain across the road.

"What do you think?" Fortis asked as he watched the Space Marines search the damaged vehicles.

"If these blue bombers destroyed an entire mechanized infantry battalion, I don't know what we can do against them. We've fought against long odds before, but this is suicide."

"Yeah, I agree. We don't need to go looking for a fight."

"Captain, this is Penny. Did that corporal mention any other survivors?"

"Negative. Why?"

"The lads found a pile of rations and hydration packs stashed in the woods. It looks like somebody is planning on coming back. We searched around but didn't find anybody."

"Maltaani?"

"I don't know, sir. Why stash it?"

"Have Doc Velez verify whether she was alone."

A few seconds later, Penny called back. *"She said she's been alone and didn't stash anything, sir."*

"If they don't come out before we move on, leave it there," Fortis said.

"Roger that."

"What do you want to do?" Ystremski asked Fortis.

"Keep moving west to the space port in Daarben and see if we can find Second Mech or MAC-M. Maybe there are other survivors who know what's going on."

The Space Marines checked the undamaged vehicles, but they couldn't get any of them started.

"I guess we're walking."

After Doc Velez fashioned a litter for Will, India Company moved out.

* * *

216 | P.A. PIATT

Three klicks down the road, they came upon the battered remains of a Space Marine. The body was headless and missing one arm, and the uniform was unrecognizable.

"Somebody left him in the middle of the road to rot," LT Young said.

"We're not leaving him for the dogs," Ystremski said. "I'll take care of it." He gathered several members of the headquarters element, and they moved the remains to a ditch on the side of the road. The ground was too hard to dig into, so they built a meter-high cairn to protect him.

Fortis found Ystremski standing on the road, staring at the pile of rocks.

"Are you good, Gunny?"

Ystremski nodded but said nothing.

"How's your gut?"

The gunny gave Fortis a sharp look. "It's good, sir. I can keep up."

The abrupt response flustered Fortis. "That's not what I meant. I mean...ah, shit, I don't know what I meant."

"Yeah, I know." Ystremski let out a big sigh. "I'm sorry, sir. This—" he gestured at the pile of rocks "—this one got to me, is all."

Fortis realized his friend had some thoughts he had to get out, so he didn't respond.

Ystremski stood over the cairn. "He was probably just a kid. Lied about his age to get into the Corps, the pride of his family back home on the farm."

"Damn, Gunny. You're getting maudlin."

"They seem so fucking young."

Suddenly, Fortis understood Ystremski's mood. His son, Petr Jr. was set to graduate from Fleet Academy soon, and he had elected to follow his father into the ISMC.

"They've always been young, Petr. We're getting older."

"What are we doing here?" Ystremski asked. "We've been fighting and dying on this planet for years, and for what?"

"Because they sent us, I guess. DINLI."

Ystremski shook his head. "DINLI, my ass." He unconsciously touched his stomach where the Maltaani ex-general had run him through with his sword.

"Have I told you how much I hate this fucking place?"

Ystremski snorted and thumped Fortis on the shoulder.

"C'mon, sir. Pity party is over; let's get back to the lads."

"Are you sure you're good?" Fortis asked.

"Never better," the gunny said with a chuckle. "Every day is a holiday, and every paycheck is a fortune."

"At least it isn't raining," Fortis added, and they laughed as they rejoined India Company.

* * * * *

Chapter Twenty-Three

Fortis called a halt when the first comms window with *Eclipse Wonder* opened. Anders called him immediately.

"What's your status, Captain?"

"We located the remains of First Mechanized Infantry Battalion on the road to Daarben. All vehicles are destroyed or inoperative. We located one survivor and brought her with us."

"One survivor? From the whole battalion?"

"Just one, sir. A lance corporal from the headquarters element named Will. She reported the convoy was attacked by what she called blue bombers, which I believe are Badaax craft with blue light rays. She also said the Badaax craft collected all the Space Marines—including the wounded and dead—and sent them west, toward Daarben.

"According to Will, Second Mech is somewhere ahead of us, so we are pushing on to try and link up with them. Any updates from the space port, sir?"

"Negative. I still don't have drones for surveillance tasking. By my estimation, Fourth Fleet should be through the gate, but I haven't heard from them yet."

"Any orders for us?"

"Stay out of sight, observe, and report. I'll be in touch during the next comms window."

"Roger that."

* * *

"General Anders, Admiral McTigue on *Invictus* calling for you. Button five," the watch commander told Anders.

Anders donned his headset and punched the button. "This is General Anders." After a short delay, McTigue responded.

"Nils, Conor McTigue here."

"Hello, Admiral. How was your jump?"

Even though Anders was a general, the admiral wore three stars to his one, and Anders didn't dare address McTigue by his first name.

"Good. The drone helped; thank you for that."

"Glad to hear it, sir. Do you want me to continue drone coverage at the gate until Sixth Division comes through, or can I redirect those assets to support ground operations on Maltaan?"

"You can redirect them, Nils. Sixth Division isn't coming."

"What?" McTigue's news stunned Anders. "What do you mean, they're not coming?"

"The Grand Council vetoed the President's decision to send them," McTigue said. *"The President resigned, along with Defense Minister Fine."*

Anders stared at his console, unseeing.

"Nils, are you still there?"

"Yes sir, I'm still here. Sorry about that. This is quite a shock."

"I imagine there are a lot of shocked people back home. Have you heard anything from General Boudreaux?"

"No sir, I haven't heard from the General since before we jumped. I sent surveillance reports, which headquarters acknowledged, but that's it. Do you have any tasking for me?"

"Are the Badaax still in orbit?"

"Yes sir. The miners reported the arrival of four additional ships in the sector two days ago, and we saw them join the other four in orbit."

"Good. I saw that report. Anything else for me?"

"I haven't been able to contact anyone on the surface, and I haven't had reconnaissance assets available, so I inserted a company of Space Marines to investigate, with orders to observe and report."

"What company? By whose authority?"

"India Company. They're an R&D company assigned to Ops and Intel. I brought them on this mission as a contingency. The drones can only give us so much information. In the absence of any other source and no contact with the surface, I decided to send them in."

"What's your plan to extract them?"

"I planned to have them link up with Sixth Division, but we can insert *Eclipse Wonder's* shuttle if necessary."

"I hope you haven't doomed those Space Marines, Nils."

"Me too, Admiral. Me too."

* * *

"Hey, Red."

"Yeah." Red forced his eyes open. He had been hoping the crash was all a bad dream, and he would wake up in his quarters on Romeo-Nine. Instead, he was still stuck in the cockpit of Fender 454 where he'd been for almost two days.

"We're almost out of hydration packs."

"Good. I'm tired of pissing in my flight suit."

The brothers laughed together, and CB patted Red's shoulder.

"I cached a bunch back at First Mech," he said. "I need to go get them."

Red felt a stab of panic. "Don't leave me!"

"What? No way, brother. I'll never leave you, but we need water."

"We gotta move this junk." Red jammed both hands under the cockpit console and heaved. "Gimme a hand."

CB shook his head. "We already tried that, Red. Just relax, I'll be back as soon as possible. It will be okay."

Red slammed his hands down on the instrument panel in frustration. Stray voltage sizzled and sparked across the wrecked electronics, and he heard a loud whine from behind him.

"Get down!"

CB rolled away just as a rocket erupted from the underwing pod. Choking white smoke flooded the cockpit, and Red hacked and coughed as he fanned it away.

Somewhere in the distance, he heard a low *boom*.

"CB, are you okay?" Red twisted around as far as he could, but he didn't see his younger brother.

CB staggered up to the cockpit and leaned against the hovercopter. His injured nose had begun to leak blood down his chin.

"What was that?" CB sputtered.

"I accidently launched a rocket. Are you okay?" Red's concern for CB became relief, and he snorted when he saw CB's face. "You look good, little brother," he said in a teasing tone.

* * *

over!"

India Company ducked into the trees on the side of the road. Fortis heard an explosion somewhere up ahead of the column.

"Command, this is First Platoon. Somebody fired a rocket across the road about a klick in front of the point."

"Was it aimed at us? Did we trigger an ambush too early?"

"There hasn't been any shooting, and the woods are clear on either side. I sent a squad to investigate where the rocket came from."

"Roger. Nice and easy, let's not wander into an ambush."

"Yes, sir."

Fortis chuckled at Penny's tone. The lieutenant knew what to do, and Fortis's guidance was unnecessary.

"I thought I heard some 'fuck off,' in that last transmission," Ystremski quipped when he joined Fortis on the side of the road.

"Bad habits are hard to break," Fortis said. He switched to the company circuit. "All stations, this is Command. Keep your eyes open and watch the skies. We don't want to get surprised by the blue bombers."

* * *

Fifteen nervous minutes later, Penny called again.

"Command, this is First Platoon. We located a crashed hovercopter near the road. Two survivors, a pilot and a corpsman. The pilot reported the rocket fired due to a system malfunction."

Fortis and Ystremski traded looks.

"A pilot?" the gunny asked.

"That's what he said. A pilot, and a corpsman."

"That sounds like the start of a bad joke."

"This ought to be interesting," Fortis said to Ystremski. He keyed his mic. "Roger that. I'm moving up to talk to them. Are they on the road?"

"Negative. The pilot is trapped in the wreck, but the lads are working on it. I'll update you when he's out."

"Roger that." Fortis turned to Ystremski. "Maybe we'll get better intel from the pilot."

* * *

Red gave CB an amused look after his brother rinsed his damaged face. "You've always had a face only our mother could love."

"Yeah, thanks. How bad is it?"

"It looks okay. Nothing that can't be fixed."

CB kicked at the bent pole lying on the ground next to the hover-copter. "What do you want to do now?"

"I don't know. I wish that thing hadn't bent because the panel was moving when you bounced on it."

"I can climb back up there and look for more stuff," CB said. "I found that about thirty meters up. Maybe there's more."

"I guess you can try. While you're doing that, I'll hang around here and try not to launch anymore rockets."

The brothers shared a chuckle, and CB turned to leave. That's when Red saw two Space Marines in strange armor kneeling on the slope above them. He traded looks with CB and saw his brother's eyes flick to the pulse rifle he'd left leaning against the wrecked hover-copter.

"We're friends," one of the newcomers said. "Take it easy."

More Space Marines emerged from the forest and formed a perimeter around the crash.

"I'm Sergeant Udoh, India Company. Who are you?"

A sense of relief washed over Red, and he choked up.

"Warrant Brumley, Fourth Aviation Battalion," he said with a croak.

"Private First Class Brumley, First Mech," CB said.

Udoh scoffed. "What are you guys, brothers or something?"

"Yeah, we are, actually," Red said.

"What are the odds of that?" Udoh tipped his head at the hovercopter. "What's going on here, Warrant?"

"I got shot down and crash landed. The instrument panel collapsed onto my lap, and I can't get out. That's how he found me."

"Are either of you injured? Besides your face," Udoh said as he gestured to CB.

"I'm good," CB said.

"I'm not sure. My left ankle hurts, but I can't tell for certain," Red added.

"Okay. Let's see what we have here." Udoh examined the cockpit and instrument panel. "You tried to move this?"

Red told him about their failed attempts to lift the panel. "I thought we had it with the lever, but it bent in half."

"Huh. Well, let's see what we can do. You're not going to shoot anymore rockets, are you?"

Red shook his head. "No. That was stray voltage. I think we're okay."

"Ferrell, Jones, Matiscik. See what you can do with this while I call the LT."

The three Space Marines positioned themselves around the cockpit. Ferrell and Jones took the sides while Matiscik climbed up and straddled the cockpit. The trio got a good grip on the instrument panel and nodded their readiness.

"On three," Ferrell said.

Veins stood out on Jones's face and a loud grunt escaped Matiscik's gritted teeth as they strained to lift the wrecked panel. There was a loud shriek as the panel began to bend back up, and two other Space Marines grabbed Red by the shoulders and pulled him free of the cockpit.

Matiscik struck a body builder pose and let out a triumphant shout from his perch atop the cockpit. "Level Ten, baby," Matiscik said and kissed his biceps.

"Get down, numb nuts, and stop shouting," Udoh admonished. The rest of the squad laughed and shook their heads as Matiscik hopped down.

CB bent over Red to check for injuries. Red pushed his hands away and pulled his brother in for a tight hug.

"Thank you, little brother," he said.

After a few seconds, Sergeant Udoh cleared his throat. "Hey, I hate to interrupt your touching family moment, but the LT wants us back down on the road most ricky-tick. We need to get moving if we're gonna make Daarben tonight."

Red tried to stand, but intense pain in his left ankle made it impossible. "Hurts like crazy, and my legs are numb."

"It might be broken," CB advised. "C'mon, I'll help you."

The squad climbed down to the road. Every bump and jolt to his ankle sent a surge of agony up Red's leg, but he bit back the urge to cry out. He almost wept with relief when they reached the road, and

CB allowed him to slump to the ground. A corpsman moved in to check him over as two other Space Marines approached and crouched next to him.

"Hey, Warrant, I'm Lieutenant Penny. The captain will be here in a minute. Maybe you can shed some light on what the fuck is going on."

Red nodded and then laid his head back and closed his eyes. Now that he was clear of the hovercopter, his whole body ached from the force of the crash. Besides his ankle and his legs, his right elbow was swollen and sore. Otherwise, he didn't feel too bad.

"Here comes the captain," Penny said.

Red opened his eyes and saw a familiar face. After a few seconds, he realized who it was.

"Captain Fortis!"

* * * * *

Chapter Twenty-Four

"Well, that was interesting," McTigue said to Ngotel as he slipped off his headset. "General Anders deployed a company of Space Marines to Maltaan to do some battlefield prep for Sixth Division."

"I thought you just said Sixth Division wasn't coming," Ngotel said.

"They're not, but Anders didn't know that when he gave the order."

"Who is General Anders, sir?"

"He's a deputy to Ellis Boudreaux of the General Staff. I met him a couple weeks before we deployed. Seemed like a decent officer. I guess he's a little rash."

"Not much we can do about it now." Ngotel gestured to the main tactical display. "It looks like we're ready for the Badaax."

"I hope so."

Ngotel glanced at McTigue.

"Pardon my asking, but where the fuck does hope fit into your plans, Admiral? 'Hope isn't a strategy.' Isn't that what you're always saying?"

"I didn't mean it like that." As a senior admiral, McTigue didn't get much dissent from his staff, and he relied on his long-time friend to be an honest voice.

"You said it, sir. If you didn't mean it, what *did* you mean?"

230 | P.A. PIATT

McTighe pursed his lips and thought for a moment. "What I meant was, there are always unknown factors that create uncertainty. We can make contingency plans, we can take steps to mitigate risk and uncertainty, but there's no way to guarantee success."

"I think the Badaax are going to have their hands full with you and all this," Ngotel said. "I don't know shit about them, but I know I'd rather be over here when the shooting starts." The warrant leaned forward and lowered his voice. "If a self-promoted commodore and a raggedy ass fleet of salvage orbit junk can destroy one of them, I think you can handle anything they throw at us."

McTigue nodded and extended his hand, and Ngotel's massive paw swallowed it as they shook.

"Aleki, we've been together a long time, and I'm proud to call you my friend."

"Me too, Skipper."

* * *

"*Command… Two.*"

Van der Cruyff had Recon Two's frequency dialed up in his left ear, and the transmission was heavy with static.

"*Station calling, this is Command, say again, over,*" van der Cruyff's comms operator replied.

"*This is Recon Two… attack… blue…*"

The circuit went dead.

"*Major, Recon Two just called, it sounded—*"

"I heard the transmission," van der Cruyff said to the comms operator. He switched to the Second Mech command circuit. "All stations, this is Command. Recon Two has been attacked, status unknown. Stand by for contact."

Van der Cruyff and Fessler stood on the edge of the road and stared east as Space Marines scrambled for their posts all around them. Anti-air was not a typical mission of the main battle mechs, but the company commanders had their Space Marines dig trenches and back their vehicles in to give them maximum elevation with their main batteries. If their sensors could detect a low-flying blue bomber, they could engage.

Infantry scattered throughout the woods on either side of the road. Many carried shoulder-fired rockets in addition to their pulse rifles. The rockets were anti-mech weapons, with armor piercing warheads, but the Space Marines figured they might be effective against the blue bombers.

"Shit!"

Fessler shoved van der Cruyff off the road as a blue bomber appeared in the western sky. The major tumbled into the underbrush on the south side of the road as the craft flooded it with blue light. He slammed his visor down and unslung his pulse rifle as he scrambled to his feet. On the road, Sergeant Major Fessler fell to his knees as the blue light washed over him.

Main battle mechs opened up on the blue bomber with their pulse cannons, and the craft glowed with unexpended energy as bolt after bolt found its mark. The craft wobbled under the barrage and drifted down the road. A squad of Space Marine infantry dashed onto the road and fired a salvo of rockets which caused the blue bomber to bank hard toward the woods on the other side of the road. A squad hidden on the south side added their rockets to the attack, and the blue bomber rolled over and crashed with a thunderous explosion.

The Space Marines cheered their victory and van der Cruyff felt a surge of excitement that turned to lead in his belly when a second blue bomber attacked from the east. This one didn't make the mistake of flying over the road and presenting a target for the battle mechs. Instead, it passed directly over the mech positions and charred the forest that concealed them. Space Marines screamed and writhed as their bodies burst into bluish flame. Some of the mechs tried to maneuver to bring their batteries to bear, but the blue bomber moved too fast, and they were unable to elevate their guns to get a shot.

Rockets soared up from infantry positions throughout the forest, but it wasn't a concentrated attack as before. Most of the weapons flew harmlessly into the sky and detonated in the distance.

Van der Cruyff dashed onto the road where Fessler knelt, but when he grabbed Fessler's shoulder to drag him clear, the sergeant major collapsed on his face and lay still. The major heard the buzz of the blue bomber's engines as it returned for another attack, and he raced back to cover.

The blue bomber made a more deliberate pass over Second Mech's position as though it recognized the battle mechs were no longer a threat. The blue ray lit up the tree line, and the forest boiled with fire as trees exploded, and thick black smoke belched skyward. Pulse rifle bolts and anti-mech rockets raced up at the attacker, to no effect.

A mismatched convoy of battle mechs, APCs, and supply trucks burst out of the burning woods and turned for Ulvaan. The blue bomber banked and lined up for an attack from the rear, and the blue ray melted the vehicles. Burning Space Marines tumbled onto the road and collapsed in sizzling piles of molten helenium.

Van der Cruyff realized he'd had no communications since the attack began, and he frantically switched circuits in search of a response from anyone. He watched in horror as a group of Space Marines broke cover from the south side of the road and fired a volley of rockets and pulse rifle bolts at the blue bomber. The craft made a tight turn, and the blue ray chased them into the trees, where they died fiery deaths. A wave of heat washed over the major, and he threw himself on the ground as oily smoke surged through the trees. He low crawled to escape the fire as the cloying stink of burning bodies penetrated his helmet, and scorching ozone coated his throat and made it impossible to breathe.

A Space Marine screamed in agony as he staggered past van der Cruyff with his hands clutched over his eyes. The heat of the blue ray had fused his body armor to his flesh, and his face was blackened and blistered. The major froze at the horror of the sight, and he watched helplessly as the man stumbled and collapsed face down on the road.

Time seemed to speed up for van der Cruyff as the savage attack continued. More Space Marines emerged from the woods to engage the blue bomber, only to die in in the searing heat of the blue light. Another group of vehicles roared onto the road and turned west, toward Daarben. When the blue bomber approached, they scattered to both sides, but their ruse was short-lived. The craft torched the woods and the vehicles before it hunted down the Space Marines that scrambled clear and tried to hide. Dead Space Marines and melted vehicles dotted the road and the surrounding hellscape.

The major came upon a Space Marine huddled in the shelter of a large boulder, and he crawled in next to him.

"Are you okay?" he asked his companion. When the other man didn't answer, van der Cruyff shook him by the shoulder. The Space Marine fell over, and the major saw his helmet visor had been shattered by a pulse rifle bolt. It took van der Cruyff a moment to realize the Space Marine had crawled behind the boulder before he put the barrel of his pulse rifle under his chin and squeezed the trigger.

A sob wracked van der Cruyff's chest, and bile burned his throat. Fear, frustration, and helplessness exploded in his mind at the utter destruction he had witnessed. Second Mech had gone from the finest mechanized infantry battalion in the Corps to a smoking ruin in less than fifteen minutes. His Space Marines were dead, his vehicles were destroyed, and they'd only managed to shoot down a single attacker. Worst of all, he had survived the annihilation by hiding in the forest instead of confronting the enemy.

Van der Cruyff's tumultuous emotions hardened into shameful anger at the scale of the defeat. He scrambled to his feet and drew his pulse pistol. With a defiant cry, he charged into the middle of the road and searched the sky for the blue bomber. When it appeared, he took careful aim and fired as fast as he could squeeze the trigger.

The enormous craft approached and bathed the road in blue light. Van der Cruyff screamed in pain as his blood boiled and his skin crackled. He was dead before he hit the ground.

* * *

"Did you hear that?" Ystremski asked Fortis as they moved forward.

"I didn't hear anything. What was it?"

"I dunno. Maybe thunder. Maybe nothing."

When Fortis and Ystremski approached First Platoon, they saw a Space Marine lying on a litter with Doc Velez working on him. LT Penny approached.

"The pilot might have a broken ankle," Penny told Fortis. "The other one, his brother, has a broken nose."

"His brother?"

"Yes sir. They're brothers."

The supine pilot propped himself up on one elbow. "Captain Fortis!"

"Red?"

"You gotta be shittin' me," Ystremski said.

Red had been Fortis's team pilot when the captain led a small team of operators against the Maltaani insurgency over a year earlier. They had lost contact when the team was dissolved, and Fortis returned to Terra Earth.

Fortis crouched next to Red and took one of his hands. "You doing okay, Red?"

"I'm good, Captain. I'm sure glad to see you." He glanced at CB, who stood next to them. "Have you met my brother, CB?"

Fortis stood and extended his hand. "Captain Fortis."

"CB...er...PFC Brumley, sir."

The corpsman who had been tending to the pilot's leg stood. "I've done everything I can for him, Captain. His leg is stable, and he can travel, but we'll have to carry him."

"Thanks, Doc."

"Unidentified aircraft inbound from the east," a lookout warned over the company circuit.

The Space Marines dragged Red with them as they scrambled for cover in the trees. A black craft flew low overhead and followed the road toward Daarben. The only sound it made was a low buzzing.

"Blue bomber." The female Space Marine on a litter next to Red spoke up. "They destroyed First Mech."

Despite their pressing need to get to Daarben, Fortis knew gleaning intelligence from Red was a higher priority. He checked the time and saw another voice comms window with *Eclipse Wonder* was twenty minutes away.

"We'll hold here for a few minutes and see what we can get from Red and the others," he told Ystremski, Penny, and Young. "I'll make a report to Anders, and then we'll move out." He turned back to Red. "That was a blue bomber?"

"I didn't know they were called blue bombers, but yeah, that's what shot down me and my wingman."

"What happened?"

"Blackjack had low lead, like this." He held his left hand palm-down, and held his right above and behind it. "I was in high trail. We approached the wreckage of First Mech from the east, but before we got there, a pair of bogeys, er, blue bombers jumped us from behind. Blackjack broke right and I broke left," he said as his hands swooped apart.

"I got around long enough for Johnson—" His voice cracked, and he cleared his throat. "For my copilot to get off a spread of rockets, but it was too fast and ended up behind me. The cockpit flashed blue, and I had nothing, no cyclic, no pedals. We hit the mountain and broke up. The next thing I knew, CB was there."

"What about you?" Fortis asked CB.

"I was on dawn patrol and got separated from my squad. I heard a bunch of firing, but by the time I got there, it was over. I hid out and watched Red and the blue bombers dogfighting. I thought everyone was dead, so I gathered up some supplies and started walking. That's when I saw his wreck. I didn't see Will."

They looked over, but the lance corporal had lapsed into unconsciousness.

"So, you haven't seen any ground troops?"

The Brumley brothers shook their heads.

"Well, here's the situation. A fleet of aliens called Badaax destroyed the support fleet and landed at the space port. We don't know exactly what they're up to. A fleet is on the way, and a division of Space Marines is right behind them. Our mission is to link up with whatever forces remain here in preparation for the division drop. Will told us Second Mech was headed for the space port. As soon as I report to the general, that's where we're going."

* * *

Fortis made contact as soon as the comms window opened. "General, we recovered another Space Marine from First Mech and a hovercopter pilot from a crash site near the road. Do you remember Red Brumley?"

"*Yes, I remember Red.*"

"Two Badaax craft ambushed him and his wingman over the Daarben-Ulvaan road. Both hovercopters went down. We found him and his brother at the crash site."

Fortis repeated everything Red had told him about the Badaax craft and their flight characteristics.

"Two of them just flew over us, and all we heard was a low buzz," he added. "I don't know what we can do about them."

"*Observe and report,*" Anders said. "*Fourth Fleet has jumped through the gate, and they'll be here soon. I have one of our drones back, so I'll get it overhead as soon as possible.*"

"That's good news, sir." There was a long moment of silence. "What's the bad news?"

"*Sixth Division isn't coming. The deployment request was denied.*"

"We're on our own?"

238 | P.A. PIATT

"No! Absolutely not. I will do everything I can to support you until the fleet gets here."

Fortis thought for a second. If there was no division on the way, there was no reason for ground-level surveillance of the space port. "What are your orders, sir?"

"There are some caves along the road that your old friend Dexter Beck hid in after the invasion. If I can locate the coordinates, maybe you can hunker down there and wait for the fleet. Alternatively, you can take up concealed positions in the forest. Or you can turn around and head for Ulvaan, and we'll figure out how to get the shuttle down to you without being detected by the Badaax. Whatever you decide, I don't want you to engage the Badaax. You're the on-scene commander; I'll leave the final decision up to you."

"Roger that, sir. I'll get with Ystremski and the platoon commanders and let you know what we're doing."

"Sounds good. We'll skip the next comms window and resume our regular schedule after that."

Fortis looked back at the company and saw Ystremski approaching. They walked over to the side of the road, and the gunny handed him a pig square.

"Are we good, sir?"

"Yeah, we're good, Gunny." Fortis bit off a chunk of freeze-dried ham. "There's been a slight change of plans."

Fortis briefed Ystremski on his call with Anders while the two men chewed their rations.

"What do you think we should do?" he asked the gunny after he finished.

"All of those options suck, sir. Hump all the way back to Ulvaan and hope the blue bombers don't shoot us down in the shuttle. Hide in a hole or camp out in the woods and wait for the fleet, but who knows when that will be. If we're lucky, the dogs and snakes won't get anyone before the fleet arrives. A whole lot of suck, sir."

"How about if we Charlie Mike?" Fortis asked. 'Charlie Mike' was Space Marine lingo for 'Continue Mission.' "We'll continue west until we find Second Mech, and then we'll take up a position that allows us to surveil the space port."

"What are you going to tell the company?" Ystremski asked.

"I don't know. I guess all of it. We're not humping to Ulvaan, and we're not waiting for rescue, either. If we press on to the space port, at least it will give them something to focus on."

"I don't think you should mention Anders gave you options. Tell them Sixth Division hasn't deployed yet, but we're still headed for the space port."

"You want me to lie to them?"

"It's approximately true, and it doesn't give anyone anything to bitch about."

The captain nodded. "Makes sense to me." He thumped Ystremski on the shoulder. "That's what the Corps pays you for, to keep us officers out of trouble."

"It's a full-time job with you, sir." Ystremski gestured to the company. "I guess we're not in a hurry anymore. Do you want to hole up and wait for dark to move out?"

"It will be harder to spot the blue bombers."

"Works both ways. I got a look at the one that went by, and it had a bright heat signature."

"Okay, let's do it. It will be dark soon. A short rest won't make much difference either way."

* * * * *

Chapter Twenty-Five

The angry buzz of Anders' communicator woke him from a deep sleep.

"Anders."

"General, it's Major Rho. I'm sorry to bother you, but four of the Badaax craft have departed Maltaan orbit. When the drone lost contact, it looked like they were headed for the Maduro Jump Gate."

"Huh." Anders let Rho's report sink in while he gave his mind a moment to clear. "Send this information to Admiral McTigue via Zulu priority message."

"Zulu, sir?"

"Those craft are on their way to engage his fleet. I'm sure of it."

"Yes sir. I've drafted the message. I'll change the priority and transmit it."

"Are the other four Badaax still in orbit?"

"Yes sir, they haven't moved."

"Good. Call me if there are any changes. If I don't hear from you, I'll be up in four hours for the drone launch."

"Yes sir."

Anders tumbled back into his bunk in search of more sleep.

* * *

Three and a half sleepless hours later, Anders slumped into his console next to Rho.

"Any changes?"

"Four Badaax ships remain in orbit. The drone crew refueled the bird, but there's a fault in the launching circuitry. The techs are working on it. They gave me an estimate of sixty minutes."

"Have we heard from Admiral McTigue?"

"No sir." Rho scowled. "But we got a message from Fleet Command regarding the Black Hole constellation. It's a no-go."

"What? What happened?"

"Apparently nothing, General. The whole situation is a complete SNAFU. When Second Division became MAC-M and our presence here drew down, responsibility for the satellites passed to the Maltaan support fleet."

"Commodore Allard."

"That's correct. Commodore Allard. Programming, crypto, maintenance, all of it, except the personnel. They returned to Terra Earth. Fleet Command referred us to her staff."

Anders sighed and shook his head. "And the satellites have been orbiting untended ever since."

"We don't know that for certain because Commodore Allard...well...since her defeat, but it's a fair assumption. Their plan was to return and recover the birds at some future date. Frankly, I'd be surprised if the orbits haven't decayed to the point where the birds burned in. We haven't seen any since we've been here."

"Huh." Ander pinched the bridge of his nose between his thumb and forefinger. "I guess I'll tell Fortis during our next comms window."

"Sir, there is one more thing. Do you recall the file we received from the *Fortuna* after they warned us when the second set of Badaax came through the warp?"

"Vaguely. Something about asteroid orbits. I didn't have time to read it in depth."

"That's the one. It's an analysis of asteroid belt orbital dynamics. Specifically, the asteroid belt where *Fortuna* was wildcatting when they observed the Badaax jump. What they saw was that the warp is located just under the edge of the belt. Because of the asteroids, it's only uncovered for approximately thirty days every eighty years. The rest of the time, it's covered by the belt."

"Interesting. Does it make sense?"

"That's hard to say without any corroborating information. There's no reason to think *Fortuna* is lying, but they could be mistaken. They're just a wildcat crew, not trained scientists. Still, if the Badaax know enough to jump through the warp, they know encountering something on the other side would be a disaster. It certainly deserves more study."

Anders squeezed his eyes shut and willed the fatigue that fogged his mind to dissipate. "I appreciate your enthusiasm, Major, but what does it mean to us?"

"The warp is uncovered right now, and the Badaax came through. It seems reasonable to believe they understand how the belt orbits, so they know their transit window will close soon. If we can predict when the asteroids will foul the gate, we can predict when the Badaax will leave."

"*If* they're leaving. They might be here to stay."

"Of course, General. If, but I think it's unlikely they would stay for eighty years without support."

244 | P.A. PIATT

"Or they might leave sooner. Now, even."

"Anything is possible, sir," Rho said in a subdued voice. Anders smiled at her.

"This is good analysis, Major. Take another look at the report to check the math, and we'll send it on to Admiral McTigue. It might make a difference in his planning." The general looked at the clock. "Let's get ready for the drone launch and the next comms window."

* * * * *

Chapter Twenty-Six

McTigue sat in his chair and forced himself to remain calm. When he'd received the warning from *Eclipse Wonder* that four of the Badaax had departed orbit and were heading in his direction, he had considered raising the alert level of the fleet but decided it was too early. Instead, he ordered frigates on both wings to deploy scout drones far ahead of the formation.

With his confidence boosted after his earlier discussion with Ngotel, the admiral was content to settle back in his seat to watch and wait while events unfolded.

"Admiral, one of the scout drones has detected an unknown contact approaching from the direction of Maltaan," the FOC watch officer announced. "It's on the big screen."

McTigue saw a white unknown contact symbol on the far edge of the strategic display, well outside maximum weapons range, in the one o'clock position.

"Do we have an ID?"

"Negative, sir."

"Thank you."

The admiral had participated in many wargames throughout his career from which he had learned two crucial lessons. First, space warfare was not for the impatient. The ranges involved meant nothing happened quickly, and the losing side was usually the one that tried to force the action.

The second lesson was the importance of ship stationing. Again, because of the ranges involved, a ship out of position when an engagement began was as out of action as if it weren't there at all. He was confident his fleet was positioned to provide maximum flexibility and mutual support, and he would be able to bring maximum firepower to bear without a lot of time-wasting maneuvers.

McTigue felt the tension in the FOC rise as the unknown ship crawled across the screen. Finally, sensors on *Tenacious* detected the ship as it approached the formation. McTigue noted it wasn't on a direct interception course with the fleet; if it maintained course and speed, it would pass ahead of the fleet, but within weapons range, before it exited the strategic display at the eight o'clock position.

"They're ranging us," McTigue said to no one in particular.

The FOC watch officer had moved to stand behind McTigue and leaned in. "Sir?"

"They're ranging us. They're testing to see the range at which we respond. Remind all ships to hold their fire."

McTigue didn't expect any of his captains to act rashly, considering the detailed planning they had engaged in, but it wouldn't hurt to let them know he was watching. After the watch officer finished transmitting his order, he smiled and nodded to her.

"Set Alert Condition Alpha throughout the fleet."

"Yes sir."

Two minutes later, McTigue's staff BWC assumed the FOC watch and reported all stations were manned and ready at Alert Condition Alpha. Two minutes after that, the last ship in the fleet reported their readiness. It surprised McTigue to note the tension in the FOC eased at the higher alert level, but it occurred to him that with the increase in readiness came the presence of the most skilled and experienced watch standers. They were the best at their assigned duties, and that knowledge gave them a degree of confidence that mitigated the strain of the situation.

"The contact is turning, sir."

Remorseless, the second frigate in the left wing, had also gained contact, and the sensor resolution between her and her sister ship *Tenacious* provided near-perfect tracking.

And targeting.

The course and speed indicator on the unknown showed the vessel in a wide left-hand turn, which would bring it across the front of McTigue's fleet at close range unless they turned. A "1" appeared under the contact, designating it Unknown One. He considered his options, but before the admiral could issue orders, a cluster of three unknowns appeared at the top of the screen.

"New contacts at one o'clock, Admiral," the BWC said.

"I see them."

The scout drone reported the new contacts closing at a high rate of speed, a speed which McTigue found difficult to believe until *Persistent,* on the right wing, gained contact and confirmed it.

"The scout drone has ceased reporting," the BWC announced. "Drone Control reports a loss of control and no communications with the bird. It looks like a mission kill."

"Order *Macau* and the left wing to kill Unknown One. Right wing, stand by to engage the other three."

At the speed they were traveling, the three unknowns would be within rail gun range in minutes. They were moving too fast to make any sharp turns to avoid the combined firepower of the right wing.

The symbol on Unknown One changed from white to red as the tactical system designated it Hostile One. Moments later, the left wing fired a full salvo of seven rail gun projectiles: three from the destroyer and two from each frigate. The course and speed indicators moved erratically as Hostile One attempted to evade, and McTigue imagined the panic aboard the enemy vessel as the rounds bore down on it. Two of the projectiles veered off into empty space, and three more disappeared, no doubt the result of countermeasures, but two made it through. Hostile One vanished.

The FOC watch standers reacted with smiles among themselves, but they remained focused on the task of engaging the other three unknowns.

"Signal Bravo Zulu to the left wing," McTigue ordered the BWC. "Designate the other three contacts as hostile."

"Bravo Zulu" was a traditional signal that meant "Well Done" in regards to an operation or action.

Even as the BWC transmitted his congratulations, McTigue did some quick math. They fired seven rail gun projectiles at Hostile One to destroy it, and the target defeated five of them. The simple answer was to fire 21 projectiles at the incoming trio,

The fleet was capable of firing 22 rail gun projectiles simultaneously. The four frigates could fire eight, the three destroyers nine, and *Invictus* added five to the total.

McTigue knew better than to believe a single full salvo would destroy their attackers. If the hostiles maintained their formation integrity, he figured their self-defense systems would be complementary and require more than 21 projectiles to overwhelm them. A full salvo would also expose the fleet to counterattack while their rail guns recharged. The recharge time varied from ship to ship, but even a few seconds' delay could leave them vulnerable.

Hostiles Two, Three, and Four continued to close the fleet and crossed into rail gun range. McTigue waited two long minutes before he issued his next orders.

"Left wing, kill Hostile Two with rail guns. Right wing, kill Hostile Four with rail guns. *Invictus* and *Marquis du Bouchet* stand by for counter-battery fire."

Two and Four turned red on the display, and the fleet engaged as ordered.

"Turn the formation ninety degrees to the right," McTigue ordered. "Slow speed to one third."

The admiral had momentarily forgotten how important it was to engage the Badaax vessels at range. Multiple symbols blossomed on the strategic display and raced toward *Duc de Nemours* on the right wing. The destroyer seemed to shudder on the display as *Persistent* and *Resolute* maneuvered to provide defensive fire with their point defense weapons.

"*Duc de Nemours* reports loss of propulsion. Shield at thirty-five percent," the BWC announced.

On the left flank, Hostile Two fired a salvo of missiles at *Tenacious* before it turned away to escape the rail gun projectiles fired by the frigate and her sister ships. Both ships disappeared from the screen at the same moment.

"Lost contact with *Tenacious!*"

"Can't be helped," McTigue muttered to himself. "Left wing, pivot to support the right wing," he ordered. "*Invictus* and *Marquis du Bouchet*, kill Hostile Three with rail guns."

There was a long moment of silence as rail gun projectiles and hostile missile symbols passed each other on the strategic display. In a spectacular display of gallantry, *Resolute* maneuvered between *Duc de*

Nemours and the incoming missiles. Half the weapons ignored the frigate and bore down on the crippled destroyer, while the other half impacted the frigate. The right wing managed to destroy four of the six inbound missiles, but the *Duc de Nemours* disappeared.

"Lost contact with *Resolute* and *Duc de Nemours.*"

By that time, *Baron de Macau* and *Remorseless* had closed to within rail gun range of Hostile Four and unleashed a full rail gun salvo at it. The enemy craft maneuvered to escape the weapons and turned to flee, even as the salvo from the flagship and her escort destroyed Hostile Three.

"Three for four!" the BWC announced in a triumphant tone as the FOC erupted in cheers. "Four is retreating!"

"Silence!" ordered McTigue. "We lost three of ours." He glared at the BWC. "Order all ships to pursue Hostile Four. I want a full status report for the remaining ships and bring up *Compassionate* to search for survivors."

The admiral forced himself to relax as the watch scrambled to obey his orders. His hands ached from gripping his armrests and his armpits felt damp, but he had a surge of euphoric pride inside.

Victory!

It had come at a steep price, but his fleet had met and defeated the Badaax. All the training and planning had paid off handsomely, and he knew Fleet Command and the Grand Council would be pleased with the victory.

McTigue logged into the digital communications system to compose a message to his higher-ups. A million thoughts raced through his mind as he stared at the blinking cursor. What he wrote next would become part of the official Fleet record and probably be released to the public on Terra Earth, so it was only appropriate he craft a succinct but profound message. He began to type.

We have met the ene—

"Hostile Four has turned back, sir."

McTigue looked up from his console, and what he saw on the screen shocked him. Hostile Four had doubled back and was heading toward the fleet at an impossible speed. Rail gun projectiles blossomed from every ship, and two missile symbols detached from the enemy craft.

"They're aimed at us, sir," the BWC announced. "Shields at one hundred percent, activating self-defense weapons."

Hostile Four disappeared under the barrage of rail gun projectiles. Suddenly, dozens of hostile missile symbols appeared on the screen and tracked toward *Invictus*.

"What the hell is that?" McTigue shouted.

"Multiple warheads," the BWC responded.

Invictus maneuvered to unmask all her self-defense batteries. *Marquis du Bouchet* tried to maintain her position relative to the flagship and provide mutual defense, but she turned away instead. A few of the incoming missiles followed the destroyer, but most of them continued inbound toward *Invictus*.

A series of violent explosions shook the ship, and the FOC went dark as the flagship lost power. Emergency lighting flickered on, and alarms sounded throughout the ship. Many of the FOC watch standers jumped up from their consoles and joined the panicked scramble for the escape hatches.

"Stay on your stations!" the BWC commanded, to no avail. Crewmembers crawled over consoles and each other in their rush to escape.

Escape to where? McTigue thought.

The forward hatch slammed open, and a wave of blue-tinged superheated air flooded the space. The people in front screamed in agony as they tried to escape the searing hell, but there was nowhere to go.

McTigue watched it all unfold for a split second until the heat slammed into him and drove him backward. He struggled to draw one final breath, but he couldn't force his lungs to work. As he collapsed to the deck, the admiral had one final thought.

Blue.

* * * * *

Chapter Twenty-Seven

Blue bombers overflew India Company's position alongside the road twice while they waited for darkness, but the Space Marines remained under cover and undetected. When Fortis was satisfied it was dark enough, the company prepared to move. Before he could give the order, Doc Velez found him in the darkness.

"Hey, Captain, before we head out, I need to tell you something about Lance Corporal Will."

"Is she okay?"

"As far as I can tell, yes sir. She's been unconscious for several hours, but her vitals are steady. She hasn't moved except when those blue bombers fly by, and then she starts squirming. I don't know what it is."

"Can she move?"

"Sure. We'll need to restrain her in case those fuckers come back while we're moving, but she can move."

"Do what you have to, Doc. We need to get moving. I'd like to find Second Mech tonight."

Refreshed from the stop, LT Penny and First Platoon pushed the pace. Fortis checked on the litter bearers and found them maintaining without effort, and it pleased Fortis to see CB keep up alongside his brother despite his broken nose. They remained alert for blue bombers but saw none.

Two hours into their westward trek, the point platoon stopped the company cold.

"Cover."

A few minutes later, Penny reported.

"Command, First Platoon. Point saw a vehicle in the road and checked it out. It looks like the remains of a recon mech, but they can't tell what unit it belonged to. It's melted into a pile of slag. There's nobody around."

"Roger that. Let's keep moving."

* * *

G eneral Anders read the message from Fleet Captain Heroux, commanding officer of *Baron de Macau,* and his blood ran cold.

Invictus, Marquis du Bouchet, Duc de Nemours, Tenacious, and *Resolute,* all destroyed. How was that possible?

He read it again, and twice more after that, as if by re-reading it, he could change the contents.

"I am holding the fleet one day from Maltaan, awaiting guidance from Fleet Command," Heroux wrote. "Given our recent experience and present force level, I believe our chances of success in continuing our engagement with the remaining enemy ships is quite low."

No Fleet officer liked to admit they were unable to meet operational tasking, and Anders noted Heroux chose his words with great care. He didn't refuse to continue the engagement, he put the onus of the decision on Fleet Command.

The general's mind raced as he considered the tactical implications of the battle. A destroyer and two frigates would not be a sufficient force to defeat the four remaining Badaax, even if they managed to surprise them.

Anders wondered how the Badaax would react to the battle. Thus far they hadn't seemed to notice the drone surveilling them in orbit, but there was no question they knew human warships were now in the sector. *Eclipse Wonder* was maintaining her position, concealed in the sensor shadow of Maltaan except for the brief comms windows, but he worried the Badaax might detect her, and she would suffer the same fate as the fleets of Allard and McTigue.

The longer he thought about it, the more he realized the sensible thing to do would be to order India Company into hiding and withdraw *Eclipse Wonder* from the area. She could monitor the drone from as far away as the jump gate, so she would have ample warning if the Badaax fleet sortied to engage.

The general checked the time and saw the next comms window with Fortis was minutes away.

* * *

India Company began to see more remains of dead Space Marines on the road as they continued west. Gunny Ystremski insisted on erecting a cairn for every set of remains they encountered, and it began to annoy Fortis. He regretted every death, of course, and it rubbed his sense of duty raw to leave the fallen behind, but India's priority had to be the living, wherever they might be. After a heated discussion on a private comms channel, the gunny made it clear that the only way he would be deterred would be if Fortis made it a formal order, and Fortis relented.

The company kept moving while Ystremski and three members of the command element fell out and piled the rocks, then raced to regain their positions in the formation. It didn't take long for Fortis to notice the point platoon telling the company to take cover soon after they passed a set of remains, and he shook his head when he realized there was no suppressing the enlisted mafia.

Fortis called a brief halt two hours later for the next comms window with *Eclipse Wonder*. India Company melted into the trees along the road to grab drinks and wait for the order to move out, while Fortis stood on the road and connected with Anders.

"I've got a drone headed for the space port; it should be overhead in twenty minutes," Anders said.

"That's good news, sir."

"I've got some bad news, too. The Black Hole constellation is not available for tasking."

"We weren't counting on it anyway." There was a long silence. "General, you're too easy to read. What's the real bad news?"

"Admiral McTigue and his fleet engaged four Badaax craft and destroyed them, but the fleet suffered heavy losses."

"The fleet isn't coming, is it?"

"They're waiting for guidance from Fleet Command. Only one destroyer and two frigates remain, and they're understandably reluctant to engage the other four Badaax in Maltaan orbit."

The enormity of Anders' words left Fortis speechless.

"Abner, are you there?"

"Yes sir."

"What's your status?"

"We're moving west at best speed, sir. I'm trying to link up with Second Mech before it gets light, if we can find them."

"I guess you decided to continue your mission?"

"I couldn't think of a reason not to. We still need to know what's happening there, with or without Sixth Division."

"Then this will be more bad news. I told you I was reserving the right to scrub the mission, and now I doing just that."

"Negative, sir. We haven't linked up with Second Mech yet."

"With what we know about First Mech, it's a safe bet Second suffered the same fate. It's not worth the risk."

Fortis fought to control the tone of his voice. "Maybe not from orbit, but from where I'm standing, it is. Sir."

"Are you disobeying a direct order, Captain Fortis?"

"No sir. You haven't given me one. Hello? Hello?"

Before Anders could respond, Fortis broke the link. When he rejoined the command element, Ystremski stood next to him.

"Everything okay with the general?"

Fortis nodded. "Yeah, it's all good. The drone should be back over the space port in twenty minutes or so."

"And?"

"There's no 'and,' Gunny. Let's move out."

* * *

General Boudreaux traded a glance with Fleet Admiral Knight as they waited outside the Minister of Defense's office. Knight's aide, Captain Phipps, stood by the door with a sick look on his face, and for a second, Boudreaux regretted not bringing his own cannon fodder.

The door jerked open, and a dour-faced man waved at them. "The Minister is waiting, gentlemen."

Boudreaux bristled at the man's attitude as he followed Admiral Knight into the office. Minister Marjorie Brooks-Green, or MBG, was a prominent member of the Peace Party and, therefore, no friend to the military. Her underlings were probably dedicated party members, but decorum demanded a minimum level of courtesy which the staffer clearly lacked.

Brooks-Green had replaced her predecessor's heavy wooden desk with a long metal and glass table positioned in front of the tall windows that made up one wall of her office. She stood behind it with arms crossed and nodded to two chairs positioned in front of it.

"Sit."

Knight and Boudreaux did as she instructed, and Phipps stood behind them.

"That's all, Captain." MBG gestured to the door. "Wait outside."

Phipps blanched and looked at Knight, but the admiral didn't react. When the captain was gone, MBG picked up a file folder from the table and waved it at the admiral and general.

"What is this?"

The folder had a bright red stripe across the top, an indicator that the contents were highly classified. Boudreaux knew it was the latest sitrep from Maltaan, detailing the defeat of Admiral McTigue, which had prompted the summons to the minister's office. He and Knight remained silent.

"What the fuck is this?" MBG repeated.

"I believe that's the latest Maltaan sitrep," Knight said.

"Don't play games with me, Admiral." MBG slapped the folder on the table. "Of course it's the sitrep. What I want to know is, what the fuck happened? How did we lose two entire fleets and a thousand Space Marines, and nobody thought to advise this office before it happened?"

"Ma'am, Minister Fine authorized the deployment of Fourth Fleet before he, uh, before the Grand Council appointed you to replace him."

"I'm aware of what transpired before I became Minister. I led the veto of Sixth Division's deployment." She tapped the folder. "It's a damn good thing I did, or there would be another half-dozen ships and six thousand Space Marines and Fleet personnel on the butcher's bill."

MBG had a well-earned reputation for straight talk and no fear of using obscenities to make her point. "What is our current status in and around Maltaan? Is it as big a clusterfuck as it sounds?"

"Minister, the destroyer *Baron de Macau* and frigates *Remorseless* and *Persistent* are in a blocking position between Maltaan and the Maduro Jump Gate. The hospital ship *Compassionate* and a handful of logistics and repair ships are loitering near the jump gate, ready to jump back in case the Badaax make a move this way. The drone surveillance vessel *Eclipse Wonder* is in orbit on the far side of Maltaan from the Badaax, and it's her drones that have provided the bulk of the intelligence on Badaax movements. She also inserted a company of Space Marines to attempt to link up with MAC-M forces on the ground, but they've had no contact thus far."

"You deployed troops? On whose authority? The Grand Council vetoed the Space Marines."

"Admiral, if I may," said Boudreaux. "Minister, before the veto, I authorized India Company to accompany General Anders aboard *Eclipse Wonder* as a contingency in case there was a need for additional troop support."

"Anders? Why does that name sound familiar?"

"Nils Anders served as the Science and Technology Advisor to the Military Attaché when you were the ambassador to Maltaan."

A look of recognition crossed MBG's face. "I remember now. He's a good man."

"Yes ma'am, he is. That's why I ordered him to deploy with *Eclipse Wonder*."

"You said they haven't made contact with MAC-M yet?"

"We haven't heard from Colonel Wisniewski since the Badaax arrived. Captain Fortis reported that India Company discovered the remains of one of two mechanized infantry battalions assigned to MAC-M."

"Fortis? I remember that name from Maltaan."

"That's correct, Minister. Fortis was present on Maltaan as well."

"Hmm." MBG paced in front of the windows and stroked her chin. "What I'm hearing is that we're on our ass. Is that a fair assessment?"

Boudreaux stifled a smile, and Knight nodded. "We are definitely on our back foot, ma'am."

"General, do you have any recommendations for how we can salvage this situation?"

"Without knowing more about their capabilities, I don't know what to recommend. We don't yet know why they appeared."

"How about you, General? What do you recommend?"

"I think we need to deploy another fleet to confront the Badaax. We've learned a great deal about their capabilities, and I believe we can use that knowledge to defeat them."

"We've lost almost two full fleets so far, including the newest ships in service, Admiral. Why should we risk even more?"

Knight stared at MBG, speechless. She looked at Boudreaux. "At least you seem to understand the situation, General Boudreaux." She gestured to the sitrep folder. "Based on this and our complete lack of original thinking, I'm going to call an emergency meeting of the Grand Council and recommend we withdraw our forces from Maltaan and perhaps the entire Maduro Sector, pending a review of the situation. Thank you, gentlemen." She turned and looked out the window.

It had been a long time since either officer had been treated so abruptly, and it took them a second to realize they'd been dismissed. They mumbled their thanks to MBG's back and left the office. When they got to the corridor outside her office, Knight let out a deep breath.

"That went well."

"She's right," Boudreaux said. "It's a clusterfuck."

"Maybe pulling back is the best thing for all of us."

"Except the Space Marines on Maltaan, you mean," Boudreaux said. "They're not going anywhere."

* * * * *

Chapter Twenty-Eight

India Company continued west through the night. The sky had begun to lighten when the point ordered a halt. LT Penny called Fortis.

"Command, this is First Platoon. There's another burned-out vehicle on the road ahead. This one looks like a main battle mech."

"This is Command, roger. Investigate and report. All stations, remain under cover."

Fortis saw Red standing next to CB and the litter bearers.

"How's the leg, Red?" Fortis asked.

"All good, Captain. I had to get up off that litter for a while." He rubbed his backside. "It's killing me."

Fortis looked at Doc Velez. "How's Will?"

"She was conscious for a few minutes during our last stop, but she's been out since then."

"Do the best you can. We'll get her out of here as soon as possible." Fortis turned to CB. "Looks like you're keeping up, CB."

The younger Brumley smiled. "No choice, Captain. Nobody is going to carry me around like my lazy brother."

LT Penny's voice on the circuit broke into the conversation.

"Command up."

Something at the front of the column required Fortis's attention, and Ystremski joined him as he trotted forward. They passed three vehicles that were burned beyond recognition before they found Penny crouched in the dark next to a destroyed main battle mech.

"What's up?" Fortis asked the lieutenant.

"This has got to be Second Mech," Penny said. "It's spread out along the road for the next couple klicks. Every vehicle is smashed, and some of them are melted into piles of slag. Everything is too crispy to tell if there are any bodies in there. There was one hell of a fight here. Even the trees are burned for fifty meters from the road. There's something in the woods on the other side that you need to see."

They crossed the road, and Penny led the way into the trees.

"We looked around over here for survivors, thinking there might have been somebody that got away, and we found this."

Penny stopped next to a Space Marine standing guard next to a tangled mess of twisted metal that lay half-buried by dirt and debris.

"What's that fucking smell?" asked the gunny.

"I don't know," said Penny. "The lads thought it might be another crashed hovercopter until they saw him."

Fortis and Ystremski peered into the wreckage and saw a bulbous blue head poking out from underneath. The eyes were closed, but the mouth hung open, and Fortis made out rows of jagged teeth.

"That's a Badaax," Fortis said.

"Yeah, that's what I figured," Penny said. "A whole battalion of mechs got smoked, but they got one."

Fortis noticed the sentry was standing with his hands clasped together over his groin.

"Are you injured?"

The Space Marine shook his head. "No sir. That thing might be radioactive, and I don't want it to roast my balls."

"Let's get out of here." Fortis led the way back to the road. "In addition to roasting our balls, that thing might be a biohazard."

"It sure smells like one," Ystremski said.

The command element and Second Platoon had moved up, and the company stared at the devastated mechs as they waited for orders.

"We need to keep moving," Ystremski said. "We can't let them dwell on this shit for too long." He gestured at the incinerated remains of the trees, barely visible through their low-light and infrared optics. "Besides, it's getting light, and there's not much cover here."

"The forest ends just beyond the last vehicle," Penny said. "The road drops down out of the hills from there."

"We'll move north inside the tree line until we're opposite the space port," Fortis ordered. "From there, we can figure out the best position from which to conduct surveillance."

First Platoon led the way into the relative safety of the forest. Their progress was slow, but it was a relief to be off the exposed road. After an hour of picking their way through the woods, Fortis called a halt for the next comms window with General Anders. He motioned for Ystremski to follow him a few meters away from the company, out of earshot.

"On my last call with Anders, he told me the fleet's not coming," he said. "They engaged the Badaax and only have three ships left."

Ystremski gave a low whistle. "Where does that leave us?"

"I'm not sure. The general wanted to abort the mission, but the comm link dropped. As far as I'm concerned, we're Charlie Mike."

"Are you going to talk to him again?"

"Affirmative. He said he would have a drone over the space port about two hours ago, and I'd like to get a look at what's going on before we get there."

266 | P.A. PIATT

"What if he orders us to abort?"

Fortis shrugged. "Comms can be unreliable sometimes. Besides, as the commander on the ground, I have the best vantage point to make that decision."

"If you say so, sir."

"We'll get into position and give it a couple days. If it doesn't look like we're getting much, we'll pull out and head for extraction in Ulvaan."

"That's a long fucking way."

"I'll make sure we go slow, so you can keep up."

"You're all heart, Captain."

Fortis found a clear spot and linked up with *Eclipse Wonder.*

"We found Second Mech near where the road comes out of the mountains and turns down toward the space port, sir. Completely destroyed, but it looks like they shot down one of the Badaax craft. There's wreckage on the south side of the road with a Badaax body inside."

"A small bit of good news," Anders said. *"Where are you?"*

"I decided to Charlie Mike. We turned south into the forest for a position opposite the space port to surveil it."

"You were supposed to abort the mission. Barring that, what you're doing isn't one of the other options we discussed."

"You said we could take up a concealed position in the forest and wait for the fleet. Now that there's no fleet, we're just waiting." Before Anders could respond, Fortis continued. "General, we've discovered two entire mechanized battalions destroyed by the Badaax. I imagine the sight of that has the lads on edge, and I don't think hiding in the woods is a good idea. I'm keeping them focused on a mission instead of what they've seen. Even if it's a mission that doesn't have a purpose, it's better than hunkering down to wait for a fleet that's not coming."

"I don't like it, but it's your call. The drone is up, and thus far, we haven't observed anything significant. The four ships are still in orbit."

The two officers agreed to lengthen the comms window interval now that Fortis and India Company were off the road and then signed off.

"Now what?" Ystremski asked when Fortis rejoined the command element.

"Do you think we're far enough away from Second Mech that we can hole up for a few hours and give the company a chance to rest?"

"Yes sir, we should be good. I'll have them post sentries and give them four hours."

* * *

While the company rested, Fortis and Penny went forward to get a look at the forest ahead of them. The tree line was a jumble of fallen logs and boulders, and it looked almost impassable. To their left, the mountains were steep and imposing, and to their right was open farmland.

"It will take a long time to get through this shit," Penny said. "I'll send a patrol upslope and see how it looks up there. Maybe there's a game trail or something we can follow."

Fortis agreed to extend their stop while the patrol searched for an easier way south. He moved among the Space Marines and stopped to talk with a few of them. It pleased him to see they all remained upbeat despite what they had seen on the road, and most seemed anxious to get some payback for their comrades. He reminded them their mission was reconnaissance but assured them that if the opportunity came, he wouldn't hesitate to strike.

The patrol found a way around the most difficult terrain, and when Fortis ordered the company to move out, India made good time as they snaked their way south along the mountain slope. By the time the next comms window began, the company was in a position almost due east of the space port, about twelve klicks across the agricultural fields that bordered the city of Daarben.

It was early evening when the company settled into their new positions, with Second Platoon to the south, First Platoon to the north, and the command element in the middle. The Space Marines didn't need encouragement to maximize cover and concealment; after what they had witnessed on the road, they knew their best chance of surviving against the Badaax was to remain undetected.

Fortis and Ystremski moved a short way up the slope to an opening in the overhead canopy for the next comms window. At the appointed time, Fortis's communicator came to life.

"Abner, the drone is up, but we're detecting no movement at the space port. We tried broadcasting on common frequencies with negative results. I just sent you the numbers so you can tap into the drone feed and watch for yourself."

"Roger that. We've taken a position in the wooded hills twelve klicks east of the space port. I'm going to do some scouting and see if there are places to set up some forward observation posts."

"Without Sixth Division, there's no need to take that risk. What do you hope to gain from it?"

"We're here to observe and report, so that's what we're going to do. My—whoa!"

Without warning, Ystremski dragged Fortis into the trees. They barely got under cover before they heard a blue bomber buzzing low overhead. It was almost invisible against the night sky.

The pair remained motionless for several long minutes until they were sure the Badaax craft had moved on.

"Holy shit," Fortis said as they untangled themselves.

"I saw the heat signature a second after it popped up overhead," Ystremski said.

"It's a good thing you did, or I would have been toast."

Fortis poked out from under cover and tried to reestablish the comms link with Anders, without success. He crawled back and rejoined Ystremski.

The gunny thumped Fortis on the shoulder. "What did the general have to say?"

"He's gonna be pissed I cut off comms with him again. The drone is up, and he sent the numbers so we can see for ourselves. Maybe we'll get some idea of what's going on at the space port. He doesn't want us to set up FOPs."

"Do you want to establish FOPs?"

"I think we have to. We're too far away to see anything from here. The drone helps, but one drone can't give us round-the-clock coverage. It's also subject to getting pulled away for other tasking. We need our own eyes on the space port."

"Roger that, sir. The platoon commanders marked some outcroppings of trees and brush that might work. After dark, we'll get some patrols out to investigate and establish the posts."

"We're gonna need all eyes on the skies while they're moving."

"Yes sir. We'll get it done."

* * * * *

Chapter Twenty-Nine

Fortis, Ystremski, Penny, and Young met to discuss the FOP situation. After a brief debate about whether it was better for the FOP teams to move rapidly or move slowly to get into position, the Space Marines decided that speed was more important than stealth. The blue bombers had a bad habit of appearing overhead when they were least expected, and nobody wanted the FOP teams to get caught in the open fields. They decided each platoon would send two two-man teams to establish FOPs in the clumps of trees and underbrush that dotted the fields adjacent to the space port.

For two tension-filled hours, they watched as the Space Marines sprinted from cover to cover across the fields until they arrived at their FOP location. The command element watch monitored the drone feed, but there was no visible reaction from the space port.

One of First Platoon's teams moved all the way up to the tree line that bordered the space port. Fortis would have called them back were it not for Ystremski.

"They're close, but they're no more exposed than the other teams," the gunny said.

Fortis agreed, and all four teams were safely in position before the sky began to brighten.

All FOPs noted negative activity at the space port in their initial reports. Fortis, Ystremski, and two members of the command element moved to the clearing so Fortis could make the next comms window with Anders.

"I thought I lost you there," Anders said when the circuit opened. *"What happened?"*

"We went to ground when a blue bomber passed overhead, and by the time we were clear, the comms window was closed."

"We need to refuel the drone, and then it will be back on task for the next six hours. I've ordered it to remain in high orbit unless there is a specific reason to descend. I'm going to have it circle the MAC-M headquarters on the way back for refueling, but I don't think there's much happening there."

"We've been monitoring the drone feed here. We established four FOPs last night, and so far, all have reported negative activity at the space port."

"I still wish you hadn't, but between the drone and your observations, we should be able to get a good handle on their operational rhythm. Make sure your lads minimize their exposure."

They agreed on the next three comms windows and signed off. When Fortis and the group returned to the command element position, he checked in with the watch to take a look at the drone imagery. One Space Marine had the drone video feed on his visor while the other two maintained a visual watch for blue bombers. If there were any significant developments, they would report to the command element watch, who also monitored communications between the FOPs and platoon commanders.

With the watch settled and a rotation established, Fortis put his back against a tree to grab the first sleep he'd had since India Company'd landed three days earlier.

* * *

LT Penny roused Fortis a short while later. *"Command, this is First Platoon. I'm sending some video from FOP One. There's a lot of movement at the space port you need to see."*

"Roger, send it," Fortis said.

The video icon on Fortis's heads-up display began to blink, and Fortis pulled it up on the inside of his visor. One of the large Badaax craft had repositioned itself at the end of the space port runway and lowered the belly ramp. Crews of Badaax ground personnel pushed two blue bombers into position at the ramp, then they slowly loaded the smaller craft aboard.

"Do you think they're leaving?" Fortis asked Penny. He forwarded the video to Ystremski, who had joined him when Penny called.

"I don't know, sir. Maybe. They could be moving to the space port at Ulvaan. Stand by."

Gunny Ystremski nodded to Fortis after he watched the video. "It looks like they're bugging out to me."

"Yeah, but to where?"

Ystremski snorted. "I hope it's not Ulvaan. I don't want to walk all the way back there."

Fortis checked the time. "There's a comms window coming up in fifteen minutes. I'll send this to Anders and see what he thinks. His drone is up there somewhere, so they should be able to see it, too."

"This is Second Platoon," LT Young said. *"FOP Four reported the Badaax are moving a caravan of Maltaani from one of the domes toward the space port. Take a look."*

Fortis watched as a long line of Maltaani trudged along, escorted by their Badaax captors. The Badaax wielded tall staffs that emitted rays of blue light, and the Maltaani walked with their heads down and

274 | P.A. PIATT

shoulders slumped forward. The caravan crawled across an open field and onto the space port where the Badaax ship waited.

"Whose view is that?" Ystremski asked. "It looks like he's up a tree."

"That's Lenoir. He stuck his helmet up in the tree to get a better look, but he's under cover."

Fortis and Ystremski traded looks and then shrugged.

"Here's another video," Penny said. *"It looks like they're lining up to board that ship."*

From the different vantage points provided by the FOPs, it was obvious the Badaax intended to load their captives onto the waiting craft.

"What the hell are they going to do with them?" Ystremski asked.

"Slaves, maybe." A feeling of dread swept over Fortis when he remembered the slaughter of the elephant they had witnessed earlier. "Anders said 'badaax' means 'harvest.'"

"You don't think they're going to eat them, do you?" Ystremski asked.

Fortis's mouth was suddenly very dry. "I don't know," he said with a croak. "I hope not." He checked the time again. "Comms window with *Eclipse Wonder* is open. Let's see what Anders has to say about it."

Five minutes later, Fortis made contact with Anders.

"Sir, the Badaax loaded two blue bombers on one of the larger ships, and now it looks like they're loading Maltaani captives. Is the drone seeing that?"

"Sorry, Abner, we had a problem with the drone launch, and it was delayed for an hour. It's up now and will be on station in the next few minutes."

"Here's what we're seeing, sir." Fortis sent the video files and waited for Anders to review them.

"Hmm. I agree they're definitely loading the Maltaani onto that ship. The question is, why?"

"I was hoping you could answer that, sir."

"I can't say for certain, but we recently received information that indicates the Badaax might be forced to withdraw from this sector soon. Perhaps this is the beginning of that movement, and they're taking their captives with them. We'll have to wait and see."

"Okay, General. Any orders?"

"Not right now. Those videos show that your Marines are a lot closer than I expected for a surveillance mission."

"The company position is too far away for meaningful observation, and there isn't enough good cover between us and the space port to reposition all of us," Fortis said. "I sent small teams forward to check it out, and they found good cover."

"You're the commander on the ground, Abner. Just understand that there's not much I can do to support you if things go sideways."

"Roger that, sir."

Ystremski saw Fortis shake his head after he signed off with Anders.

"Good news?"

Fortis snorted. "There's not much I can do if things go sideways," he said in his best Anders voice.

"Fuck 'em. We don't need 'em anyhow."

"He did say the drone will be back up any minute if you want to notify the watch. He also said they have information that the Badaax might be in the process of withdrawing from the sector."

"Is it something we said?"

Fortis chuckled. "He didn't say." A wide yawn escaped his mouth.

"Tell you what, sir. I'll go check on the watch and see what the platoons are up to. You get comfy and do some more officer stuff," Ystremski said as he stood. "Just remember to stay under cover. I don't want the blue boogeyman to get you."

"Yes, Mom."

Two hours later, Ystremski shook Fortis awake.

"Hey, Captain. They finished loading the Maltaani onto that ship, and it looks like they're preparing to launch. Check your visor vid."

Fortis sat up and started the video. He watched the last of the Maltaani shamble up the ramp before it closed behind them. The video ended, and Fortis looked out over the fields toward the space port twelve klicks away.

"How are they going to launch?" Ystremski asked. "That thing is too big for the runway."

Before Fortis could answer, they heard a faint *whoomph* and saw a bright flash in the direction of the space port. The craft hurtled down the runway at an impossible speed, and a muffled *boom* reached their ears as it broke the sound barrier before it took flight. It climbed straight up into the Maltaani sky and disappeared in seconds.

* * * * *

Chapter Thirty

General Anders watched the feed from the Alpha Bird after it arrived back in high orbit over the space port. The tail end of the column of Maltaani and animals trudged up into the belly of the Badaax ship before the ramp closed. He saw a bright blue flash from the rear of the craft and watched in surprise as it accelerated down the runway and climbed out of view.

"That was fast," Major Rho commended from the console next to him.

"It's amazing how they generate enough thrust to move a craft that large so fast. I'd like to get my hands on the technology to see how they do it."

"I'd like to never see them again."

"Agreed, but in the interim, let's watch the Bravo feed to see that ship rendezvous with the rest in orbit."

"Excuse me, General. High priority message from General Boudreaux." The *Eclipse Wonder* crewmember gestured to his console. "It's available on your screen."

From: General Staff Director of Operations

To: Deputy Director for Operations and Intelligence

In accordance with the UNT Charter, in the absence of a duly elected President, the Grand Council has assumed operational control of Terran armed forces. All units on and around

278 | P.A. PIATT

Maltaan are ordered to disengage with the Badaax and stand down. Take no offensive action. Military force is authorized for self-defense only after all other measures fail.

Acknowledge receipt immediately.

"Bad news, sir?" Rho asked.

"No, not necessarily. In fact, it doesn't mean much since it looks like the Badaax are withdrawing."

"What about the drones?"

"I think we can maintain our posture without violating the spirit of the Grand Council's orders. When I acknowledge this message to General Boudreaux, I'll inform him we have to keep eyes on their fleet to avoid surprises. I'll order Captain Fortis to withdraw his FOPs and wait for exfil by shuttle."

They lapsed into silence as Bravo Bird transmitted images of the Badaax landing craft approach the orbiting fleet. Without anything to give them scale, it was difficult to remember that the lander was three hundred meters long and the mother ships were four times longer than that.

Massive doors opened on the belly of a mother ship, and the lander moved into position underneath. The smaller craft rose into the mother ship as if guided by invisible hands, and the doors swung shut. The entire evolution took less than ten minutes. Moments later, the mother ship pivoted and moved out of orbit. The rear of the craft glowed blue and it disappeared from camera view.

"Trajectory indicates it is headed for the gate coordinates passed to us by *Fortuna*," Rho said.

"Good. Notify her there is a ship headed their way." Anders checked the time. "The next comms window is coming up. I need to acknowledge this message from General Boudreaux and then talk to Fortis."

* * *

Fortis answered promptly when Anders called.

"General, the Badaax finished loading their first ship, and it took off."

"Roger that. We watched it on the drone feed," Anders said. *"It arrived in orbit with the rest of the Badaax fleet. A mother ship recovered it before it departed in the direction of the unmapped warp."*

"That's good news. It looks like they're really leaving. They moved another ship into position on the tarmac. I'm guessing they'll load another pair of blue bombers and more prisoners."

"Agreed. I've got an important update for you. The Grand Council has directed that all UNT forces disengage with the Badaax and stand down. That includes your FOPs. Only self-defense is authorized."

"Roger that, sir. Is it in our best interest to break surveillance on the space port before they're gone?"

"The directive doesn't leave any wiggle room. 'Disengage, stand down, and take no offensive action.' Pull them back."

"I'll have to wait until dark before I can get them out, General."

"Understood."

The pair agreed to talk during the next comms window and then signed off.

"That's it, then," Fortis said to Ystremski. "The general said they're leaving, and the Grand Council ordered all UNT forces to disengage and stand down. No offensive action. He ordered me to pull back the FOPs."

"Huh. Who will be watching the space port, the drone?"

"I didn't think to ask."

"You know, sir, I have a theory about the blue light," Ystremski said.

"I'm all ears."

"It's a mind control ray. Those Maltaani captives move like their brains have been scrambled. Even the elephants are sleepwalking, and they're as docile as babies. But it's more than that. It has a destruction mode, too. Red said he was shot down by a blue ray. Second Mech was melted into piles of slag."

"What about First Mech? A lot of their stuff was sitting on the road, like they parked it there."

"Maybe if you don't fight back, they don't melt you. From what CB and Will told us, the Badaax surprised them, and there wasn't much resistance. It's possible Second Mech knew an attack was coming and had a chance to prepare. They shot down one of the blue bombers, remember?"

Fortis nodded. "That's a fair theory. How do we use it?"

"I'm just the idea guy, sir. You officers can figure that out. Until you do, I'm going to hole up here in the woods."

"Figures." Fortis chuckled. "I'd like to get a look inside those domes and see how many prisoners they're holding."

The gunny gave him a look of disbelief. "Did you hit your head while I wasn't looking? We can't go down there for that."

"No. I said I'd like to; I didn't say we would. It would be suicide. Besides, by the time this is over, we'll know for sure because we will have watched them load all their prisoners."

"Command, this is Second Platoon. FOP Four reported the Badaax are positioning two more blue bombers for loading. Do you want the video?"

"Negative," Fortis replied. "Not unless there's something notable on it." He turned to Ystremski. "Anders said they watched a Badaax mother ship recover the first lander before it left orbit and headed back the way they came."

"Too bad we don't have Black Hole. We could blast the runway to stop them."

"And trap them down here with us? Now who's talking like he hit his head? Why would you want to do that?"

"There are a couple mechanized infantry battalions that need some payback," the gunny said in a grim tone.

Fortis felt his face redden. "Damn, I forgot all about them."

"That happens to a lot of Space Marines here on Maltaan, sir. They're forgotten, I mean."

The captain thought for a long moment before he nodded. "Maybe so, but we're no match for the blue bombers. The fleet has a better chance against them than we do. We'll have to wait and see what happens."

"DINLI."

"DINLI, indeed."

* * *

The Space Marines watched as the Badaax loaded a second ship with blue bombers and a stream of Maltaani and their animals. The engines fired, and the craft went supersonic before it shot straight into the sky. They lined up the third ship and repeated the process before it, too, blasted off. As night fell, activity at the space port ceased.

"Looks like they're done for the day," Fortis said to Ystremski.

"They don't seem to like working at night. Kind of like the Maltaani."

Fortis pulled off his helmet and rubbed his head. "That's okay with me. They'll be out of here first thing in the morning, and then maybe we can hitch a ride on the shuttle."

The gunny also removed his helmet. "I don't know, sir. I'm not big on omens and all that, but it doesn't feel like we're getting out of here any time soon."

"Oh, my God, don't say that." Fortis shook his head. "Have I told you how much I hate this fucking place?"

"Only every day, sir. How long do you want to wait before we bring the FOPs in?"

"I've been thinking about that, and I want to leave them out for the night. It looks like the Badaax will be gone in the morning, and the FOPs are well-concealed. It seems to me there's more risk in moving them back than leaving them there for a few more hours. What do you think?"

"It makes sense to me, but what are you going to tell the general?"

"If he doesn't ask, I won't tell him. If he does, I'll explain it exactly like I did to you."

"Fair enough, sir. If he gets mad, what's the worst that can happen? We get sent to Maltaan?"

* * * * *

Chapter Thirty-One

Ystremski leaned against the same tree Fortis had used to get some rest. The captain moved up and down their position to check on the men and talk with the platoon commanders. It was obvious to everyone the Badaax were withdrawing, and the mood was light as their thoughts turned to going home. Fortis tried to share their enthusiasm, but after Ystremski's remark, he wondered if they'd really be leaving soon.

I'd feel a lot better if Sixth Division were here to take over.

He found Red and CB with Doc Velez and Will. Red's legs were bruised a deep purple where the hovercopter console had folded down over his lap, but he was able to bend them and even stand for brief periods without assistance.

"No broken bones in my legs," the pilot told Fortis. "Sore as anything, but Doc says that will fade. The ankle's another story."

"That's good news, Red. Rest up, heal up, and you'll be back in the cockpit in no time." Fortis looked at CB and smiled. His face was still swollen, and he had dark circles around both eyes, like a Terran raccoon. "What's up, chicken butt?" he asked the private.

CB gave him a pained expression. "That's messed up, sir," he said as Red and Fortis laughed. "Using my line against me."

"How's your nose feeling?" Fortis asked. "It doesn't look as bad as it did."

283

"The swelling is down. It's still tender, but it's okay. Thanks for asking, sir."

Fortis pointed to Will, who was unconscious on a litter next to Red. "How's she doing, Doc?"

"No change, sir," Velez said. "It's like she's asleep, but I can't wake her up. I've been able to keep fluids in her, but I don't have any vitamin IV packs."

"If this last Badaax ship takes off in the morning, maybe we can get her out of here tomorrow," Fortis said.

Fortis completed his tour of India Company's position and returned to the command element. The rest of the night passed without incident, punctuated by quiet radio checks with the FOPs.

An hour before daylight, Ystremski joined Fortis in the command post.

"Did I miss anything, sir?"

"No movement reported," Fortis said.

"They don't seem to be in a hurry, but it seems so. Here's hoping, anyway."

"It looks like they're going to enjoy one last meal on the hoof before they go. Pull up Lenoir's helmet video. You can just see them on the edge of the screen." Fortis switched views and shuddered as he rewatched the Badaax slaughtering an elephant and biting into still-quivering chunks of the beast with gusto. "Eating one of those filthy bastards is bad enough, but raw?" He watched the video feed for several seconds. "I count thirteen of them left."

Ystremski nodded. "That was my count, too. There might be a couple on the ship, but there aren't many left. They only loaded one blue bomber on the third ship, so there's two of them left. If it weren't for them, we could probably take 'em."

As if on cue, a blue bomber flew over the space port, circled, and touched down. The craft taxied to a position behind the fourth craft, stopped, and a pair of Badaax emerged.

"Fifteen," Fortis said absentmindedly.

"And only one blue bomber."

"Maybe they lost another one we don't know about?"

The Badaax pushed the blue bomber to the ramp, and it slowly disappeared inside the lander.

"Hey, Captain, what's this about leaving today? All the men are talking about it. Did you tell them that, sir?"

"No, I—ah shit. I told Doc Velez we might get Will out of here today. It was just a random remark."

An alarmed voice came over the company circuit. *"Command, this is Doc Velez. Corporal Will is missing."*

"What do you mean, missing?" Ystremski asked.

"She was asleep on her litter next to Warrant Brumley when I checked on them a couple hours ago. I went back just now, and she's gone."

"She's probably taking a leak," the gunny said.

"I don't think so, Gunny. Me and Doc Brumley searched the latrines and all around, and she's not here."

Fortis and Ystremski traded looks. "A snake?" Fortis mouthed, and Ystremski shrugged in response.

"I'm on my way." The gunny stood. "I'll get this sorted out—"

"Command, Second Platoon. We found Will," LT Young said. *"She's down by FOP Four."*

"What? What's she doing down there?" Fortis asked.

"I don't know, sir. The FOP reported some movement, and when they got a good visual, it was Will. She's walking toward the space port. They tried calling

286 | P.A. PIATT

out to her, but she's not responding. Do you want them to break cover and stop her?"

Ystremski shook his head emphatically.

"Negative," Fortis said.

"Too late, sir."

* * *

Corporals Aiyuk and Lenoir of Second Platoon had established FOP Four close to the south end of the space port, where they had a clear view of the end of the runway and the domes. Lenoir had put his helmet up in the branches of a tree so the camera could capture images of activity around the domes, and then the pair had settled back into their hole. FOP duty sucked, and the pair was happy the Badaax looked like they were withdrawing from Maltaan.

"Hey, Lenny, I've got movement in the field behind us," Aiyuk whispered.

Lenoir strained his eyes, but it was too dark.

"I can't see. What is it? It's not a dog, is it?"

"I don't think so. Too tall."

"Elephant?"

"Shit! It's a human. Hang on, let me call this in."

Lenoir rose to his knees. "I see her now. It's that driver from First Mech." As the sky lightened, he could make out Will stumbling across the field with her head down as though she were sleepwalking. "What's she doing?"

"I don't know. Stand by; Penny is talking to Command," Aiyuk said.

"We gotta get her."

"Lenny, wait!"

Lenoir moved at a low crouch to intercept Will. He grabbed her arm, but she pulled free and continued to trudge toward the spaceport. He tackled her and tried to drag her toward their hiding spot, but Will curled into the fetal position and began to scream.

* * *

"What the fuck's going on?" Fortis demanded, but he got no response. "Penny!"

"Lenoir broke cover to get her, and they're wrestling," Penny said.

"Get him back under cover!"

"This is FOP Three. Badaax headed for FOP Four!"

Ystremski tapped Fortis on the shoulder. "It's too late, sir. Look at the video."

Fortis pulled up the FOP Four video from Lenoir's helmet and saw two Badaax walking toward the border of the space port. It was obvious they had detected Will and Lenoir. It didn't take long for them to clear the buildings and move out of the field of view.

"Switch to Aiyuk's video," Penny said.

Fortis changed his display and saw the backs of the two Badaax as they crouched over the Space Marines. The first alien wielded a tall staff with an orb at the top that bathed the scene in blue light. Lenoir and Will got to their feet and stood with their shoulders hunched and their heads hanging down. Suddenly, the camera view jostled as Aiyuk stood and opened up with his pulse rifle.

"Oh shit!" Ystremski exclaimed.

Plasma bolts stitched up the back of one of the Badaax, and it dropped to its knees. The other Badaax turned and focused the blue rays from its staff on Aiyuk, but he kept firing. Meanwhile, the first Badaax had climbed back to its feet, and it lashed out with a whip. Aiyuk's video jerked skyward and then tumbled into the grass before it went black.

"What the fuck happened?"

Fortis switched back to Lenoir's helmet video. When he did, he could see the two Badaax returning to the space port. Will and Lenoir trudged behind them, bathed in blue light, dragging Aiyuk's body between them. At the space port, the other Badaax had finished their meal and dispersed toward the domes. They didn't seem concerned with the capture of three more humans.

"What do we do, Command?" LT Penny asked.

"Stand by," Fortis ordered. He looked at Ystremski. "What do you think, Gunny?"

"They're loading the ship," Penny reported. *"This time, they've got humans."*

The Space Marines stared in horror as a long column of humans emerged from the domes, escorted by Badaax carrying blue light staffs. The front of the column was all civilians, but they were followed by Space Marines clad in the familiar coveralls and battle armor of mech drivers and infantry.

"We can't just let the Badaax have them," Ystremski said. "Not without trying to stop them."

Fortis swore under his breath. "All right, gimme a minute and let me tell Anders what we're gonna do." He switched to the company circuit. "All stations, this is Command. I'm calling the general to tell him what's going on down here, and then I'll tell you what we're going to do. Stand by."

Fortis dialed up the circuit to *Eclipse Wonder.*

"Ah, Abner, good. I was just about to call you," Anders said when he came on. *"I've got news about the fleet. Three of the four ships that were in orbit have departed, and it looks like the fourth is waiting for the last of them down there. The Badaax are definitely withdrawing."*

"Sorry, General, but that doesn't matter right now. We have more immediate issues down here," Fortis said. "The Badaax discovered one of our FOPs. They killed a Space Marine and captured two more."

"You were supposed to pull the FOPs back last night. What hap—"

The captain cut him off. "They're loading the last ship, sir." Fortis felt his face flush as his temper rose, and he was almost shouting. "They're loading *humans* aboard the last ship. There must be two thousand people, including several hundred Space Marines, marching up the ramp. We can't let them launch, sir."

"I'll notify Baron de Macau. Maybe they can catch them in orbit."

"Negative, sir. What the fuck are they going to do, attack the ship? They'll kill the prisoners if they do. We have stop the Badaax from down here. Now. Fortis, out."

He switched off the satellite circuit before Anders could reply and yanked off his helmet. He scowled and shook his head.

"He doesn't get it," Fortis said to Ystremski. "It's like he thinks that because the Badaax are leaving, we've won."

"What are we going to do, sir?"

"We're going to get our people back."

After a moment to assess the situation, Fortis got on the company circuit.

"This is Captain Fortis. It looks like the Badaax are withdrawing. I just got news that the rest of their fleet has retreated back to where they came from. As you all know, they're loading their last ship and taking a bunch of human prisoners with them, including several hundred Space Marines. I'm not going to let that happen without a fight."

Fortis paused for a moment and looked at Lenoir's video feed. The column had almost reached the tarmac. He took a deep breath.

"We're going to cross the fields at a double time and hit the Badaax before they finish loading. It's about twelve klicks, and you're all fully speed enhanced, so I figure we can get over there in ten minutes. They're big bastards, but there's only fifteen of them. I like our odds.

"We will advance in a single wave, with First Platoon on the left and Second Platoon on the right. Maintain your alignment on the command element. When we engage them, keep your visors down and kill everything that's blue. Watch out for the prisoners."

Fortis looked at Ystremski, who gave him a thumbs up.

"You have one minute to get ready. Let's do the deed, lads."

Fortis turned and saw CB Brumley standing behind him, holding his pulse rifle.

"Where do you think you're going?" Ystremski asked.

"To the space port," Brumley replied. "I'm not fully speed enhanced, but I'll keep up."

Fortis shook his head. "Not this time. I appreciate your spirit, CB, but I need you to stay here and look after Red. Doc Velez is coming with us."

CB's face fell, and Fortis felt a twinge of guilt for dashing his hope for battle glory.

"Here." He reached inside the neck of his battle armor and pulled his Maltaani dog tooth necklace up over his head. CB's hand trembled as Fortis gave it to him. "Hold on to this until we get back. I don't want to lose it."

The young corpsman's face broke into a wide grin, and he saluted. "Yes sir. I'll guard it with my life."

"Carry on," Fortis said as he returned the salute. He turned back to Ystremski. "You ready?"

"Born ready, sir."

* * *

"Fortis! Captain Fortis!" Anders shouted into his microphone. When there was no response, he tore off his headset and threw it down in disgust. "Fuck!"

Rho's eyes widened with surprise at the general's uncharacteristic outburst.

"What happened, sir?"

"The Badaax attacked one of his FOPS, and now they're loading humans onto the last ship."

"Humans?"

"The last column is civilians and Space Marines."

"What is Fortis going to do?"

"He's going to do something stupid," Anders said. "He disregarded my order to pull back the FOPs, and now, it sounds like he's going to attack the space port with a company of Space Marines."

"What are you going to do, General?"

Anders gestured at the drone displays. "Watch. And pray."

* * *

India Company stepped out from the tree line into the bright Maltaan daylight and formed a line abreast. Fortis checked the alignment before he nodded to Ystremski.

"Gunny, sound the charge."

"India Company, forward at a double time, charge!"

The Space Marines surged forward and broke into a run. Several of them whooped as they raced across the open fields toward the space port. Fortis felt naked after so many hours concealed in the forest, and his combat instincts screamed at him to take cover.

The entire scene had a surreal feeling to it. The Space Marines barely broke stride to hurdle low bushes and irrigation ditches, and Fortis couldn't believe the Badaax hadn't seen them as every step brought them closer to the far edge of the fields. The Space Marines in the FOPs jumped up and joined the charge as the wave passed them by.

It seemed improbable to Fortis they would make it all the way without detection, but they almost did. When they were fifty meters from the cluster of buildings and domes at the edge of the space port, the Badaax reacted.

"Here they come!" a Space Marine warned.

Several Badaax emerged from among the buildings in front of Second Platoon. The Space Marines opened fire with pulse rifles and grenades, and the ground around the aliens exploded in dirt and bursts of energy bolts. The Badaax responded with blue rays from their staffs, and several Space Marines went down. One of the aliens wailed in agony when a frag went off next to its head, and it dropped to the ground. First Platoon began to veer to the right as they edged forward to get into the fight in support of Second.

"First Platoon, maintain your alignment," Ystremski ordered with a growl. "You'll get your chance."

As if on cue, four Badaax appeared in front of First Platoon on the left, and the Space Marines delivered a devastating barrage of pulse rifle fire and grenades.

Fortis noted the Badaax seemed almost impervious to the pulse rifle fire from the Space Marines. Many of the plasma bolts hit the blue light rays and veered off as if the light created a shield or force field. The bolts that got through didn't seem to do much visible damage.

On the right, Second Platoon halted and took up positions along the edge of the field. Several Space Marines were down, and the rest poured fire on the remaining Badaax. The Badaax advanced to within a few meters, and Fortis watched one of them lash out with a whip. It tangled around a Marine's IEBS and jerked him off his feet, and the Badaax stomped him before another blasted the fallen Marine with rays from its staff. The rest of the platoon responded with a barrage of pulse rifle fire which drove the Badaax backward, but they didn't go down. Another Space Marine stepped up to defend his comrade, and flames *whooshed* from his FGU and engulfed the Badaax. The Badaax let out an ear-piercing shriek as it twisted and turned in a macabre dance to escape the flames. The second Badaax focused its blue rays on the fire-wielding Space Marine, and he dropped in a smoking mass of flesh, metal, and dancing blue flames.

First Platoon was having less success against the aliens. Both attackers and defenders seemed to realize they had to focus their attacks on a single enemy at a time, but the Badaax appeared almost invulnerable as they stacked up and combined their blue light shields to close in. Fortis saw two Badaax go down, but the remaining two had killed or wounded almost half of First Platoon. A volley of smoke grenades engulfed the Badaax in choking smoke and gave the Space Marines a chance to regroup and resume their attack. Tongues of fire lapped at another Badaax through the smoke, and the Space Marines claimed another enemy dead.

Suddenly, the remaining Badaax on both flanks turned and loped back toward the space port. The surviving Space Marines let out a ragged cheer at tthe retreat.

"This isn't over by a long shot!" Fortis jumped to his feet. "They're headed for their ship. We can't let them get there. Follow me!"

* * * * *

Chapter Thirty-Two

Anders and Rho watched the Space Marines charge across the field in stunned silence. Just when it looked like they would reach the space port undetected, several Badaax turned away from loading their captives and headed for the Space Marines.

A confused melee ensued on the edge of the fields. Blue rays and pulse rifle bolts flew in all directions, and puffs of smoke revealed the explosions of grenades. The Space Marines were no match for the Badaax one on one, but their FGUs evened the odds.

While the battle raged, the unengaged Badaax continued to shepherd their captives aboard the ship. Then the Badaax fighting the Space Marines disengaged and headed for the lander.

"That's got to be it," Rho said.

She no sooner got the words out of her mouth before the Space Marines jumped up in pursuit of the fleeing Badaax.

The blue rays over the line of captives winked out, and the entire column collapsed. The Badaax retreated up the ramp and into their ship, with the Space Marines hard on their heels.

* * *

The surviving Space Marines of India Company followed Fortis as he weaved through the buildings and onto the tarmac. He saw the Badaax shepherding their captives up the ramp into the ship, and that's when Fortis got a real sense of the enormity of the craft.

The Badaax turned at their approach and then the blue light rays that bathed the prisoners went out. The entire line collapsed in a long row of bodies as the aliens made for their craft.

"Come on!" Fortis shouted. "We can't let them escape!"

The Space Marines sprinted for the Badaax craft as Badaax kicked dead humans off the ramp to close it. The grenadiers fired salvos of grenades that exploded all around the ramp, and the Badaax retreated inside. A blizzard of pulse rifle bolts followed them into the dark interior.

The ponderous craft had begun to turn to line up with the runway when the Space Marines arrived.

"Blow that ramp! We've got to stop it!"

The Space Marines scrambled to follow Fortis's orders. Sappers ducked underneath the lander and slapped breaching charges onto the body. Dozens of grenades exploded inside as grenadiers fired a salvo into the still-open ramp, and the left side of the ramp collapsed and began to drag on the ground. Blue rays flashed from inside, and two Space Marines went down without a sound.

Heedless of the human captives inside the lander, one of the sappers stuck the nozzle of his FGU into the damaged ramp and unleashed his entire load of fuel inside the craft. Fortis heard familiar screams of Badaax agony, and one tumbled onto the tarmac and landed in a writhing heap of thick, oily smoke and orange flames.

The left side of the ramp hung askew as the Badaax ship lined up for takeoff. There was a loud grinding noise and the shriek of metal tearing as the Badaax tried to raise it, but it wouldn't shut. Fortis stared as the lander lined up on the runway, seemingly intending to launch.

Gunny Ystremski grabbed Fortis by the shoulder and dragged him sideways. "We gotta get the fuck out of here before that thing hits the boosters."

The Space Marines clambered clear of the blast from the alien engines just in time. The *whoomph* of the engines was deafening at close range, and they threw themselves down on the tarmac. The craft hurtled down the runway just as the first of the breaching charges detonated on the hull, followed by a string of explosions down the side. The charges weren't large, but their combined effect was enough to tear a hole in the skin of the spacecraft. Instead of a sonic boom, Fortis heard the screech of metal on pavement as the craft slewed wildly before violently tumbling. Chunks of fuselage flew in all directions as the ship disintegrated.

A massive blue light flashed a millisecond before a thunderous boom reached his ears, and the ground trembled. A pinnacle of bluish-white fire raced skyward and exploded into a shower of blue and white sparks that glittered and glinted as they fell.

Around the tarmac, Space Marines struggled to their feet and moved to attend to their wounded comrades.

"Look!"

High above them, a drone pinwheeled downward, trailing smoke from the fuselage where its left wing used to be. It took half a minute for it to fall from altitude before it crashed on the tarmac two hundred meters away in a brilliant orange fireball.

After the shock of all he had witnessed wore off, Fortis looked around to take stock of their situation.

"Platoon commanders, report."

298 | P.A. PIATT

A minute later, LT Young called. *"This is Second Platoon. I've got twenty-seven effectives present on the tarmac, with no KIA/WIA. I sent my platoon sergeant to check on casualties back in the field."*

"This is Command, roger. First Platoon, report." Silence greeted his order. "LT Penny, report."

"Sir, uh, this is Sergeant Udoh. LT Penny went down in the field. He's still back there, as far as I know."

Before Fortis could respond, Ystremski tapped Fortis on the shoulder and cut in. *"You're the senior man, Sergeant. Get your Space Marines together and make a report."* He looked at Fortis. "Command element is all secure. I'll get First Platoon sorted out," he said before he trotted away.

Fortis went over to the grotesque mass of bodies at the end of the runway. Space Marines, civilians, and even a few Maltaani were heaped in a jumbled line that stretched back toward the domes where they'd been held captive.

"How many do you think there are, sir?" Sergeant Connolly had approached unnoticed and stood next to Fortis.

Fortis shook his head. "I don't know. A thousand. Maybe more."

"Sir, First Platoon has thirty-three effectives," Ystremski reported. *"Sergeant Udoh is the acting platoon commander."*

"Roger that. Muster the company at the space port; I'm going to report to General Anders."

When Fortis dialed up the circuit to *Eclipse Wonder,* Anders answered immediately.

"General, we've driven the Badaax from the space port and destroyed their last landing ship."

"I watched your charge, Captain. That was foolhardy, not to mention in direct violation of my orders. They were leaving."

"Leaving with human captives, sir."

"I saw it. I was watching on the drone until you shot it down," Anders said.

"Collateral damage, sir. Couldn't be helped."

"What's your status?"

"Sixty effectives, unknown number of WIA. The company is mustering now."

"Any civilian casualties?"

Fortis glanced at the line of bodies. "They're all dead, sir. Everyone the Badaax captured is dead. They were lined up to board that ship when we attacked, and when they turned the blue light off, all the prisoners fell. It's a fucking mess."

There was a long moment of silence before Anders spoke.

"It was a tough call, Abner."

"We couldn't just let them be taken."

"The remaining alien ships have fled toward the warp they came through. The last ship in orbit departed just now."

"That's good news. What are your orders for us?"

"Secure the space port and stand by for reinforcements and follow-on orders. Unless there's a more senior officer down there, you're now acting MAC-M."

* * *

Fortis, Ystremski, and the platoon commanders set about organizing India Company to secure the space port. They established sentry posts, guard duty bills, fighting positions, and a command post.

When that was all completed, the Space Marines broke for a long overdue meal of pig squares and hydration packs. Ystremski nodded and led Fortis out of earshot of the men.

"Next task is to deal with the casualties," the gunny said as he munched on a bite of dehydrated pork steak. "Some of them were in bad shape before, and it's not going to get better with age."

As if to punctuate his point, a slight breeze carried the odor of decomposition to Fortis's nose, and he got a thick feeling in his throat.

"We have to bury them," Fortis said. "Bury them and mark them for Graves Registration."

Ystremski nodded. "As soon as the lads finish eating, I'll get them organized. It's gonna take a mighty big hole."

"No choice. DINLI."

"DINLI."

The Space Marines discovered earthmoving equipment in one of the domes, which greatly sped up the grim task of burying the dead. Each dead Space Marine got his own grave, and Fortis carefully recorded the information on their identity tags to forward up the chain of command. None of the civilians carried identification, so the Space Marines took pictures of each one as they laid them side by side in a long common grave.

They counted nine hundred and sixty-two bodies, including four hundred and twelve Space Marines from MAC-M, First and Second Mech, and India Company. Fortis and Ystremski acknowledged there was no practical way to recognize each individual Space Marine as they were buried, so the gunny ordered a corporal from the command element to bang two pipes together in place of a bell as the dirt was pushed over their bodies.

Red Brumley insisted on attending the interment, and he leaned on a crutch and hugged CB as his brother wept while the casualties from First Mech were buried. Fortis struggled to control his emotions at the poignant scene, and he had to clear his throat more than once to choke down a sob.

When they completed their grisly duty, morale among the Space Marines was as low as Fortis had ever seen during his ISMC career. Ystremski tapped him on the arm and motioned for him to follow.

"I have something to show you that might cheer you up."

The gunny led Fortis to one of the space port hangers and slid open the door. It was empty except for a thick pole approximately eight meters long, with a bright blue stone at one end.

"Is that what I think it is?" Fortis asked as he approached the object.

"Yes sir, it is. We found it in the field next to one of those dead fuckers. There are two whips with it, too."

Fortis stopped five meters from the staff. "Is it on?"

"No idea, sir. I had them stash it in here before one of these monkeys started fucking with it and fried all our brains."

"Let's get out of here."

"I'm going to post a sentry here," Ystremski said.

"Thanks, Gunny. That's a good find."

"Not so fast, sir. I have one more thing for you."

They walked over to the mess tent, which was half-collapsed. Ystremski picked his way through the rubble until they arrived at a rear storage room. He patted three barrels and gave Fortis an expectant smile.

"DINLI?" Fortis asked.

"Six hundred liters. The Space Marines posted here at the space port must have been brewing night and day."

"Is it any good?"

Ystremski winked. "I might have sampled a bit, just to be sure." He handed Fortis a mug that had been stashed behind the barrels. "Give it a taste."

Fortis took a sip. The hootch went down smooth, and the sweetness masked the raw alcohol burn, but it still made him gasp.

"Damn, that is good," Fortis said as he passed the mug back to Ystremski.

"Best part of being on this fucking planet is the fruit. It makes the best DINLI I've ever had," Ystremski said. "With your permission, I'd like to issue one of these barrels to the troops tonight so they can let off a little steam. They're feeling pretty low right now, and the nightmare of burying those bodies can't be the last thing on their minds when they go to sleep tonight. This stuff will make sure it isn't."

"Permission granted. Just make sure the guard roster is set."

* * *

General Anders read the message from General Boudreaux twice to let the words sink in.

From: General Staff Director of Operations

To: General Nils Anders

EYES ONLY

Nils, the Grand Council invoked Article Forty-Seven of the UNT Charter when the President resigned, and they appointed Councilor Brooks-Green as the new Minister of Defense. You might remember her as the former ambassador to Maltaan?

MoD has empaneled a committee to conduct a full investigation of "the most recent Maltaani debacle," as she refers to the situation there. You are hereby ordered to remain on station,

preserve all records, and cooperate with the investigation until you're released. This order extends to all Fleet personnel and Space Marines on/around Maltaan.

I'll send official orders via separate correspondence.—Ellis

"Is everything okay, General?" Major Rho, seated next to Anders, must have sensed his unease.

He motioned to the screen. "Have a look."

Rho let out a low whistle after she read Boudreaux's message. "I guess we're going to be here for a while."

"Bet on it."

"Do you want me to forward it to Captain Fortis?"

"No. I need to give him this news in person. Schedule a shuttle run to the surface tomorrow morning."

* * *

Fortis and Ystremski waited on the tarmac as *Eclipse Wonder's* shuttle taxied to a stop near the hangars. When the ramp dropped, Major Rho stepped down and waved them over.

"The general is waiting for you in the passenger compartment." She lowered her voice. "You're being recorded."

The pair exchanged mystified looks as they followed the major aboard the shuttle and met the general in the passenger compartment. Anders returned their salutes but didn't shake their hands.

"Captain Fortis, the Minister of Defense has ordered a complete investigation into the recent events on the surface and in the space surrounding Maltaan. General Boudreaux has directed India Company to remain in place until the investigation is complete."

"Stay here?" Ystremski blurted.

The general nodded. "Affirmative. You will prepare a detailed report of your actions, and you are to protect all evidence including logs, records, and recordings. Do you understand your orders?"

"Yes sir, I understand."

"Good." Anders stood and motioned for Fortis and Ystremski to follow him. He walked down the ramp and stopped on the tarmac along with Major Rho.

"Sorry about that, gents, but it's necessary for your protection, and mine."

"What's going on, General?"

"After the president resigned, the Grand Council invoked Article Forty-Seven of the UNT Charter. They appointed Councilor Melawi Brooks-Green as the new Minister of Defense. Do you remember her?"

"Yes sir." Fortis turned to Ystremski. "She was the ambassador here, before we evacuated."

"Exactly. After the evacuation, there were some who tried to lay the blame for the evacuation at her feet. We invaded and won easily, and everything that happened before was forgotten. Now, her party appointed her MoD, and I believe she's anxious to ensure the blame for our losses lands anywhere but on her. Hence the investigation."

"What about MAC-M? They're sending more troops and someone to take over, aren't they?" Fortis asked.

"No decision has been made at this point, so you're it."

"What do we do if the Badaax return?"

"Good question. I recently read an unofficial analysis of the warp they came through. It's positioned next to an asteroid belt, and apparently, the asteroid rotation fouls it except for a brief window approximately every eighty years."

"So, we didn't chase the Badaax off, they left on their own?"

"That's what it looks like, yes. This is all unofficial, you understand. We'll know more after the Ministry of Science has a chance to study the asteroid belt."

"General, I'm sorry to interrupt, but we have six Space Marines who require more medical care than we can give them here," the gunny said. "Any chance of a medevac?"

Anders nodded. "Affirmative. *Compassionate* is in orbit, along with the remainder of Fourth Fleet. Load them on the shuttle, and we'll take them up with us."

"I'll make it happen, Captain," Ystremski said and then strode toward the medical tent.

"On a positive note, General Boudreaux was able to get an Alien Material Exploitation Team included in the investigation team, so between the wreckage and the bodies you recovered, we might be able to glean some insights into the Badaax."

"We burned the Badaax bodies, sir. They smelled so bad, some of the men got sick, and I didn't want to risk exposing them to an unidentified biohazard."

"Pity," Rho said.

"Ma'am, if you're interested, we found the wreck of a blue bomber with a body in it just beyond the eastern border of the space port. I can also give you coordinates for another blue bomber that Second Mech shot down. We left the body there, too."

"I'll make sure to pass them on to the AMET," Rho said.

"Major, would you go see if Gunny Ystremski needs any help?"

"But sir, I think—"

306 | P.A. PIATT

"Major, just go. I want to speak to Captain Fortis in private."

A disappointed look crossed Rho's face, but she did as Anders ordered.

"Abner, I want you to know the responsibility for what happened here is on me, not you. I'm the one that authorized your drop."

"Sir, I practically demanded the drop, and I'm the one that continued our mission even after we knew Sixth Division wasn't coming. If I remember correctly, you wanted us to hide until the Badaax left."

"That's all for the investigation to sort out. There's no denying you disobeyed my orders and the orders of the Grand Council, but you were the commander on the ground. Just be forthright with the investigators and let the chips fall where they may." He clapped Fortis on the shoulder. "My guess is the ultimate responsibility will land on Colonel Wisniewski, Commodore Allard, and Admiral McTigue."

"Blame the dead guys," Fortis said with deep bitterness.

"It's how the game is played, Captain." They stopped and looked at the remains of the space port. "There's something else I want to talk to you about. Big changes are coming to the government and the ISMC. The great Maltaani experiment has become symbolic of the failure of the former president and his party. We're obligated by regulations to remain apolitical, but that doesn't mean Minister Brooks-Green and the Peace Party are our friends."

Fortis nodded. "I think I understand, sir. Thank you."

Major Rho and Gunny Ystremski returned with a group of Space Marines carrying wounded comrades toward the shuttle.

"There's only five, Gunny," Fortis said. "I thought you said six."

"Warrant Brumley refuses to leave," Ystremski replied. "He won't leave his brother behind, and we can't let CB go. We need every swinging dick—er, excuse me ma'am—every able-bodied Space Marine we can get."

"Doc thinks his ankle is broken," Fortis told Anders. "The scanner here was damaged in the fighting, so we don't know for sure."

"Is his health in danger, or does his presence affect your readiness?"

"No sir. In fact, there are two hovercopters in the hangars that are undamaged, and he thinks he can get them back in the air."

"Then he stays. Load up the rest, and we'll get out of your hair, Captain."

They traded salutes, then Anders and Rho followed the injured Space Marines into the shuttle. The craft raced down the runway and straight into the sky.

"Muster the company and let's give them the bad news, Gunny." Fortis sighed. "Have I told you how much I hate this fucking place?"

Ystremski scoffed. "Only every day, dickhead. DINLI."

"DINLI, indeed."

* * * * *

Epilogue

Ogre met DeeDee and his drilling crew in *Fortuna's* cavernous hangar after the drilling rig was secured and the hangar was repressurized.

"How did it go?" the master asked.

"You guys get cleaned up and have some chow," DeeDee told his crew. "We've got plenty of time to get the rig squared away before we get home." He turned to Ogre. His eyes glowed with excitement. "Can we talk in private?"

Ogre was intrigued by his tone, so she nodded and led the foreman to her stateroom that doubled as her office. She closed the door behind them.

"What's up?"

DeeDee dug into a satchel he had slung over his shoulder and pulled out a chunk of grey metal bigger than both his fists put together. "You know what this is?"

Ogre turned it over in her hands. "I dunno. A rock?"

He gave her a triumphant smile. "Helenium ore."

"Really? Wow." She hefted the ore. She guessed the weight to be about two kilos. "Heavy."

"That's because it's ninety-four percent pure."

Ogre tried to do some quick math in her head, but she didn't know the market price for helenium.

DeeDee chuckled. "Fifty-five thousand credits per kilo of pure helenium. That sample weighs two point four kilos. At ninety-four percent pure, that's about one hundred and twenty-four thousand credits worth of helenium."

Ogre handed the sample back to DeeDee, and he put it back in his satchel.

"Please tell me there's more," she said.

"What if I told you we found an entire asteroid of the stuff? Ten million metric tons, at least."

Ogre's knees grew weak and she steadied herself with a hand on her desk before she sank into her chair. "Ten million? Are you sure?"

"Give or take. I only got some rough measurements, but it worked out to about ten million, yeah."

The GRC paid a wildcat drilling crew ten percent of the current market price for their discoveries and ten percent went to the support ship. Ogre's heart raced and her head swam. She fumbled at her keyboard to do the math, but DeeDee stopped her.

"Five hundred and seventeen trillion credits worth of helenium. Ten percent of that is—"

"Fifty-one trillion, seven hundred million credits," Ogre said breathlessly. Her face broke into a smile so wide it hurt, and tears of joy spilled down her cheeks. "Fifty-one trillion, seven hundred million."

"Yeah, and that's not the best part. We drilled four boreholes in the first asteroid and then jumped to the next one, where we found the exact same thing. Solid helenium."

Ogre could only stare. *Another helenium asteroid?*

"After I saw the second set of samples, I did spectrographic surveys on smaller asteroids nearby. All helenium. The whole fucking belt."

Ogre's body went numb. Processing a fifty-one trillion credit payday had been hard enough, but ten percent of an entire asteroid belt of helenium? It was beyond comprehension.

Ogre pointed to the satchel. "Who knows about this?"

DeeDee shrugged. "Officially, just me and the assistant rig foreman. I told her not to say anything, but you know how that goes."

Ogre punched a button on her desktop communicator. "Elvis, shut down all outgoing communications, especially the P2P."

"Yes, ma'am."

P2P, or point-to-point terminals, were circuits installed on many space-going craft that permitted crewmembers to send and receive text, voice, and video messages from other terminals in space or back home on Terra Earth.

"Why did you do that?" DeeDee asked.

"We don't want word of this to get off the ship," Ogre said. "Not before the GRC can get here to defend their claim. Every wildcat crew in the galaxy will be headed this way."

"How soon can you get us home?"

"Home? You want to go all the way to Terra Earth? Why not meet the core runner at the gate?"

The GRC sent a ship from jump gate to jump gate on a regular basis to collect ore samples from deep-space wildcat ships so they could stay out longer.

"Not a chance. I'm personally going to deliver this bag and the rest of our samples to the chief assayer, and I'm not giving them the coordinates until he finishes testing. They're not screwing me this time."

"Us."

"Yeah, us." DeeDee walked to the door, and Ogre followed him. He turned, and she was a half-meter away. "Speaking of us, how about after I drop off the samples, we fly this thing to Eros-28, drop off the rig for overhaul, and head on over the Eros-69 for a few days of fun? Just us."

"Gee, DeeDee, that sounds tempting."

He brushed away a lock of her hair that had escaped her ponytail and gave her a leer. "I'm a pretty wealthy guy now, you know."

Ogre pushed his hand away. "Don't be a pig. I wouldn't go to Eros-69 with you if I was flat broke."

A look of amused disappointment crossed his face. "Your loss," he said as he led the way out of her stateroom.

"I've got fifty-one trillion reasons to get over it."

# # # # #

About the Author

Paul A. Piatt was born and raised in western Pennsylvania. After his first attempt at college, he joined the Navy to see the world. He started writing as a hobby when he retired in 2005 and published his first novel in 2018. His published works include the Abner Fortis, International Space Marine mil-sf series, the Walter Bailey Misadventures urban fantasy trilogy, and other full-length thrillers in both science fiction and horror. All of his novels and published short stories can be found on Amazon. You can find him on Facebook, MeWe, and on the internet at www(dot)papiattauthor(dot)com, or you can contact him directly at paulpiattauthor(at)gmail(dot)com.

* * * * *

Get the **free** Four Horsemen prelude story **"Shattered Crucible"**

and discover other titles by Theogony Books at:

http://chriskennedypublishing.com/

* * * * *

Meet the author and other CKP authors on the Factory Floor:

https://www.facebook.com/groups/461794864654198

* * * * *

Did you like this book?
Please write a review!

* * * * *

The following is an

Excerpt from Book One of The Prince of Britannia Saga:

The Prince Awakens

Fred Hughes

Available from Theogony Books

eBook, Paperback, and (soon) Audio

.

Excerpt from "The Prince Awakens:"

Sixth Fleet was in chaos. Fortunately, all the heavy units were deployed forward toward the attacking fleet and were directing all the defensive fire they had downrange at the enemy. More than thirteen thousand Swarm attack ships were bearing down on a fleet of twenty-six heavy escorts and the single monitor. The monitor crew had faith in their shields and guns, but could they survive against this many? They would soon find out.

Luckily, they didn't have to face all the Swarm ships. Historically, Swarm forces engaged major threats first, then went after the escorts. Which was why the monitor had to be considered the biggest threat in the battle.

Then the Swarm forces deviated from their usual pattern. The Imperial plan was suddenly irrelevant as the Swarm attack ships divided into fifteen groups and attacked the escorts, which didn't last long. When the last dreadnought died in a nuclear fireball, the Swarm attack ships turned and moved toward the next fleet in the column, Fourth Fleet, leaving the monitor behind.

The entire plan was in shambles. But, more importantly, the whole fleet was at risk of being defeated. The admiral's only option now was to save as many as he could.

"Signal to the Third, Fifth, and Seventh Fleets. The monitors are to execute Withdrawal Plan Beta."

The huge monitors had eight fleet tugs that were magnetically attached to the hull when not in use. Together, the eight tugs could get the monitors into hyperspace. However, this process took time, due to the time it took for the eight tugs to generate a warp field large enough to encompass the enormous ship. It could take up to an hour to accomplish, and they didn't have an hour.

Plan Bravo would use six heavy cruisers to accomplish the same thing. The cruisers' larger fusion engines meant the field could be generated within ten minutes, assuming no one was shooting at them. "The remaining fleet units will move to join First Fleet. Admiral

Mason in First Fleet will take command of the combined force and deploy it for combat."

The fleet admiral continued giving orders.

"I want Second Fleet to do the same, but I want heavy cruiser Squadron Twenty-Three to merge with First Fleet. Admiral Conyers, I want you to coordinate with the Eighth, Ninth, and Tenth Fleets. I want their monitors to perform a normal Alpha Withdrawal. As they're preparing to do that, have their escorts combine into a single fleet. Figure out which admiral is senior and assign him local command to organize them." He pointed at the single icon indicating the only ship left in Sixth Fleet. "Signal *Prometheus* to move at best speed to join First Fleet. That covers everything for now. I fear there's not much we can do for Fourth Fleet."

The icons were already moving on the tactical display as orders were transmitted and implemented.

"I've given the fleets in the planet's orbit their orders, Admiral," the chief of staff informed him. "The other fleets are on the move now. The Swarm should contact Fourth Fleet in approximately ten minutes. Based on their attack of Sixth Fleet, the battle will last about twenty minutes. With fifteen minutes for them to reorganize and travel to First Fleet, we're looking at forty-five minutes to engagement with the Swarm."

"What are the estimates on the rest of the fleets moving to join up with First?"

"Twenty minutes, Admiral. However, *Prometheus* is going to take at least forty-five and will arrive about the same time as the enemy."

"Organize six heavies from Seventh Fleet and have them coordinate a rendezvous with *Prometheus*, earliest possible timing," the admiral ordered. "Then execute a Beta jump. Unless the Swarm forces divert, they should have enough time. Then find out how many ships have the upgraded forty-millimeter rail gun systems and form them into a single force. O'Riley said that converting the guns to barrage fire was a simple program update. Brevet Commodore O'Riley will be in command of the newly created Task Force Twenty-Three. They are to form a wall of steel which the fleet will form behind. I am not sure if we can win this, but we need to bleed these bastards if we can't. If they win, they'll still have to make up those losses, and that will delay the next attack."

* * * * *

Get "The Prince Awakens" here: https://www.amazon.com/dp/B0BK232YT2.

Find out more about Fred Hughes at: https://chriskennedypublishing.com.

* * * * *

The following is an
Excerpt from Book One of The Last Marines:

Gods of War

————————————————

William S. Frisbee, Jr.

Available from Theogony Books

eBook, Audio, and Paperback

Excerpt from "Gods of War:"

"Yes, sir," Mathison said. Sometimes it was worth arguing, sometimes it wasn't. Stevenson wasn't a butter bar. He was a veteran from a line infantry platoon that had made it through Critical Skills Operator School and earned his Raider pin. He was also on the short list for captain. Major Beckett might pin the railroad tracks on Stevenson's collar before they left for space.

"Well, enough chatting," Stevenson said, the smile in his voice grating on Mathison's nerves. "Gotta go check our boys."

"Yes, sir," Mathison said, and later he would check on the men while the lieutenant rested. "Please keep your head down, sir. Don't leave me in charge of this cluster fuck. I would be tempted to tell that company commander to go fuck a duck."

"No, you won't. You will do your job and take care of our Marines, but I'll keep my head down," Stevenson said. "Asian socialists aren't good enough to kill me. It's going to have to be some green alien bastard that kills me."

"Yes, sir," Mathison said as the lieutenant tapped on Jennings' shoulder and pointed up. The lance corporal understood and cupped his hands together to boost the lieutenant out of the hole. He launched the lieutenant out of the hole and went back to digging as Mathison went back to looking at the spy eyes scrutinizing the distant jungle.

A shot rang out. On Mathison's heads-up display, the icon for Lieutenant Stevenson flashed and went red, indicating death.

"You are now acting platoon commander," Freya reported.

* * * * *

Get "Gods of War" now at: https://www.amazon.com/dp/B0B5WJB2MY.

Find out more about William S. Frisbee, Jr. at: https://chriskennedypublishing.com.

* * * * *